THE INNER SHRINE

A NOVEL OF TODAY

BASIL KING

The Inner Shrine

Basil King

© 1st World Library – Literary Society, 2004
PO Box 2211
Fairfield, IA 52556
www.1stworldlibrary.org
First Edition

LCCN: 2005901135

Softcover ISBN: 1-4218-1113-8
Hardcover ISBN: 1-4218-1013-1
eBook ISBN: 1-4218-1213-4

Purchase *"The Inner Shrine"*
as a traditional bound book at:
www.1stWorldLibrary.org/purchase.asp?ISBN=1-4218-1113-8

1st World Library Literary Society is a nonprofit organization dedicated to promoting literacy by:

- Creating a free internet library accessible from any computer worldwide.
- Hosting writing competitions and offering book publishing scholarships.

Readers interested in supporting literacy
through sponsorship, donations or
membership please contact:
literacy@1stworldlibrary.org
Check us out at: www.1stworldlibrary.ORG
and start downloading free ebooks today.

The Inner Shrine
contributed by Tim, Ed & Rodney
in support of
1st World Library Literary Society

I

Though she had counted the strokes of every hour since midnight, Mrs. Eveleth had no thought of going to bed. When she was not sitting bolt upright, indifferent to comfort, in one of the stiff-backed, gilded chairs, she was limping, with the aid of her cane, up and down the long suite of salons, listening for the sound of wheels. She knew that George and Diane would be surprised to find her waiting up for them, and that they might even be annoyed; but in her state of dread it was impossible to yield to small considerations.

She could hardly tell how this presentiment of disaster had taken hold upon her, for the beginning of it must have come as imperceptibly as the first flicker of dusk across the radiance of an afternoon. Looking back, she could almost make herself believe that she had seen its shadow over her early satisfaction in her son's marriage to Diane. Certainly she had felt it there before their honeymoon was over. The four years that had passed since then had been spent - or, at least, she would have said so now - in waiting for the peril to present itself.

And yet, had she been called on to explain why she saw it stalking through the darkness of this particular June night, she would have found it difficult to give coherent statement to her fear. Everything about her was pursuing its normally restless round, with scarcely a hint of the exceptional. If life in Paris was working up again to that feverish climax in which the season dies, it was only what she had witnessed every year since the last days of the Second Empire. If Diane's gayety was that of excitement rather than of youth, if George's depression was that of jaded effort rather than of satiated pleasure, it was no more than she had seen in them at other times. She acknowledged that she had few facts to go upon - that she had indeed little more than the terrified prescience which warns the animal of a storm.

There were moments of her vigil when she tried to reassure herself with the very tenuity of her reasons for alarm. It was a comfort to think how little there was that she could state with the definiteness of knowledge. In all that met the eye George's relation to Diane was not less happy than in the first days of their life together. If, on Diane's part, the spontaneity of wedded love had gradually become the adroitness of domestic tact, there was nothing to affirm it but Mrs. Eveleth's own power of divination. If George submitted with a blinder obedience than ever to each new extravagance of Diane's Parisian caprice, there was nothing to show that he lived beyond his means but Mrs. Eveleth's maternal apprehension. His income was undoubtedly large, and, for all she knew, it justified the sumptuous style Diane and he kept up. Where the purchasing power of money began and ended was something she had never known. Disorder was so frequent in her own affairs that when George grew up she had been glad to resign them to his keeping, taking what he told her was her income. As for Diane, her fortune was so small as to be a negligible quantity in such housekeeping as they maintained - a poverty of *dot* which had been the chief reason why her noble kinsfolk had consented to her marriage with an American. Looking round the splendid house, Mrs. Eveleth was aware that her husband could never have lived in it, still less have built it; while she wondered more than ever how George, who led the life of a Parisian man of fashion, could have found the means of doing both.

Not that her anxiety centred on material things; they were too remote from the general activities of her thought for that. She distilled her fear out of the living atmosphere around her. She was no novice in this brilliant, dissolute society, or in the meanings hidden behind its apparently trivial concerns. Hints that would have had slight significance for one less expert she

BASIL KING

found luminous with suggestion; and she read by signs as faint as those in which the redskin detects the passage of his foe across the grass. The odd smile with which Diane went out! The dull silence in which George came home! The manufactured conversation! The forced gayety! The startling pause! The effort to begin again, and keep the tone to one of common intercourse! The long defile of guests! The strangers who came, grew intimate, and disappeared! The glances that followed Diane when she crossed a room! The shrug, the whisper, the suggestive grimace, at the mention of her name! All these were as an alphabet in which Mrs. Eveleth, grown skilful by long years of observation, read what had become not less familiar than her mother-tongue.

The fact that her misgivings were not new made it the more difficult to understand why they had focussed themselves tonight into this great fear. There had been nothing unusual about the day, except that she had seen little of Diane, while George had remained shut up in his room, writing letters and arranging or destroying papers. There had been nothing out of the common in either of them - not even the frown of care on George's forehead, or the excited light in Diane's eyes - as they drove away in the evening, to dine at the Spanish Embassy. They had kissed her tenderly, but it was not till after they had gone that it seemed to her as if they had been taking a farewell. Then, too, other little tokens suddenly became ominous; while something within herself seemed to say, "The hour is at hand!"

The hour is at hand! Standing in the middle of one of the gorgeous rooms, she repeated the words softly, marking as she did so their incongruity to herself and her surroundings. The note of fatality jarred on the harmony of this well-ordered life. It was preposterous, that she, who had always been hedged round and sheltered by pomp and circumstance, should now in her middle age be menaced with calamity. She dragged herself over to one of the long mirrors and gazed at her reflection pityingly.

The twitter of birds startled her with the knowledge that it was dawn. From the Embassy George and Diane were to go on to two or three great houses, but surely they should be home by this time! The reflection meant the renewal of her fear. Where was her son? Was he really with his wife, or had the moment come when he must take the law into his own hands, after their French manner, to avenge himself or her? She knew nothing about duelling, but she had the Anglo-Saxon mother's dread of it. She had always hoped that, notwithstanding the social code under which he lived, George would keep clear of any such brutal senselessness; but lately she had begun to fear that the conventions of the world would prove the stronger, and that the time when they would do so was not far away.

Pulling back the curtains from one of the windows, she opened it and stepped out on a balcony, where the long strip of the Quai d'Orsay stretched below her, in gray and silent emptiness. On the swift, leaden-colored current of the Seine, spanned here and there by ghostly bridges, mysterious barges plied weirdly through the twilight. Up on the left the Arc de Triomphe began to emerge dimly out of night, while down on the right the line of the Louvre lay, black and sinister, beneath the towers and spires that faintly detached themselves against the growing saffron of the morning. High above all else, the domes of the Sacred Heart were white with the rays of the unrisen sun, like those of the City which came down from God.

It was so different from the cheerful Paris of broad daylight that she was drawing back with a shudder, when over the Pont de la Concorde she discerned the approach of a motor-brougham.

Closing the window, she hurried to the stairway. It was still night within the house, and the one electric light left burning drew forth dull gleams from the wrought-metal arabesques of the splendidly sweeping balustrades. When, on the ringing of the bell, the door opened and she went down, she had the strange sensation of entering on a new era in her life.

Though she recalled that impression in after years, for the moment she saw nothing but Diane, all in vivid red, in the act of letting the voluminous black cloak fall from her shoulders into the sleepy footman's hands.

"Bonjour, petite mere!" Diane called, with a nervous laugh, as Mrs. Eveleth paused on the lower steps of the stairs.

"Where is George?"

She could not keep the tone of anxiety out of her voice, but Diane answered, with ready briskness:

"George? I don't know. Hasn't he come home?"

"You must know he hasn't come home. Weren't you together?"

"We were together till - let me see! - whose house was it? - till after the cotillon at Madame de Vaudreuil's. He left me there and went to the Jockey Club with Monsieur de Melcourt, while I drove on to the Rochefoucaulds'."

She turned away toward the dining-room, but it was impossible not to catch the tremor in her voice over the last words. In her ready English there was a slight foreign intonation, as well as that trace of an Irish accent which quickly yields to emotion. Standing at the table in the dining-room where refreshments had been laid, she poured out a glass of wine, and Mrs. Eveleth could see from the threshold that she drank it thirstily, as one who before everything else needs a stimulant to keep her up. At the entrance of her mother-in-law she was on her guard again, and sank languidly into the nearest chair. "Oh, I'm so hungry!" she yawned, pulling off her gloves, and pretending to nibble at a sandwich. "Do sit down," she went on, as Mrs. Eveleth remained standing. "I should think you'd be hungry, too."

"Aren't you surprised to see me sitting up, Diane?"

"I wasn't, but I can be, if that's my cue," Diane laughed.

At the nonchalance of the reply Mrs. Eveleth was, for a second, half deceived. Was it possible that she had only conjured up a waking nightmare, and that there was nothing to be afraid of, after all? Possessing the French quality of frankness to an unusual degree, it was difficult for Diane to act a part at any time. With all her Parisian finesse her nature was as direct as lightning, while her glance had that fulness of candor which can never be assumed. Looking at her now, with her elbows on the table, and the sandwich daintily poised between the thumb and forefinger of her right hand, it was hard to connect her with tragic possibilities. There were pearls around her neck and diamonds in her hair; but to the wholesomeness of her personality jewels were no more than dew on the freshness of a summer morning.

"I thought you'd be surprised to find me sitting up," Mrs. Eveleth began again; "but the truth is, I couldn't go to bed while - "

"I'm glad you didn't," Diane broke in, with an evident intention to keep the conversation in her own hands. "I'm not in the least sleepy. I could sit here and talk till morning - though I suppose it's morning now. Really the time to live is between midnight and six o'clock. One has a whole set of emotions then that never come into play during the other eighteen hours of the day. They say it's the minute when the soul comes nearest to parting with the body, so I suppose that's the reason we can see things, during the wee sma' hours, by the light of the invisible spheres."

"I should be quite content with the light of this world - "

"Oh, I shouldn't," Diane broke in, with renewed eagerness to talk against time. "It's like being content with words, and having no need of music. It's like being satisfied with photographs, and never wanting real pictures."

BASIL KING

"Diane," Mrs. Eveleth interrupted, "I insist that you let me speak."

"Speak, petite mère? What are you doing but speaking now? I'm scarcely saying a word. I'm too tired to talk. If you'd spent the last eight or ten hours trying to get yourself down to the conversational level of your partners, you'd know what I've been through. We women must be made of steel to stand it. If you had only seen me this evening - "

"Listen to me, Diane; don't joke. This is no time for that."

"Joke! I never felt less like joking in my life, and - "

She broke off with a little hysterical gasp, so that Mrs. Eveleth got another chance.

"I know you don't feel like joking, and still less do I. There's something wrong."

"Is there? What?" Diane made an effort to recover herself. "I hope it isn't indiscreet to ask, because I need the bracing effect of a little scandal."

"Isn't it for you to tell me? You're concealing something of which - "

"Oh, petite mère, is that quite honest? First, you say there's something wrong; and then, when I'm all agog to hear it, you saddle me with the secret. That's what you call in English a sell, isn't it? A sell! What a funny little word! I often wonder who invents the slang. Parrots pass it along, of course, but it must take some cleverness to start it. And isn't it curious," she went on, breathlessly, "how a new bit of slang always fills a vacant place in the language? The minute you hear it you know it's what you've always wanted. I suppose the reason we're obliged to use the current phrase is because it expresses the current need. When the hour passes, the need passes with it, and something new must be coined to meet the new situation. I should think a most interesting book might be written on the Psychology of Slang, and if I wasn't so busy with other things - "

"Diane, I entreat you to answer me. Where is George?"

"Why, I must have forgotten to tell you that he went to the Jockey Club with Monsieur de Melcourt - "

"You did tell me so; but that isn't all. Has he gone anywhere else?"

"How should I know, petite mere? Where should he go but come home?"

"Has he gone to fight a duel?"

The question surprised Diane into partially dropping her mask. For an instant she was puzzled for an answer.

"Men who fight duels," she said, at last, "don't generally tell their wives beforehand."

"But did George tell you?"

Again Diane hesitated before speaking.

"What a queer question!" was all she could find to say.

"It's a question I have a right to ask."

"But have I a right to answer?"

"If you don't answer, you leave me to infer that he has."

"Of course I can't keep you from inferring, but isn't that what they call meeting trouble half-way?"

"I must meet trouble as it comes to me."

"But not before it comes. That's my point."

"It has come. It's here. I'm sure of it. He's gone to fight. You know it. You've sent him. Oh, Diane, if he comes to harm his blood will be on your head."

Diane shrugged her shoulders, and took another sandwich.

"I don't see that. In the first place, it's quite unlikely there'll be any blood at all - or more than a very little. One of the things I admire in men - our men, especially - is the maximum of courage with which they avenge their honor, coupled with the minimum of damage they work in doing it. It must require a great deal of skill. I know I should never have the nerve for it. I should kill my man every time he didn't kill me. But they hardly ever do."

"How can you say that? Wasn't Monsieur de Cretteville killed? And Monsieur Lalanne?"

"That makes two cases. I implied that it happens sometimes - generally by inadvertence. But it isn't likely to do so in this instance - at least not to George. He's an excellent shot - and I believe it was to be pistols."

"Then it's true! Oh, my God, I know I shall lose him!"

Mrs. Eveleth flung her cane to the floor and dropped into a seat, leaning on the table and covering her face with her hands. For a minute she moaned harshly, but when she looked up her eyes were tearless.

"And this is my reward," she cried, "for the kindness I've shown you! After all, you are nothing but a wanton."

Diane kept her self-control, but she grew pale.

"That's odd," was all she permitted herself to say, delicately flicking the crumbs from her fingertips; "because it was to prove the contrary that George called Monsieur de Bienville out."

"Bienville! You've stooped to *him?*"

"Did I say so?" Diane asked, with a sudden significant lifting of the head.

" There's no need to say so. There must have been something - "

"There was something - something Monsieur de Bienville invented."

"Wasn't it a pity for him to go to the trouble of invention - ?"

"When he could have found so much that was true," Diane finished, with dangerous quietness. "That's what you were going to say, isn't it?"

"You have no right to ascribe words to me that I haven't uttered. I never said so."

"No; that's true; I prefer to say it for you. It's safer, in that it leaves me nothing to resent."

"Oh, what shall I do! What shall I do!" Mrs. Eveleth moaned, wringing her hands. "My boy is gone from me. He will never come back. I've always been sure that if he ever did this, it would be the end. It's my fault for having brought him up among your foolish, hot-headed people. He will have thrown his life away - and for nothing!"

"No; not that," Diane corrected; "not even if the worst comes to the worst."

"What do you mean? If the worst comes to the worst, he will have sacrificed himself - "

"For my honor; and George himself would be the first to tell you that it's worth dying for."

Diane rose as she spoke, Mrs. Eveleth following her example. For a brief instant they stood as if measuring each other's strength, till they started with a simultaneous shock at the sharp call of the telephone from an adjoining room. With a smothered cry Diane sprang to answer it, while Mrs. Eveleth, helpless with dread, remained standing, as though frozen to the spot.

"Oui - oui - oui," came Diane's voice, speaking eagerly. "Oui, c'est bien Madame George Eveleth. Oui, oui. Non. Je comprends. C'est Monsieur de Melcourt. Oui - oui - Dites-le-moi tout de suite - j'insiste - Oui - oui. Ah-h-h!"

The last, prolonged, choking exclamation came as the cry of one who sinks, smitten to the heart. Mrs. Eveleth was able to move at last. When she reached the other room, Diane was crouched in a little heap on the floor.

"He's dead? He's dead?" the mother cried, in frenzied questioning.

But Diane, with glazed eyes and parted lips, could only nod her head in affirmation.

II

During the days immediately following George Eveleth's death the two women who loved him found themselves separated by the very quality of their grief. While Diane's heart was clamorous with remorse, the mother's was poignantly calm. It was generally remarked, in the Franco-American circles where the tragedy was talked of, that Mrs. Eveleth displayed unexpected strength of character. It was a matter of common knowledge that she shrank from none of the terrible details it was necessary to supervise, and that she was capable of giving her attention to her son's practical affairs.

It was not till a fortnight had passed that the two women came face to face alone. The few occasions on which they had met hitherto had been those of solemn public mourning, when the great questions between them necessarily remained untouched. The desire to keep apart was common to both, for neither was sufficiently mistress of herself to be ready for a meeting.

The first move came from Diane. During her long, speechless days of self-upbraiding certain thoughts had been slowly forming themselves into resolutions; but it was on impulse rather than reflection that, at last, she summoned up strength to knock at Mrs. Eveleth's door.

She entered timidly, expecting to find some manifestation of grief similar to her own. She was surprised, therefore, to see her mother-in-law sitting at her desk, with a number of business-like papers before her. She held a pencil between her fingers, and was evidently in the act of adding up long rows of figures.

"Oh, come in," she said, briefly, as Diane appeared. "Excuse me a minute. Sit down."

Diane seated herself by an open window looking out on the garden. It was a hot morning toward the end of June, and from the neighboring streets came the dull rumble of Paris. Beyond the garden, through an opening, she could see a procession of carriages - probably a wedding on its way to Sainte-Clotilde. It was her first realizing glimpse of the outside world since that gray morning when she had driven home alone, and the very fact that it could be pursuing its round indifferent to her calamity impelled her to turn her gaze away.

It was then that she had time to note the changes wrought in Mrs. Eveleth; and it was like finding winter where she expected no more than the first genial touch of autumn. The softnesses of lingering youth had disappeared, stricken out by the hard, straight lines of gravity. Never having known her mother-in-law as other than a woman of fashion, Diane was awed by this dignified, sorrowing matron, who carried the sword of motherhood in her heart.

It was a long time before Mrs. Eveleth laid her pencil down and raised her head. For a few minutes neither had the power of words, but it was Diane who spoke at last.

"I can understand," she faltered, "that you don't want to see me; but I've come to tell you that I'm going away."

"You're going away? Where?"

The words were spoken gently and as if in some absence of mind. As a matter of fact, Mrs. Eveleth was scarcely thinking of Diane's words - she was so intent on the poor little, tear-worn face before her. She had always known that Diane's attractions were those of coloring and vivacity, and now that she had lost these she was like an extinguished lamp.

"I haven't made up my mind yet," Diane replied, "but I want

you to know that you'll be freed from my presence."

"What makes you think I want to be - freed?"

"You must know that I killed George. You said that night that his blood would be on my head - and it is."

" If I said that, I spoke under the stress of terror and excitement - "

"You needn't try to take back the words; they were quite true."

"True in what sense?"

"In almost every sense; certainly in every sense that's vital. If it hadn't been for me, George would be here now."

"It's never wise to speculate on what might have happened if it hadn't been for us. There's no end to the useless torture we can inflict on ourselves in that way."

"I don't think there ought to be an end to it."

"Have you anything in particular to reproach yourself with?"

"I've everything."

"That means, then, that there's no one incident - or person - I didn't know but - " She hesitated, and Diane took up the sentence.

"You didn't know but what I had given George specific reason for his act. I may as well tell you that I never did - at least not in the sense in which you mean it. George always knew that I loved him, and that I was true to him. He trusted me, and was justified in doing so. It wasn't that. It was the whole thing - the whole life. There was nothing worthy in it from the beginning to the end. I played with fire, and while George knew it was only playing, it was fire all the same."

"But you say you were never - burnt."

"If I wasn't, others were. I led men on till they thought - till they thought - I don't know how to say it - "

"Till they thought you should have led them further?"

"Precisely; and Bienville was one of them. It wasn't entirely his fault. I allowed him to think - to think - oh, all sorts of things! - and then when I was tired of him, I turned him into ridicule. I took advantage of his folly to make him the laughing-stock of Paris; and to avenge himself he lied. He said I had been his - No; I can't tell you."

"I understand. You needn't tell me. You needn't tell me any more."

"There isn't much more to tell that I can put into words. It was always - just like that - just as it was with Bienville. He wasn't the only one. I made coquetry a game - but a game in which I cheated. I was never fair to any of them. It's only the fact that the others were more honorable than Bienville that's kept what has happened now from having happened long ago. It might have come at any time. I thought it a fine thing to be able to trifle with passion. I didn't know I was only trifling with death. Oh, if I had been a good woman, George would have been with us still!"

"You mustn't blame yourself," the mother-in-law said, speaking with some difficulty, "for more than your own share of our troubles. I want to talk to you quite frankly, and tell you things you've never known. The beginning of the sorrows that have come to us dates very far back - back to a time before you were born."

"Oh?"

Diane's brown eyes, swimming in tears, opened wide in a sort of mournful curiosity.

"I admit," Mrs. Eveleth continued, "that in the first hours of our - our bereavement I had some such thoughts about you as you've just expressed. It seemed to me that if you had lived differently, George might have been spared to us. It took reflection to show me that if you *had* lived differently, George himself wouldn't have been satisfied. The life you led was the one he cared for - the one I taught him to care for. The origin of the wrong has to be traced back to me."

"To you?" Diane uttered the words in increasing wonder. It was strange that a first role in the drama could be played by any one but herself.

"I've always thought it a little odd," Mrs. Eveleth observed, after a brief pause, "that you've never been interested to hear about our family."

"I didn't know there was anything to tell," Diane answered, innocently.

"I suppose there isn't, from your European point of view; but, as we Americans see things, there's a good deal that's significant. Foreigners care so little about who or what we are, so long as we have money."

Diane raised her hand in a gesture of deprecation, intimating that such was not her attitude of mind.

"And I've never wanted to bore you with what, after all, wasn't necessary for you to hear. I shouldn't do so now if it had not become important. There's a great deal to settle and arrange."

"I can understand that there must be business affairs," Diane murmured, for the sake of saying something.

"Exactly; and in order to make them clear to you, I must take you a little further back into our history than you've ever gone before. I want you to see how much more responsible I am than you for our calamity. You were born into this life of Paris, while I came into it of my own accord. You did nothing but yield naturally to the influences around you, while I accepted them after having been fully warned. If you knew a little more of our American ideals I should find it easier to explain."

"I should like to hear about them," Diane said, sympathetically. The new interest was beginning to take her out of herself.

"My husband and I," Mrs. Eveleth went on again, "belong to that New York element which dates back to the time when the city was New Amsterdam, and the State, the New Netherlands. To you that means nothing, but in America it tells much. I was Naomi de Ruyter; my husband, on his mother's side, was a Van Tromp."

"Really?" Diane murmured, feeling that Mrs. Eveleth's tone of pride required a response. "I know there's a Mr. van Tromp here - the American banker."

"He is of the same family as my husband's mother. For nearly three hundred years they've lived on the island of Manhattan, and seen their farms and pastures grow into the second city in the world. The world has poured in on them, literally in millions. It would have submerged them if there hadn't been something in that old stock that couldn't be kept down. However high the tide rose, they floated on the top. My people were thrifty and industrious. They worked hard, saved money, and lived in simple ways. They cared little for pleasure, for beauty, or for any of the forms of art; but, on the contrary, they lived for work, for religion, for learning, and all the other high and serious pursuits. It was fine; but I hated it."

"Naturally."

"I longed to get away from it, and when I married I persuaded my husband to give up his profession and his home in order to establish himself here."

"But surely you can't regret that? You were free."

"Only the selfish and the useless are ever free. Those who are worth anything in this world are bound by a hundred claims upon them. They must either stay caught in the meshes of love and duty, or wrench themselves away - and that's what I did. Perhaps I suffered less than many people in doing the same thing; but I cannot say that I haven't suffered at all."

"But you've had a happy life - till now."

"I've had what I wanted - which may be happiness, or may not be."

"I've heard that you were very much admired. Madame de Nohant has told me that when you appeared at the Tuileries, no one was more graceful, not even the Empress herself."

"I had what I wanted," Mrs. Eveleth repeated, with a sigh. "I don't deny that I enjoyed it; and yet I question now if I did right. When my husband died, and George was a little boy, my friends made one last effort to induce me to take him back, and bring him up in his own country. I ignored their opinions, because all their views were so different from mine. I was young and independent, and enamoured of the life I had begun to lead. I had scruples of conscience from time to time; but when George grew up and developed the tastes I had bred in him, I let other considerations go. I was pleased with his success in the little world of Paris, just as I had been flattered by my own. When he fell in love with you I urged him to marry you, not because of anything in yourself, but because you were Mademoiselle de la Ferronaise, the last of an illustrious family. I looked upon the match as a useful alliance for him and for me. I encouraged George in extravagance. I encouraged him when he began to live in a style far more expensive than anything to which he had been accustomed. I encouraged him when he built this house. I wanted to impress you; I wanted you to see that the American could give you a more splendid home than any European you were likely to marry, however exalted his rank. I was not without fears that George was spending too much money; but we've always had plenty for whatever we wanted to do; and so I let him go on when I should have stopped him. It was my vanity. It wasn't his fault. He inherited a large fortune; and if I had only brought him up wisely, it would have been enough."

"And wasn't it enough?"

In spite of her growing dread, Diane brought out the question firmly. Mrs. Eveleth sat one long minute motionless, with hands clasped, with lips parted, and with suspended breath.

"No."

The monosyllable seemed to fill the room. It echoed and re-echoed in Diane's ears like the boom of a cannon. While her outward vision took in such details as the despair in Mrs. Eveleth's face, the folds of crape on her gown, the Watteau picture on the panel of moss-green and gold that formed the background, all the realities of life seemed to be dissolving into chaos, as the glories of the sunset sink into a black and formless mass. When Mrs. Eveleth spoke again, her voice sounded as though it came from far away.

"I want to take all the blame upon myself. If it hadn't been for me, George would never have gone to such extremes."

"Extremes?"

Diane spoke not so much from the desire to speak as from the necessity of forcing her reeling intelligence back to the world of fact.

"I'm afraid there's no other word for it."

"Do you mean that there are debts?"

"A great many debts."

"Can't they be paid?"

"Most of them can be paid - perhaps all; but when that is done I'm afraid there will be very little left."

"But surely we haven't lived so extravagantly as that. I know I've spent a great deal of money - "

"It hasn't been altogether the style of living. When my poor boy saw that he was going beyond his means he tried to recoup himself by speculation. Do you know what that is?"

"I know it's something by which people lose money."

"He had no experience of anything of the kind, and his men of business tell me he went into it wildly. He had that optimistic temperament which always believes that the next thing will be a success, even though the present one is a failure. Then, too, he fell into the hands of unscrupulous men, who made him think that great fortunes were to be made out of what they call wildcat schemes, when all the time they were leading him to ruin."

Ruin! The word appealed to Diane's memory and imagination alike. It came to her from her remotest childhood, when she could remember hearing it applied to her grandfather, the old Comte de la Ferronaise. After that she could recollect leaving the great chateau in which she was born, and living with her parents, first in one European capital, and then in another. Finally they settled for a few years in Ireland, her mother's country, where both her parents died. During all this time, as well as in the subsequent years in a convent at Auteuil, she was never free from the sense of ruin hanging over her. Though she understood well enough that her way of escape lay in making a rich marriage, it was impressed upon her that the meagreness of her *dot* would make her efforts in this direction difficult. When, within a few months of leaving the convent, she was asked by George Eveleth to become his wife, it seemed as if she had reached the end of her cares. She had the less scruple in accepting what he had to give in that she honestly liked the generous, easy-going man who lived but to gratify her whims. During the four years of her married life she had spent money, not merely for the love of spending, but from sheer joy in the sense that Poverty, the arch-enemy, had been defeated; and lo! he was springing at her again.

"Ruin!" she echoed, when Mrs. Eveleth had let fall the word. "Do you mean that we're - ruined?"

"It depends on how you look at it. You will always have your own small fortune, on which you can live with economy."

"But you will have yours, too."

Mrs. Eveleth smiled faintly.

"No; I'm afraid that's gone. It was in George's hands, and I can see he tried to increase it for me, by doing with it - as he did with his own. I'm not blaming him. The worst of which he can be accused is a lack of judgment."

"But there's this house!" Diane urged, "and all this furniture! - and these pictures!"

She glanced up at the Watteau, the Boucher, and the Fragonard, which gave the key to the decorations of the dainty boudoir. The faint smile still lingered on Mrs. Eveleth's lips, as it lingers on the face of the dead.

"There'll be very little left," she repeated.

"But I don't understand," Diane protested, with a perplexed movement of the hand across her brow. "I don't know much about business, but if it were explained to me I think I could follow."

"Come and sit beside me at the desk," Mrs. Eveleth suggested. "You will understand better if you see the figures just as they stand."

She went over the main points, one by one, using the same untechnical simplicity of language which George's men of business had employed with herself. The facts could be stated broadly but comprehensively. When all was settled the Eveleth estate would have disappeared. Diane would possess her small inheritance, which was a thing apart. Mrs. Eveleth would have a few jewels and other minor personal belongings, but nothing more. The very completeness of the story rendered it easy in the telling, though the largeness of the facts made it impossible for Diane to take them in. It was an almost unreasonable tax on credulity to attempt to think of the tall, fragile woman sitting before her, with luxurious nurture in every pose of the figure, in every habit of the mind, as penniless. It was trying to account for daylight without a sun.

"It can't be!" Diane cried, when she had done her best to weigh the facts just placed before her.

Mrs. Eveleth shook her head, the glimmering smile fixed on her lips as on a mask.

"It is so, dear, I'm afraid. We must do our best to get used to it."

"I shall never get used to it," Diane cried, springing to her feet - "never, never!"

"It will be hard for you to do without all you've had - when you've had so much - but - "

"Oh, it isn't that," Diane broke in, fiercely. "It isn't for me. I can do well enough. It's for you."

"Don't worry about me, dear. I can work."

The words were spoken in a matter-of-fact tone, but Diane recoiled at them as at a sword-thrust.

"You can - what?"

It was the last touch, not only of the horror of the situation, but of its ludicrous irony.

"I can work, dear," Mrs. Eveleth repeated, with the poignant tranquillity that smote Diane more cruelly than grief. "There are many things I could do - "

"Oh, don't!" Diane wailed, with pleading gestures of the hands. "Oh, don't! I can't bear it. Don't say such things. They kill me. There must be some mistake. All that money can't have gone. Even if it was only a few hundred thousand francs, it would be something. I will not believe it. It's too soon to judge. I've heard it took a long time to settle up estates. How can they have done it yet?"

"They haven't. They've only seen its possibilities - and impossibilities."

"I will never believe it," Diane burst out again. "I will see those men. I will tell them. I am positive that it cannot be. Such injustice would not be permitted. There must be laws - there must be something - to prevent such outrage - especially on you!" She spoke vehemently, striding to and fro in the little room, and brushing back from time to time the heavy brown hair that in her excitement fell in disordered locks on her forehead. "It's too wicked. It's too monstrous. It's intolerable. God doesn't allow such things to happen on earth, otherwise He wouldn't be God! No, no; you cannot make me think that such things happen. You work! The Mater Dolorosa herself was not called upon to bear such humiliation. If God reigns, as they say He does - "

"But, Diane dear," Mrs. Eveleth interrupted, gently, "isn't it true that we owe it to George's memory to bear our troubles bravely?"

"I'm ready to bear anything bravely - but this."

"But isn't this the case, above all others, in which you and I should be unflinching? Doesn't any lack of courage on our parts imply a reflection on him?"

"That's true," Diane said, stopping abruptly.

"I don't know how far you honor George's memory - ?"

"George's memory? Why shouldn't I honor it?"

"I didn't know. Some women - after what you've just discovered - "

"I am not - some women! I am Diane Eveleth. Whatever George did I shared it, and I share it still."

"Then you forgive him?"

"Forgive him? - I? - forgive him? No! What have I to forgive? Anything he did he did for me and in order to have the more to give me - and I love him and honor him as I never did till now."

Mrs. Eveleth rose and stood unsteadily beside her desk.

"God bless you for saying that, Diane."

"There's no reason why He should bless me for saying anything so obvious."

"It isn't obvious to me, Diane; and you must let *me* bless you - bless you with the mother's blessing, which, I think, must be next to God's."

Then opening her arms wide, she sobbed the one word "Come!" and they had at last the comfort, dear to women, of weeping in each other's arms.

III

In the private office of the great Franco-American banking-house of Van Tromp & Co., the partners, having finished their conference, were about to separate.

"That's all, I think," said Mr. Grimston. He rose with a jerky movement, which gave him the appearance of a little figure shot out of a box.

Mr. van Tromp remained seated at the broad, flat-topped desk, his head bent at an angle which gave Mr. Grimston a view of the tips of shaggy eyebrows, a broad nose, and that peculiar kind of protruding lower lip before which timid people quail. As there was no response, Mr. Grimston looked round vaguely on the sombre, handsome furnishings, fixing his gaze at last on the lithographed portrait of Mr. van Tromp senior, the founder of the house, hanging above the mantelpiece.

"That's all, I think," Mr. Grimston repeated, raising his voice slightly in order to drown the rumble that came through the open windows from the rue Auber.

Suddenly Mr. van Tromp looked up.

"I've just had a letter," he said, in a tone indicating an entirely new order of discussion, "from a person who signs herself Diana - or is it Diane? - Eveleth."

"Oh, Diane! She's written to you, has she?" came from Mr. Grimston, as his partner searched with short-sighted eyes for the letter in question among the papers on the desk.

"You know her, then?"

"Of course I know her. You ought to know her, too. You would, if you didn't shut yourself up in the office, away from the world."

"N-no, I don't recall that I've ever met the lady. Ah, here's the note, just sit down a minute while I read it."

Mr. Grimston shot back into his seat again, while Mr. van Tromp wiped his large, circular glasses.

"'Dear Mr. van Tromp,' she begins, 'I am most anxious to talk to you on very important business, and would take it as a favor if you would let me call on Tuesday morning and see you very privately. Yours sincerely, Diane Eveleth.' That's all. Now, what do you make of it?"

The straight smile, which was all the facial expression Mr. Grimston ever allowed himself, became visible between the lines of his closely clipped mustache and beard. He took his time before speaking, enjoying the knowledge that this was one of those social junctures in which he had his senior partner so conspicuously at a disadvantage.

"It's a bad business, I'm afraid," he said, as though summing up rather than beginning.

"What does the woman want with me?"

"That, I fear, is painfully evident. You must have heard of the Eveleth smash a couple of months ago. Or - let me see! - I think it was just when you were in New York. No; you'd be likely not to hear of it. The Eveleths have so carefully cut their American acquaintance for so many years that they've created a kind of vacuum around themselves, out of which the noise of their doings doesn't easily penetrate. They belong to that class

BASIL KING

of American Parisians who pose for going only into French society."

"I know the kind."

"Mrs. Grimston could tell you all about them, of course. Equally at home as she is in the best French and American circles, she hears a great many things she'd rather not hear."

"She needn't listen to 'em."

"Unfortunately a woman in her position, with a daughter like Marion, is obliged to listen. But that's rather the end of the story - "

"And I want the beginning, Grimston, if you don't mind. I want to know why this Diane should be after me."

"She's after money," Mr. Grimston declared, bluntly. "She's after money, and you'd better let me manage her. It would save you the trouble of the refusal you'll be obliged to make."

"Well, tell me about her and I'll see."

Mr. Grimston stiffened himself in his chair and cleared his throat.

"Diane Eveleth," he stated, with slow, significant emphasis, "is an extremely fascinating woman. She has probably turned more men round her little finger than any other woman in Paris."

"Is that to her credit or her discredit?"

"I don't want to say anything against Mrs. Eveleth," Mr. Grimston protested. "I wish she hadn't come near us at all. As it is, you must be forewarned."

"I'm not particular about that, if you'll give me the facts."

"That's not so easy. Where facts are so deucedly disagreeable, a fellow finds it hard to trot out any poor little woman in her weaknesses. I must make it clear beforehand that I don't want to say anything against her."

"It's in confidence - privileged, as the lawyers say. I sha'n't think the worse of her - that is, not much."

"Poor Diane," Mr. Grimston began again, sententiously, "is one of the bits of human wreckage that have drifted down to us from the pre-revolutionary days of French society. Her grandfather, the old Comte de la Ferronaise, belonged to that order of irreconcilable royalists who persist in dashing themselves to pieces against the rising wall of democracy. I remember him perfectly - a handsome old fellow, who had lost an arm in the Crimea. He used to do business with us when I was with Hargous in the rue de Provence. Having impoverished himself in a plot in favor of the Comte de Chambord, somewhere about 1872, he came utterly to grief in raising funds for the Boulanger craze, in the train of the Duchesse d'Uzes. He died shortly afterward, one of the last to break his heart over the hopeless Bourbon cause."

"That, I understand you to say, was the grandfather of the young woman who is after money. She's a Frenchwoman, then?"

"She's half French. That was her grandfather. The father was of much the same type, but a lighter weight. He married an Irish beauty, a Miss O'Hara, as poor as himself. He died young, I believe, and I'd lost sight of the lot, till this Mademoiselle Diane de la Ferronaise floated into view, some five years ago, in the train of the Nohant family. Her marriage to George Eveleth, which took place almost at once, was looked upon as an excellent thing all round. It rid the Nohants of a poor relation, and helped to establish the Eveleths in the heart of the old aristocracy. Since then Diane has been going the pace."

"What pace?"

BASIL KING

"The pace the Eveleth money couldn't keep up with; the pace that made her the most-talked-of woman in a society where women are talked of more than enough; the pace that led George Eveleth to put a bullet through his head under pretence of fighting a duel."

"Dear me! Dear me! A most unusual young woman! Do you tell me that her husband actually put an end to himself?"

"So I understand. The affair was a curious one; but Bienville swears he fired into the air, and I believe him. Besides, George Eveleth was found shot through the temple, and no one but himself could have inflicted a wound like that. To make it conclusive, Melcourt and Vernois, who were seconds, testify to having seen the act, without having the time to prevent it. You can see that it is a relief to me to be able to take this view of the case - on poor Marion's account."

"Marion - your daughter! Was she mixed up in the affair?"

"Mixed up is a little to much to say. I don't mind telling you in confidence that there was something between her and Bienville. I don't know where it mightn't have ended; but of course when all this happened, and we got wind of Bienville's entanglement with Mrs. Eveleth, we had to put a stop to the thing, and pack her off to America. She'll stay there with her aunt, Mrs. Bayford, till it blows over."

"And your friend Bienville? Hasn't he brought himself within the clutches of the law?"

"George Eveleth was officially declared a suicide. He had every reason to be one - though I don't want to say anything against Mrs. Eveleth. When Bienville refused to put an end to him, he evidently decided to do it himself. His family know nothing about that, so please don't let it slip out if you see Diane. With her notions, the husband fallen in her cause has perished on the field of honor; and if that's any comfort to her, let her keep it. As for Bienville, he's joined young Persigny, the explorer, in

South America. By the time he returns the affair will have been forgotten. He's a nice young fellow, and it's a thousand pities he should have fallen into the net of a woman like Mrs. Eveleth. I don't want to say anything against her, you understand - "

"Oh, quite!"

"But - "

Mr. Grimston pronounced the word with a hard-drawn breath, and presented the appearance of a man who restrains himself. He was still endeavoring to maintain this attitude of repression when a discreet tap on the door called from Mr. van Tromp a gruff "Come in." A young man entered with a card.

"She's here," the banker grunted, reading the name.

Mr. Grimston shot up again.

"Better let me see her," he insisted, in a warning tone.

"No, no. I'll have a look at her myself. Bring the lady in," he added, to the young man in waiting.

"Then I'll skip," said Mr. Grimston, suiting the action to the word by disappearing in one direction as Diane entered from another.

Mr. van Tromp rose heavily, and surveyed her as she crossed the floor toward him. He had been expecting some such seductive French beauty as he had occasionally seen on the stage on the rare occasions when he went to a play; so that the trimness of this little figure in widow's dress, with white bands and cuffs, after the English fashion, somewhat disconcerted him. Unaccustomed to the ways of banks, Diane half offered her hand, but, as he was on his guard against taking it, she stood still before him.

"Mrs. Eveleth, I believe," he said, when he had surveyed her well. "Have the goodness to sit down, and tell me what I can do for you."

Diane took the seat he indicated, which left a discreet space between them. The heavy black satchel she carried she placed on the floor beside her. When she raised her veil, Mr. van Tromp observed to himself that the pale face, touching in expression, and the brown eyes, in which there seemed to lurk a gentle reproach against the world for having treated her so badly, were exactly what he would have expected in a woman coming to borrow money.

"I've come to you, Mr. van Tromp," Diane began, timidly, "because I thought that perhaps - you might know - who I am."

"I don't know anything at all about you," was the not encouraging response.

"Of course there's no reason why you should - " Diane hastened to say, apologetically.

"None whatever," he assured her.

"Only that a good many people do know us - "

"I dare say. I haven't the honor to be among the number."

"And I thought that possibly - just possibly - you might be predisposed in my favor."

"A banker is never predisposed in favor of any one - not even his own flesh and blood."

"I didn't know that," Diane persisted, bravely, "otherwise I might just as well have gone to anybody else."

"Just as well."

"Would you like me to go now?"

The question took him by surprise, and before replying he looked at her again with queer, bulgy eyes peering through big circular glasses, in a way that made Diane think of an ogre in a fairy tale.

"You're not here for what I like," he said at last, "but for what you want yourself."

"That's true," Diane admitted, ruefully, "but I might go away. I *will* go away, if you say so."

"You'll please yourself. I didn't send for you, and I'll not tell you to go. How old are you?"

It was Diane's turn to be surprised, but she brought out her age promptly.

"Twenty-four."

"You look older."

"That's because I've had so much trouble, perhaps. It's because we're in trouble that I've come to you, Mr. van Tromp."

"I dare say. I didn't suppose you'd come to ask me to dinner. There are not many days go by without some one expecting me to pull him out of the scrape he would never have got into if it hadn't been for his own fault."

"I'm afraid that's very like my case."

"It's like a good many cases. You're no exception to the rule."

"And what do you do at such times, if I may ask?"

"You may ask, but I'll not tell you. You're here on your own business, I presume, and not on mine."

BASIL KING

"I thought that perhaps you'd be good enough to make mine yours. Though we've never met, I have seen you at various times, and it always seemed to me that you looked kind; and so - "

"Stop right there, ma'am!" he cried, putting up a warning hand. "'Most important business,' was what you said in your note, otherwise I shouldn't have consented to see you. If you have any business, state it, and I'll say yes or no, as it strikes me. But I'll tell you beforehand that there isn't a chance in a thousand but what it'll be no."

"I did come because I thought you looked kind," Diane declared, indignantly, "and if you think it was for any other reason whatever, you're absolutely mistaken."

"Then we'll let it be. I can't help my looks, nor what you think about them. The point is that you're here for something; so let's know what it is."

"You make it very hard for me," Diane said, almost tearfully, "but I'll try. I must tell you, first of all, that we've lost a great deal of money."

"That's no new situation."

"It is to me; and it's even more so to my poor mother-in-law. I should think you must have heard of her at least. She is Mrs. Arthur Eveleth. Her maiden name was Naomi de Ruyter, of New York."

"Very likely."

"Her husband was related, on his mother's side, to the Van Tromps - the same family as your own."

"That's more likely still. There are as many Van Tromps in New York as there are shrimps on the Breton coast, and they're all related to me, because I'm supposed to have a little money."

"I sha'n't let you offend me," Diane said, stoutly, "because I want your help."

"That's a very good reason."

"But since you take so little interest in us I will not attempt to explain how it is that we've come to such misfortune."

"I'll take that for granted."

"The blow has fallen more heavily on my mother-in-law than on me. She has lost everything she had in the world; while I have still my own money - my *dot* - and a little over from the sale of my jewels."

"Well?"

"If you'd ever seen her, you would know how terrible, how impossible, such a situation is for her. She's the sort of woman who ought to have money - who *must* have money. And so I thought if I came to you - "

"I'd give her some."

"No," Diane said, quickly, with a renewed touch of indignation, "but that you'd help me to do it."

He looked at her with an odd, upward glance under his shaggy, overhanging brows, while the protruding lower lip went a shade further out.

"Help you to do it? How?"

"By letting her have mine."

Again he looked at her, almost suspiciously.

"You've got plenty to give away, I suppose?"

"On the contrary, I've pitifully little; but such as it is, I want her to have it all. She could live on it - with economy; or at least she says I could."

"And can't you?"

"I don't want to. As there isn't enough for two, I wish to settle it on her. Isn't that the word? - settle?"

"It'll do as well as another. And what do you propose to do yourself?"

"Work."

Diane forced the word in a little gasp of humiliation, but she got it out.

"And what'll you work at?"

"I don't know yet, exactly. I shall have to see. My mother-in-law is going to America; and when she does I'll join her."

"Humph! My good woman, you wouldn't do more than just keep ahead of starvation."

"Oh, I shouldn't expect to do more. If I succeeded in that - I should live."

"How much money have you got?"

"It's all here," she answered, picking up the black satchel and opening it. "These are my securities, and I'm told they're very good."

"And do you take them round with you every time you go shopping?"

"No," Diane smiled, somewhat wanly. "They've been in the hands of the Messrs. Hargous for a good many years past. They are entirely at my own disposal - not in trust, they said; so that I had a right to take them away. I thought I would just bring them to you."

"What for?"

"To keep them for my mother-in-law and pay her the interest, or whatever it is."

"Why didn't you leave them with Hargous?"

"I was afraid, from some things he said, he would object to what I wanted to do."

"And what made you think I wouldn't object to it, too?"

"Two or three reasons. First, Monsieur Hargous is not an American, and you are; and I'd been told that Americans always like to help one another - "

"I don't know who could have put that notion into your head."

"And, then, from the few glimpses I've had of you - I *will* say it! - I thought you looked kind."

"Well, now that you've had a better look, you see I don't. How much money have you got? You haven't told me that yet."

"Here's the memorandum. They said they were mostly bonds, and very good ones."

With the slip of paper in his hand the banker leaned back in the chair, and took a longer time than was necessary to scan the poor little list. In reality he was turning over in his mind the unexpected features of the case, venturing a peep at Diane as she sat meekly awaiting the end of his perusal.

"Hasn't it occurred to you," he asked, at last, "that you could leave your affairs in Hargous' hands, and still turn over to your mother-in-law whatever sums he paid you?"

"Yes; but she wouldn't take the money unless she thought it was her very own."

"But it isn't her very own. It's yours."

"I want to make it hers. I want to transfer it to her absolutely - so that no one else, not even I, shall have a claim upon it. There must be ways of doing that."

"There are ways of doing that, but as far as she's concerned it comes to the same thing. If she won't touch the income, she will refuse to accept the principal."

"I've thought of that, too; and it's among the reasons why I've come to you. I hoped you'd help me - "

"To tell a lie about it."

"I should think it might be done without that. My mother-in-law is a very simple woman in business affairs. She has been used all her life to having money paid into her account, when she had only the vaguest idea as to where it came from. If you should write to her now and say that some small funds in her name were in your hands, and that you would pay her the income at stated intervals, nothing would seem more natural to her. She would probably attribute it to some act of foresight on her son's part, and never think I had anything to do with it at all."

For three or four minutes he sat in meditation, still glancing at her furtively under his shaggy brows, while she waited for his decision.

"I don't approve of it at all," he said, at last.

"Don't say that," she pleaded. "I've hoped so much that you'd - "

"At the same time I won't say that the thing isn't feasible. I'll just verify these bonds and certificates, and - "

He took them, one by one, from the bag, and, having compared them with the list, replaced them.

"And," he continued, "you can come and see me again at this time to-morrow."

"Oh, thank you!"

"You can thank me when I've done something - not before. Very likely I sha'n't do anything at all. But in the mean while you may leave your satchel here, and not run the risk of being robbed in the street. If I refuse you to-morrow - as is probable I shall - I'll send a man with you to see you and your money safely back to Hargous."

He touched a bell, and a young man entered. On directions from the banker the clerk left the room, taking the bag with him; while Diane, feeling that her errand had been largely accomplished, rose to leave.

"You can't go without the receipt for your securities. How do you know I'm not stealing them from you? What right would you have to claim them when you came again? Sit down now and tell me something more about yourself."

Half smiling, half tearfully, Diane complied. Before the clerk returned she had given a brief outline of her life, agreeing in all but the tone of telling with much of what Mr. Grimston had stated half an hour earlier.

"It has been all my fault," she declared, as the young man re-entered. "There's been nobody to blame but me."

BASIL KING

"I see that well enough," the old man agreed, and once more she prepared to depart.

"Look at your receipt. Compare it with the list there on the desk." Diane obeyed, though her eyes swam so that she could not tell one word from another. "Is it all right? Then so much the better. You'll find me at the same time to-morrow - if you're not late."

"Since you won't let me thank you, I must go without doing so," she began, tremulously, "but I assure you - "

"You needn't assure me of anything, but just come again to-morrow."

She smiled through the mist over her eyes, and bowed.

"I shall not be - late," was all she ventured to say, and turned to leave him.

She had reached the door, and half opened it, when she heard his voice behind her.

"Stay! Just a minute! I'd like to shake hands with you, young woman."

Diane turned and allowed him to take her hand in a grip that hurt her. She was so astounded by the suddenness of the act, as well as by the rapidity with which he closed the door behind her, that her tears did not actually fall until she found herself in the public department of the bank, outside.

IV

On board the *Picardie*, steaming to New York, Mrs. Eveleth and Diane were beginning to realize the gravity of the step they had taken. As long as they remained in Paris, battling with the sordid details of financial downfall, America had seemed the land of hope and reconstruction, where the ruined would find to their hands the means with which to begin again. The illusion had sustained them all through the first months of living on little, and stood by them till the very hour of departure. It faded just when they had most need of it - when the last cliffs of France went suddenly out of sight in a thick fog-bank of nothingness; and the cold, empty void, through which the steamer crept cautiously, roaring from minute to minute like a leviathan in pain, seemed all that the universe henceforth had to offer them. They would have been astonished to know that, beyond the fog, Fate was getting the New World ready for their reception, by creating among the rich those misfortunes out of which not infrequently proceed the blessings of the poor.

When that excellent aged lady, Miss Regina van Tromp, sister to the well-known Paris banker, was felled by a stroke of apoplexy, the personal calamity might, by a mind taking all things into account, have been considered balanced by the circumstance that it was affording employment to some refined woman of reduced means, capable of taking care of the invalid. It had the further advantage that, coming suddenly as it did, it absorbed the attention of Miss Lucilla van Tromp, the sick lady's companion and niece, who became unable henceforth to give to the household of her cousin, Derek Pruyn, that general supervision which a kindly old maid can exercise in the home of a young and prosperous widower. Were Destiny on the lookout for still another opening, she could have found it in the fact that Miss Dorothea Pruyn, whose father's discipline came by fits and starts, while his indulgence was continuous, had reached a point in motherless maidenhood where, according to Miss Lucilla, "something ought to be done." There was thus unrest, and a straining after new conditions, in that very family toward which Mrs. Eveleth's imagination turned from this dreary, leaden sea as to a possible haven.

Since the wonderful morning when the banker had brought her the news of her little inheritance her thoughts had dwelt much on Van Tromps and Pruyns, as representatives of that old New York clan with which she deigned to claim alliance; and she found no small comfort in going over, again and again, the details of the interview which had brought her once more into contact with her kin. James van Tromp, she informed Diane, as they lay covered with rugs in their steamer-chairs, had been gruff in manner, but kind in heart, like all the Van Tromps she had ever heard of. He had not scrupled to dwell upon her past extravagance, but he had tempered his remarks by commending her resolution to return to her old home and friends. In the matter of friends, he assured her, she would find herself with very few. She would be forgotten by some and ignored by others; while those who still took an interest in her would resent the fact that in the days of her prosperity she had neglected them. In any case, she must have the meekness of the suppliant. As her means at most would be small, she must be grateful if any of her relatives would take her without wages, as a sort of superior lady's maid, and save her the expense of board and lodging.

"And so you see, dear," she finished, humbly, "it's going to be all right. George thought of me; and far more than any money, I value that. James van Tromp said that this sum had been placed in his hands some time ago to be specially used for me, and I couldn't help understanding what that meant. When my boy saw the disaster coming he did his best to protect me; and it will be my part now to show that he did enough."

If Diane listened to these familiar remarks, it was only to take a dull satisfaction in the working of her scheme; but Mrs. Eveleth's next words startled her into sudden attention.

"Haven't I heard you say that you knew James van Tromp's nephew, Derek Pruyn?"

"I did know him," Diane answered, with a trace of hesitation.

"You knew him well?"

"Not exactly; it was different from - well."

"Different? How? Did you meet him often?"

"Never often; but when we did meet - "

The possibilities implied in Diane's pause induced Mrs. Eveleth to turn in her chair and look at her.

"You've never told me about that."

"There wasn't much to tell. Don't you know what it is to have met, just a few times in your life, some one who leaves behind a memory out of proportion to the degree of the acquaintance? It was something like that with this Mr. Pruyn."

"Where was it? In Paris?"

"I met him first in Ireland. He was staying with some friends of ours the last year mamma and I lived at Kilrowan. What I remember about him was that he seemed so young to be a widower - scarcely more than a boy."

"Is that all?"

"It's very nearly all; but there *is* something more. He said one day when we were talking intimately - we always seemed to talk intimately when we were together - that if ever I was in trouble, I was to remember him."

"How extraordinary!"

"Yes, it was. I reminded him of it when we met again. That was the year I was going out with Marie de Nohant, just before George and I were married."

"And what did he say then?"

"That he repeated the request."

"Extraordinary!" Mrs. Eveleth commented again. "Are you going to do anything about it?"

"I've thought of it," Diane admitted, "but I don't believe I can."

"Wouldn't it be a pity to neglect so good an opportunity?"

"It might rather be a pity to avail one's self of it. There are things in life too pleasant to put to the test."

"He might like you to do it. After all, he's a connection."

Not caring to continue the subject, Diane murmured something about feeling cold, and rose for a little exercise. Having advanced as far forward as she could go, she turned her back upon her fellow-passengers, stretched in mute misery in their chairs or huddled in cheerful groups behind sheltering projections, and stood watching the dip and rise of the steamer's bow as it drove onward into the mist. Whither was she going, and to what? With a desperate sense of her ignorance and impotence, she strained her eyes into the white, dimly translucent bank, from which stray drops repeatedly lashed her face, as though its vaporous wall alone stood between her and the knowledge of her future.

*   *   *   *   *

If she could have seen beyond the fog and carried her vision over the intervening leagues of ocean, so as to look into a large, old-fashioned New York house in Gramercy Park, she would have found Derek Pruyn and Lucilla van Tromp discussing one of the cardinal points on which that future was to turn.

That it was not an amusing conversation would have been clear from the agitation of Derek's manner as he strode up and down the room, as well as from the rigidity with which his cousin, usually a limp person, held herself erect, in the attitude of a woman who has no intention of retiring from the stand she has taken.

"You force me to speak more plainly than I like, Derek," she was saying, "because you make yourself so obtuse. You seem to forget that years have a way of passing, and that Dorothea is no longer a very little girl."

"She's barely seventeen - no more than a child."

"But a motherless child, and one who has been allowed a great deal of liberty."

"Is there any reason why a girl shouldn't be a free creature?"

"Only the reason why a boy shouldn't be one."

"That's different. A boy would be getting into mischief."

"Even a girl isn't proof against that possibility. It mayn't be a boy's kind of mischief, but it's a kind of her own."

Unwilling to credit this statement, and yet unable to contradict it, Pruyn continued his march for a minute or two in silence, while Miss Lucilla waited nervously for him to speak again. It was one of the few points in the round of daily existence on which she was prepared to give him battle. It was part of the ridiculous irony of life that Derek, with the domestic incompetency natural to a banker and a club-man, should have a daughter to train, while she whose instinct was so passionately maternal must be doomed to spinsterhood. She had never made any secret of the fact that to watch Derek bringing up Dorothea made her as fidgety as if she had seen him trimming hats, though she recognized the futility of trying to snatch the task from his hands in order to do it properly. The utmost she had been able to accomplish was to be allowed to plod daily from Gramercy Park to Fifth Avenue, in the hope of keeping bad from becoming worse; and even this insufficient oversight must be discontinued now, since Aunt Regina would monopolize her care. If she took the matter to heart, it was no more, she thought, than she had a right to do, seeing that Derek was almost like a younger brother, and, with the exception of Uncle James in Paris, and Aunt Regina in New York, her nearest relative in the world.

As she glanced up at him from time to time she reflected, with some pride, that no one could have taken him for anything but what he was - a rising young New York banker of some hereditary line. As in certain English portraits there is an inborn aptitude for statesmanship, so in Derek Pruyn there was that air, almost inseparable from the Van Tromp kinship, of one accustomed to possess money, to make money, to spend money, and to support moneyed responsibilities. The face, slightly stern by nature, slightly grave by habit, and tanned by outdoor exercise, was that of a man who wields his special kind of power with a due sense of its importance, and yet wields it easily. Nature having endowed the Van Tromps with every excellence but that of good looks, it was Miss Lucilla's tendency to depreciate beauty; but she was too much a woman not to be sensible of the charms of six feet two, with proportionate width of shoulder, and a way of standing straight and looking straight, incompatible with anything but "acting straight," that was full of a fine dominance. That he should be carefully dressed was but a detail in the exactitude which was the main element in his character; while his daily custom of wearing in his button-hole a dark-red carnation, a token of some never-explained memory of his dead wife, indicated a capacity for sober romance which she did not find displeasing.

"Then what would you do about it?" he asked, at last, pausing abruptly in his walk and confronting her.

"There isn't much choice, Derek. Human society is so constituted as to leave us very little opportunity for striking into original paths. Aunt Regina has told you many a time what was possible, and you didn't like it; but I'll repeat it if you wish. You could send her to a good boarding-school - "

Never!

"Or you could have a lady to chaperon her properly."

"Rubbish!"

"Well, there you are, Derek. You refuse the only means that could help you in your situation; and so you leave Dorothea a prey to a woman like Mrs. Wappinger. You'll excuse me for mentioning it; but - "

"I'd excuse you for mentioning anything; but even Mrs. Wappinger ought to have justice. You know as well as I do that Uncle James wanted to marry her, and that it was only her own common-sense that saved us from having her as an aunt. You may not admire her type, but you can't deny that it's one which has a legitimate place in American civilization. Ours isn't a society that can afford to exclude the self-made man, or his widow."

"That may be quite true, Derek; only in that case you have also to reckon with - his son."

Derek bounded away once more, making manifest efforts to control himself before he spoke again.

"You know this subject is most distasteful to me, Lucilla," he said, severely.

"I know it is; and it's equally so to me. But I see what's going on, and you don't - there's the difference. What should a young man like you know about bringing up a school-girl? To see you intrusted with her at all makes me very nearly doubt the wisdom of the ends of Providence. She's a good little girl by nature, but your indulgence would spoil an angel."

"I don't indulge her. I've forbidden her to do lots of things."

"Exactly; you come down on the poor thing when she's not doing any harm, and you put no restrictions on the things in which she's wilful. If there's a girl on earth who is being brought up backward, it's Dorothea Pruyn."

"She's my child. I presume I've got a right to do what I like with her."

"You'll find that you've done what you don't like with her, when you've allowed her to get into a ridiculous, unmaidenly flirtation with the young man Wappinger."

"I shouldn't let that distress me if I were you. As far as Dorothea is concerned, your young man Wappinger doesn't exist."

"That's as it may be," Miss Lucilla sniffed, now on the brink of tears.

"That's as it is," he insisted, picking up his hat.

"It's to be regretted," he added, with dignity, as he took his leave, "that on this subject you and I cannot see alike; but I think you may trust me not to endanger the happiness of my child."

* * * * *

Even if Diane could have transcended space to assist at this brief interview, she would probably have missed its bearing on herself; but had she transported her spirit at the same instant to still another scene, the effect would have been more enlightening. While she still stood watching the rise and dip of the steamer's bow, Mrs. Wappinger, in a larger and more elaborate mansion than the old-fashioned house in Gramercy Park, was reading to her son such portions of a letter from James van Tromp as she considered it discreet for him to hear. A stout, florid lady, in jovial middle age, her appearance as an agent in her affairs would certainly have surprised Diane, had the vision been vouchsafed to her.

Passing over those sentences in which the old man admitted the wisdom of her decision in rejecting his proposals, on the ground that he saw now that the married state would not have suited him, Mrs. Wappinger came to what was of common interest.

"'... You will remember, my good friend,'" she read, with a strong Western accent, "'that both at the time of, and since, your husband's death I have been helpful to you in your business affairs, and laid you under some obligation to me. I have, therefore, no scruple in asking you to fulfil a few wishes of mine, in token of such gratitude as I conceive you to feel. There will arrive in your city by the steamer *Picardie*, on the twenty-eighth day of this month, two foolish women, answering to the name of Eveleth - mother-in-law and daughter-in-law - both widows - and presenting the sorry spectacle of Naomi and Ruth returning to the Land of Promise, after a ruinous sojourn in a foreign country - with whose history you are familiar from your reading of the Scriptures.'"

"Is there a Bible in the house, mother?" Carli Wappinger asked, swinging himself on the piano-stool.

"I think there must be - somewhere. There used to be one. But, hush! Let me go on. 'They will descend,'" she continued to read, "'at a modest French hostelry in University Place, to which I have commended them, as being within their means. I desire, first, that you will make their acquaintance at your

BASIL KING

earliest possible convenience. I desire, next, that you will invite them to your house on some occasion, presumably in the afternoon, when you can also ask my nephew, Derek Pruyn, and Lucilla van Tromp, my niece, to meet them. I desire, furthermore, that though you may use my name to the Mesdames Eveleth, as a passport to their presence, you will in no wise speak of me to my relatives in question, or give them to understand that I have inspired the invitation you will accord them...."'

Mrs. Wappinger threw down the letter with the emphasis of gesture which was one of her characteristics.

"There!" she exclaimed, in a loud, hearty voice, not without a note of triumph; "that's what I call a chance."

"Chance for what, mother?"

"Chance for a good many things - and first of all for bearding Lucilla van Tromp right in her own den."

"I don't see - "

"No; but I do. We're on to a big thing. I've got to go right there; and she's got to come right here. She's held off, and she's kept me off; but now the ice'll be broken with a regular thaw."

"Still, I don't see. It's one thing to invite her, to oblige old man Van Tromp; but it's another thing to get her to come."

"She'll come fast enough - this time; she'll come as if she was shot here by a secret spring. There is a secret spring, you may take my word for it. I don't know what it is, and I don't care; it's enough for me to know that it's in good working order - which it is, if James van Tromp has got his hand on it. James van Tromp may look like a fool and talk like a fool, but he isn't a fool - No, sir!"

It is commonly believed that a woman never thinks otherwise than gently of the man who has wanted to marry her; and if this be the rule, Mrs. Wappinger was no exception to it. As she sat on the sofa in her son's room, the mere mention of the old man's name, attended by the kindly opinion she had just expressed, sent her off into sudden reverie. While it was quite true that, in her own phrase, she "would no more have married him than she would have married a mole," it was none the less flattering to have been desired. The onlooker, like Lucilla van Tromp or Derek Pruyn, might wonder what were those hidden forces of affinity which led a man to single Mrs. Wappinger out of all the women in the world; but to Mrs. Wappinger herself the circumstance could not be otherwise than pleasing.

Seeing her pensive, Carli swung himself back to the keyboard again, pounding out a few bars of the dance music in Strauss' *Salome*, of which the score lay open before him. He was a good-looking young man of twenty-two, of whom any mother, not too exacting, might be proud. Very blond - with well-chiselled features and waving hair - not so tall as to make his excessive slimness seem disproportionate - there was something in the perfection with which he was "turned out" that gave him the air of a "creation." Mrs. Wappinger's joy in him was the more satisfying because of the fact that, relative to herself, he was in the line of progress. He was the blossom of culture, travel, and sport, borne by her own strenuous generation of successful material effort. To the things to which he had attained she felt that in a certain sense she had attained herself, on the principle of *facit per alium, facit per se*. In the social position she had reached it was a pleasure to know that Harvard, Europe, and money had given Carli a refinement that made up in some measure for her own deficiencies.

"Well, what are you going to do about it?" he asked, breaking off in the midst of the cruel ecstasy of the daughter of Herodias, and swinging himself back, so as to confront her.

"I'm going to give a little tea," Mrs. Wappinger answered, with decision; "a *tay antime,* as the French say. I shall have these two Eveleths - or whatever their name is - Lucilla van Tromp, and Derek and Dorothea Pruyn."

"You may accomplish the first and the last. You'll find it difficult to fill in the middle. To say nothing of the old girl, Derek Pruyn is too busy for teas - *intime,* or otherwise."

"I'm going to have him," she stated, with energy.

"You go round and tell Dorothea she's got to bring him - she's just got to, that's all. He'll come - I know he will. There are forces at work here that you and I don't see, and if something doesn't happen, my name isn't Clara Wappinger."

With this mysterious saying she rose, to leave Carli to his music.

"How very occult!" he laughed.

"Nobody knows James van Tromp better than I do," she declared, with pride, turning on the threshold, "and he doesn't write that way unless he has a plan in mind. You tell Dorothea what I say. Let me see! To-day is Tuesday; the *Picardie* will get in on Saturday; you'll see Dorothea on Sunday; and we'll have the tea on Thursday next."

With her habitual air of triumphant decision Mrs. Wappinger departed, and the incident closed.

V

It must be admitted that Diane Eveleth found her entry into the Land of Promise rather disappointing. To outward things she paid comparatively little heed. The general aspect of New York was what she had seen in pictures and expected. That habits and customs should be strange to her she took as a matter of course; and she was too eager for a welcome to be critical. As a Frenchwoman, she was neither curious nor analytical regarding that which lay outside her immediate sphere of interest, and she instituted no comparisons between Broadway and the boulevards, or any of the tall buildings and Notre Dame. It may be confessed that her thoughts went scarcely beyond the human element, with its possible bearing on her fortunes.

In this respect she made the discovery that Mrs. Eveleth was not to be taken as an authority. She had given Diane to understand that the return of Naomi de Ruyter to New York would be a matter of civic interest, "especially among the old families," and that they would scarcely have landed before finding themselves amid people whom she knew. But forty years had made a difference, and Mrs. Eveleth recognized no familiar faces in the crowd congregated on the dock. When it became further evident that not only was Naomi de Ruyter forgotten in the city of her birth, but that the very landmarks she remembered had been swept away, there was a moment of disillusion, not free from tears.

To Diane the discovery meant only that, more than she had supposed, she would have to depend upon herself. This, to her, was the appalling fact that dwarfed all other considerations. To be alone, while the crowds surged hurriedly by her, was one thing; to be obliged to press in among them and make room for herself was another. As she walked aimlessly about the streets during the few days following her arrival she had the forlorn conviction that in these serried ranks there could be no place for one so insignificant as she. The knowledge that she must make such a place, or go without food and shelter, only served to paralyze her energies and reduce her to a state of nerveless inefficiency.

She had gone forth one day with the letters of introduction she hoped would help her, only to find that none of the persons to whom they were addressed had returned to town for the winter. Tired and discouraged, she was endeavoring on her return to cheer Mrs. Eveleth with such bits of forced humor as she could squeeze out of the commonplace happenings of the day, when cards were brought in, bearing the unknown name of Mrs. Wappinger.

That in this huge, overwhelming town any one could desire to make their acquaintance was in itself a surprise; but in the interview that followed Diane felt as though she had been caught up in a whirlwind and carried away. Mrs. Wappinger's autocratic breeziness was so novel in character that she had no more thought of resisting it than of resisting a summer storm. She could only let it blow over her and bear her whither it listed. In the end she felt like some wayfarer in the *Arabian Nights*, who has been wafted by kindly *jinn* across unknown miles of space, and set down again many leagues farther on in his career.

Never in her life did Diane receive in the same amount of time so much personal information as Mrs. Wappinger conveyed in the thirty minutes her visit lasted. She began by explaining that she was a friend of James van Tromp's - a very great friend. In fact, her husband had been at one time a partner in the Van Tromp banking-house; but it was an old business, and what they call conservative, while Mr. Wappinger was from the West. The West was a long way ahead of New York, though

Mrs. Wappinger had "lived East" so long that she had dropped into walking pace like the rest. She traced her rise from a comparatively obscure position in Indiana to her present eminence, and gave details as to Mr. Wappinger's courtship and the number of children she had lost. Left now with one, she had spent a good deal of money on him, and was happy to say that he showed it. While she preferred not to name names, she made no secret of the fact that Carli was in love; though for her own part a feeling of wounded pride induced her to hope that he would never enter a family where he wasn't wanted. The transition of topic having thus become easy, the invitation to tea was given, and its acceptance taken as a matter of course.

"It'll only be a *tay antime*," she declared, in answer to Diane's faint protests, "so you needn't be afraid to come; and as I never do things by halves, I shall send one of my automobiles for the old lady and you at a little after four to-morrow." With these words and a hearty shake of the hand, she bustled away as suddenly as she had come, leaving Diane with a bewildering sense of having beheld an apparition.

* * * * *

It was not less surprising to Diane to find herself, on the following afternoon, face to face with Derek Pruyn. Though she had expected, in so far as she thought of him at all, that chance would one day throw them together, she had not supposed that the event would occur so soon. The lack of preparation, the change in her fortunes, and the necessity to explain, combined to bring about one of those rare moments in which she found herself at a loss.

On his side, Pruyn had come to the house with a very special purpose. In spite of the stoutness of his protest when young Wappinger's name was coupled with his child's, he was not without some inward misgivings, which he resolved to allay once and for all. He would dispel them by seeing with his own eyes that they had no force, while he would convict Miss

Lucilla of groundless alarm by ocular demonstration. It would be enough, he was sure, to watch the young people together to prove beyond cavil that Dorothea was aware of the gulf between the son of Mrs. Wappinger, worthy woman though she might be, and a daughter of the Pruyns. He had, therefore, astonished every one not only by accepting the invitation himself, but by insisting that Miss Lucilla should do the same, forcing her thus to become a witness to the vindication of his wisdom.

Arrived on the spot, however, it vexed him to find that instead of being a mere spectator, permitted to take notes at his ease, he was passed from lady to lady - Mrs. Wappinger, Miss Lucilla, Mrs. Eveleth, in turn - only to find himself settled down at last with a strange young woman in widow's weeds, in a dim corner of the drawing-room. The meeting was the more abrupt owing to the circumstance that Diane, unaware of his arrival, had just emerged from the adjoining ball-room, which was decorated for a dance. Mrs. Wappinger, coming forward at that minute with a cup of tea for her, pronounced their names with hurried indistinctness, and left them together.

With her quick eye for small social indications, Diane saw that, owing to the dimness of the room and the nature of her dress, he did not know her, while he resented the necessity for talking to one person, when he was obviously looking about for another. With her tea-cup in her hand she slipped into a chair, so that he had no choice but to sit down beside her.

He was not what is called a lady's man, and in the most fluent of moods his supply of easy conversation was small. On the present occasion he felt the urgency of speech without inspiration to meet the need. With a furtive flutter of the eyelids, while she sipped her tea, she took in the salient changes the last five years had produced in him, noting in particular that though slightly older he had improved in looks, and that the dark-red carnation still held its place in his buttonhole.

"Very unseasonable weather for the time of year," he managed to stammer, at last.

"Is it? I hadn't noticed."

His manner took on a shade of dignity still more severe, as he wondered whether this reply was a snub or a mere ineptitude.

"You don't worry about such trifles as the weather," he struggled on.

"Not often."

"May I ask how you escape the necessity?"

"By having more pressing things to think about." With the finality of this reply the brief conversation dropped, though the perception on Derek's part that it was not from her inability to carry it on stirred him to an unusual feeling of pique. Most of the women he met were ready to entertain him without putting him to any exertion whatever. They even went so far as to manifest a disposition to be agreeable, before which he often found it necessary to retire. Without being fatuous on the point, he could not be unaware of the general conviction that a wealthy widower, who could still call himself young, must be in want of a wife; and as long as he was unconscious of the need himself, he judged it wise to be as little as possible in feminine society. On the rare occasions when he ventured therein he was not able to complain of a lack of welcome; nor could he remember an instance in which his hesitating, somewhat scornful, advances had not been cordially met, until to-day. The immediate effect was to cause him to look at Diane with a closer, if somewhat haughty, attention, their eyes meeting as he did so. Her voice, with its blending of French and Irish elements, had already made its appeal to his memory, so that the minute was one in which the presentiment of recognition came before the recognition itself. In his surprise he half arose from his chair, resuming his seat as he exclaimed:

"It's Mademoiselle de la Ferronaise!"

His astonished tone and awe-struck manner called to Diane's lips a little smile.

"It used to be," she said, trying to speak naturally; "it's Mrs. Eveleth now."

"Yes," he responded, with the absent air of a man getting his wits together; "I remember; that was the name."

"You knew, then, that I'd been married?"

"Yes; but I didn't know - "

His glance at her dress finished the sentence, and she hastened to reply.

"No; of course not. My husband died at the beginning of last summer - six months ago. I hoped some one would have told you before we met. But we have not many common acquaintances, have we?"

"I hope we may have more now - if you're making a visit to New York."

"I'm making more than a visit; I expect to stay."

"Oh! Do you think you'll like that?"

"It isn't a question of liking; it's a question of living. I may as well tell you at once that since my husband's death I have my own bread to earn."

To no Frenchwoman of her rank in life could this statement have been an easy one, but by making it with a certain quiet outspokenness she hoped to cover up her foolish sense of shame. The moment was not made less difficult for her by the astonishment, mingled with embarrassment, with which he took her remark.

"You!" he cried. "You!"

"It isn't anything very unusual, is it?" she smiled.

"I'm not the first person in the world to make the attempt."

"And may I ask if you're succeeding?"

"I haven't begun yet. I only arrived a few days ago.

"Oh, I see. You've come here - "

"In the hope of finding employment - just like the rest of the disinherited of the earth. I hope to give French lessons, and - "

"There's always an opening to any one who can," he interrupted, encouragingly. "I'm not without influence in one or two good schools that my daughter has attended - "

"Is that your daughter?" she asked, glad to escape from her subject, now that it was stated plainly - "the very pretty girl in red?"

The question gave Pruyn the excuse he wanted or looking about him.

"I believe she's in red - but I don't see her."

He searched the dimly lighted room, where Mrs. Wappinger sat, silent and satisfied, behind her tea-table, while Mrs. Eveleth was conversing with Lucilla on Knickerbocker genealogy; but neither of the young people was to be seen. His look of anxiety did not escape Diane, who responded to it with her usual straightforward promptness.

"I fancy she's still in the ball-room with young Mr. Wappinger," she explained. "We were all there a few minutes ago, looking at the decorations for the dance Mrs. Wappinger is giving to-night. It was before you came."

The shadow that shot across his face was a thing to be noticed only by one accustomed to read the most trivial signs in the social sky. In an instant she took in the main points of the case as accurately as if Mrs. Wappinger had named those names over which she had shown such laudable reserve.

"Wouldn't you like to see them? - the decorations? They're very pretty. It's just in here."

She rose as she spoke, with a gesture of the hand toward the ball-room. He followed, because she led the way, but without seeing the meaning of the move until they were actually on the polished dancing-floor. Owing to the darkness of the December afternoon, the large empty room was lit up as brilliantly as at night. For a minute they stood on the threshold, looking absently at the palms grouped in the corners and the garlands festooning the walls. It was only then that Pruyn saw the motive of her coming; and for an instant he forgot his worry in the perception that this woman had divined his thought.

"There's no one here," he said, at last, in a tone of relief, which betrayed him once more.

"No," Diane replied, half turning round. "Perhaps we had better go back to the drawing-room. My mother-in-law will be getting tired."

"Wait," he said, imperiously. "Isn't that - ?"

He was again conscious of having admitted her into a sort of confidence; but he had scarcely time to regret it before there was a flash of red between the tall potted shrubs that screened an alcove. Dorothea sauntered into view, with Carli Wappinger, bending slightly over her, walking by her side. They were too deep in conversation to know themselves observed; but the earnestness with which the young man spoke became evident when he put out his hand and laid it gently on the muff Dorothea held before her. In the act, from which Dorothea did not draw back, there was nothing beyond the admission of a certain degree of intimacy; but Diane felt, through all her highly trained subconscious sensibilities, the shock it produced in Derek's mind.

The situation belonged too entirely to the classic repertoire of life to present any difficulties to a woman who knew that catastrophe is often averted by keeping close to the commonplace.

"Isn't she pretty!" she exclaimed, in a tone of polite enthusiasm. "Mayn't I speak to her? I haven't met her yet."

Before she had finished the concluding words, or Wappinger had withdrawn his hand from Dorothea's muff, she had glided across the floor, and disturbed the young people from their absorption in each other.

"Mr. Wappinger," Derek heard her say, as he approached, "I want you to introduce me to Miss Pruyn. I'm Mrs. Eveleth, Miss Pruyn," she continued, without waiting for Carli's intermediary offices. "I couldn't go away without saying just a word to you."

If she supposed she was coming to Dorothea's rescue in a moment which might be one of embarrassment, she found herself mistaken. No experienced dowager could have been more amiable to a nice governess than Dorothea Pruyn to a lady in reduced circumstances. A facility in adapting herself to other people's manners enabled Diane to accept her cue; and presently all four were on their way back to the drawing-room, where farewells were spoken.

While Miss Lucilla was making Mrs. Eveleth renew her promise to come and see her, and "bring young Mrs. Eveleth with her , " Pruyn found an opportunity for another word with Diane.

"You must understand," he said, in a tone which he tried to make one of explanation for her enlightenment rather than of apology for Dorothea - "you must understand that girls have a good deal of liberty in America."

"They have everywhere," she rejoined. "Even in France, where they've been kept so strictly, the old law of Purdah has been more or less relaxed."

"If you take up teaching as a work, you'll naturally be thrown among our young people; and you may see things to which it will be difficult to adjust your mind."

"I've had a good deal of practice in adjusting my mind. It often seems to me as movable as if it was on a pivot. I'm rather ashamed of it."

"You needn't be. On the contrary, you'll find it especially useful in this country, where foreigners are often eager to convert us to their customs, while we are tenacious of our own."

"Thank you," she said, in the spirit of meekness his didactic attitude seemed to require. "I'll try to remember that, and not fall into the mistake."

"And if I can do anything for you," he went on, awkwardly, "in the way of schools - or - or - recommendations - you know I promised long ago that if you ever needed any one - "

"Thank you once more," she said, hurriedly, before he had time to go on. "I know I can count on your help; and if I require a good word, I shall not hesitate to ask you for it."

As she slipped away, Pruyn was left with the uncomfortable sense of having appeared to a disadvantage. He had been stilted and patronizing, when he had meant to be cordial and kind. On the other hand, he resented the quickness with which she had read his thoughts, as well as her perception that he had ground for uneasiness regarding his child. That she should penetrate the inner shrine of reserve he kept closed against those who stood nearest to him in the world gave him a sense of injury; and he turned this feeling to account during the next few hours in trying to deaden the echo of the French voice with the Irish intonation that haunted his inner hearing, as well as to banish the memory of the plaintive smile in which, as he feared, meekness was blended with amusement at his expense.

VI

If the secret spring worked by James van Tromp had been an active agency in bringing Diane and Derek Pruyn once more together, as well as in creating the intimacy that sprang up during the next two months between Miss Lucilla and the elder Mrs. Eveleth, it had certainly nothing to do with the South American complications in the business of Van Tromp & Co., which made Pruyn's departure for Rio de Janeiro a possibility of the near future. He had long foreseen that he would be obliged to make the journey sooner or later, but that he should have to do it just now was particularly inconvenient. There was but one aspect in which the expedition might prove a blessing in disguise - he might take Dorothea with him.

During the six or eight weeks following the afternoon at Mrs. Wappinger's he had bestowed upon Dorothea no small measure of attention, obtaining much the same result as a mastiff might gain from his investigation of the ways of a bird of paradise. He informed himself as to her diversions and her dancing-classes, making the discovery that what other girls' mothers did for them, Dorothea was doing for herself. As far as he could see, she was bringing herself up with the aid of a chosen band of eligible, well-conducted young men, varying in age from nineteen to twenty-two, whom she was training as a sort of body-guard against the day of her "coming out." On the occasions when he had opportunities for observation he noted the skill with which she managed them, as well as the chivalry with which they treated her; and yet there was in the situation an indefinable element that displeased him. It was something of a shock to learn that the flower he thought he was cultivating in secluded sweetness under glass had taken root of its own accord in the midst of young New York's great, gay parterre. Aware of the possibilities of this soil to produce over-stimulated growth, he could think of nothing better than to pluck it up and, temporarily at least, transplant it elsewhere. Having come to the decision overnight, he made the proposition when they met at breakfast in the morning.

A prettier object than Miss Dorothea Pruyn, at the head of her father's table, it would have been difficult to find in the whole range of "dainty rogues in porcelain." From the top of her bronze-colored hair to the tip of her bronze-colored shoes she was as complete as taste could make her. The flash of her eyes as she lifted them suddenly, and as suddenly dropped them, over her task among the coffee-cups was like that of summer waters; while the rapture of youth was in her smile, and a becoming school-girl shyness in her fleeting blushes. In the floral language of American society, she was "not a bud"; she was only that small, hard, green thing out of which the bud is to unfold itself, but which does not lack a beauty of promise specially its own. If any criticism could be passed upon her, it was that which her father made - that there was danger of the promise being anticipated by a rather premature fulfilment, and the flower that needed time forced into a hurried, hot-house bloom.

"What! And leave my friends!" she exclaimed, when Derek, with some hesitation, had asked her how she would like the journey.

"They would keep."

"That's just what they wouldn't do. When I came back I should find them in all sorts of new combinations, out of which I should be dropped. You've got to be on the spot to keep in your set, otherwise you're lost."

"Why should you be in a set? Why shouldn't you be independent?"

"That just shows how much you understand, father," she said, pityingly. "A girl who isn't in a set is as much an outsider as a Hindoo who isn't in a caste. I must know people; and I must know the right people; and I must know no one but the right people. It's perfectly simple."

"Oh, perfectly. I can't help wondering, though, how you recognize the right people when you see them."

"By instinct. You couldn't make a mistake about that, any more than one pigeon could make a mistake about another, or take it for a crow."

"And is young Wappinger one of the right people?"

It was with an effort that Derek made up his mind to broach this subject, but Dorothea's self-possession was not disturbed.

"Certainly," she replied, briefly, with perhaps a slight accentuation of her maiden dignity.

"I'm rather surprised at that."

"Yes; you should be," she conceded; "but I couldn't make you understand it, any more than you could make me understand banking."

"I'm not convinced of the impossibility of either," he objected, knocking the top off an egg. "Suppose you were to try."

Dorothea shook her head.

"It wouldn't be of any use. The fact is, I really don't understand it myself. What's more, I don't suppose anybody else does. Carli Wappinger belongs to the right people because the right people say he does; and there is no more to be said about it."

"I should think that Mrs. Wappinger might be a - drawback."

"Not if the right people don't think so; and they don't. They've taken her up, and they ask her everywhere; but they couldn't tell you why they do it, any more than birds could tell you why they migrate. As a matter of fact, they don't care. They just do it, and let it be."

"That sort of election and predestination may be very convenient for Mrs. Wappinger, but I should think you might have reasons for not caring to indorse it."

"I haven't. Why should I, more than anybody else."

"You've so much social perspicacity that I hoped you would see without my having to tell you. It's chiefly a question of antecedents."

Dorothea looked thoughtful, her head tipped to one side, as she buttered a bit of toast.

"I know that's an important point," she admitted, "but it isn't everything. You've got to look at things all round, and not mistake your shadow for your bone."

"I'm glad you see there is a shadow."

"I see there is only a shadow."

"A shadow on - what?"

Pruyn meant this for a leading question, and as such Dorothea took it. She gazed at him for a minute with the clear eyes and straightforward expression that were so essential a part of her dainty, self-reliant personality. If she was bracing herself for an effort, there was no external sign of it.

"I may as well tell you, father," she said, "that Carli Wappinger has asked me to marry him."

For a long minute Derek sat with body seemingly stunned, but with mind busily searching for the wisest way in which to take this astounding bit of information. At the end of many seconds of silence he exploded in loud laughter, choosing this method of treating Dorothea's confidence in order to impress her with the ludicrous aspect of the affair, as it must appear to the grown-up mind.

"Funny, isn't it?" she remarked, dryly, when he thought it advisable to grow calmer.

"It's not only funny; it's the drollest thing I ever heard in my life."

"I thought it might strike you that way. That's why I told you."

"And what did you tell him, if I may ask?"

"I told him it was out of the question - for the present."

"For the present! That's good. But why the reservation?"

"I couldn't tell him it would be out of the question always, because I didn't know. As long as he didn't ask me for a definite answer, I didn't feel obliged to give him one."

"I think you might have committed yourself as far as that."

"I prefer not to commit myself at all. I'm very young and inexperienced - "

"I'm glad you see that."

"Though neither so inexperienced nor so young as mamma was when she married you. And you were only twenty-one yourself, father, while Carli is nearly twenty-three."

"I wouldn't compare the two instances if I were you."

"I don't. I merely state the facts. I want to make it plain that, though we're both very young, we're not so young as to make the case exceptional."

"But I understood you to say that there was no - case."

"There is to this extent: that while I'm free, Carli considers himself bound. That's the way we've left it."

"That is to say, he's engaged, but you aren't."

"That's what Carli thinks."

"Then I refuse to consent to it."

"But, father dear," Dorothea asked, arching her pretty eyebrows, "do you have to consent to what Carli thinks about himself? Can't he do that just as he likes?"

"He can't become a hanger-on of my family without my permission."

"He says he's not going to hang on, but to stand off. He's going to allow me full liberty of action and fair play."

"That's very kind of him."

"Only, when I choose to come back to him I shall find him waiting."

"I might suggest that you never go back to him at all, only that there's a better way of meeting the situation. That is to put a stop to the nonsense now; and I shall take steps to do it."

Dorothea preserved her self-control, but two tiny hectic spots began to burn in her cheeks, while she kept her eyes persistently lowered, as though to veil the spirit of determination glowing there.

"Hadn't you better leave that to me?" she asked, after a brief pause.

"I will, if you promise to put it through."

"You see," she answered, in a reasoning tone, "my whole object is not to promise anything - yet. I should think the advantage of that would strike you, if only from the point of view of business. It's like having the refusal of a picture or a piece of property. You may never want them; but it does no harm to know that nobody else can get them till you decide."

"Neither does it do any harm to let somebody else have a chance, when you know that you can't take them."

"Of course not; but I couldn't say that now. I quite realize that I'm too young to know my own mind; and it's only reasonable to consider things all round. Carli is rich and good-looking. He has a cultivated mind and a kind heart. There are lots of men, to whom you'd have no objection whatever, who wouldn't possess all those qualifications, or perhaps any of them."

"Nevertheless, I should imagine that the fact that I have objections would have its weight with you."

"Naturally; and yet you would neither force me into what I didn't like to do, nor refuse me what I wanted."

With this definition of his parental attitude Dorothea pushed back her chair and moved sedately from the room.

Physically, Derek was able to go on with his breakfast and finish it, but mentally he was like a man, accustomed to action, who suddenly finds himself paralyzed. To the best of his knowledge he had never before been put in a position in which he had no idea whatever as to what to do. He had been placed in some puzzling dilemmas in private life, and had passed through some serious crises in financial affairs, but he had always been able to take some course, even if it was a mistaken one. It had been reserved for Dorothea to checkmate him in such a way that he could not move at all.

* * * * *

That the feminine mind possessed resources which his own did not was a claim Derek had made it a principle to deny. The theory on which he had brought up Dorothea had been based on his belief in his own insight into his daughter's character. Though he was far from abjuring that confidence even yet, nevertheless, when the succeeding days brought no enlightenment of counsel, and the long journey to South America became more imminent, he was forced once more to turn his steps toward Gramercy Park, and seek inspiration from the great, eternal mother-spirit of mankind, as represented by his cousin.

Miss Lucilla van Tromp passed among her friends as a sort of diffident Minerva. Though deficient in outward charms, she was considered to possess intellectual ability; and, having once been told that her profile resembled George Eliot's, she made the pursuit of learning, music, and Knickerbocker genealogy her special aims. Derek had, all his life, felt for her a special tenderness; and having neither mother, wife, nor sister, he was in the habit of coming to her with his cares.

"You're a woman," he declared, now, in summing up his case. "You're a woman. If you'd been married, you would probably have had children. You ought to be able to tell me exactly what to do."

Flushes of shy rapture illumined and softened her ill-assorted features on being cited as the type of maternity and sex, so that when she replied it was with an air of authority.

"I can tell you what to do, Derek; but I've done it already, and you wouldn't listen. You should send her to a good school - "

"It's too late for that. She wouldn't go."

"Then you should have some woman to live in your house who would be wise enough to manage her."

He jerked out the monosyllable, and began, according to his custom when puzzled or annoyed, to stride up and down the library.

"That is," Miss Lucilla went on, "you wouldn't like it. It would bore you to see a stranger in the house."

"Naturally."

"And so you would sacrifice Dorothea to your personal convenience."

"I wouldn't, if there was a woman competent to take the place; but there isn't."

"There is. There's Diane Eveleth."

"Who?"

The dark flush that swept into his face made it clear to Lucilla that his question was not put for purposes of information. She had remarked in Derek during the past few weeks a manner of fighting shy of Diane at variance with his usual method with women. Safety in flight was the course he commonly adopted; but since Diane appeared on the scene, Lucilla had noticed that it was flight with a curious tendency to looking backward.

"I said Diane Eveleth," she replied, in tactful answer to his superfluous question; "and I assure you she's fully equal to the duties you would require of her. I suppose you've never noticed her especially - ?"

"I used to know her a little," he said, in an offhand manner. "I've seen her here. That's all."

"If a woman could have been made on purpose for what you want, it's she."

"Dear me! You don't say so!"

"It's no use trying to be sarcastic about it, Derek. She's not the one to suffer by it; it's Dorothea. Though, when it comes to suffering, she has her share, poor thing."

"I suppose no decent woman who has just lost her husband is expected to be absolutely hilarious over the event."

"She hasn't *just* lost him; it's getting on toward a year. And, besides, it isn't only that. As a matter of fact, I don't believe she ever loved him as she could love the man to whom she gave her heart. If grief was her only trouble, I am sure the poor thing could bear it."

"And can't she bear it as it is?"

"The fact that she does bear it shows that she can; but it must be hard for a woman, who has lived as she has, to be brought to want."

"Want? Isn't that a strong word? One isn't in want unless one is without food and shelter."

"She has the shelter for the time being; I'm not sure that she always has the food."

"What? You don't know what you're saying."

"I know exactly what I'm saying; and I mean exactly what I say. There have been days when I've suspected that she's pinching in the essentials of meat and drink."

"But she has pupils."

"She has two; but they must pay her very little. It's dreadful for people who have as much as we to have to look on at the tragedy of others going hungry - "

"Good Lord! Don't pile it on."

Striding to a window, he stood with his back to her, staring out.

"I'm not piling it on, Derek. I wish I were."

"Well, can't we do something? If it's as you say, they mustn't be left like that."

"It's a very delicate matter. The mother-in-law has money of her own; but Diane has nothing. It's difficult to see what to do, except to find her a situation."

"Then find her one."

"I have; but you won't take her."

"In any case," he said, in the aggressive tone of a man putting forward a weak final argument, "you couldn't leave the mother-in-law all alone."

"I'd take her," Lucilla said, promptly. "You have no idea how much I want her, in this big, empty house. It's getting to be more than I can do to take care of Aunt Regina all alone."

Minutes went by in silence; but when Derek turned from the window and spoke, Lucilla shrank with constitutional fear from the responsibility she had assumed.

"Go and ring them up, and tell young Mrs. Eveleth I'm waiting to see her here."

"But, Derek, are you sure - ?"

"I'm quite sure. Please go and ring them up."

"But, Derek, you're so startling. Have you reflected?"

"It's quite decided. Please do as I say, and call them up."

"But if anything were to go wrong in the future you'd think it was my - "

"I shall think nothing of the kind. Don't say any more about it, but please go and tell Diane I'm waiting."

The use of this name being more convincing to Lucilla than pledges of assurance, she sped away to do his bidding; but it was not till after she had gone that Derek recognized the fact that the word had passed his lips.

VII

During the half-hour before the arrival of Mrs. Eveleth and Diane, Miss Lucilla's tact allowed Derek to have the library to himself. He was thus enabled to co-ordinate his thoughts, and enact the laws which must henceforth regulate his domestic life. It was easy to silence the voice that for an instant accused him of taking this step in order to provide Diane Eveleth with a home; for Dorothea's need of a strong hand over her was imperative. He had reached the point where that circumstance could no longer be ignored. The avowal that the child had passed beyond his control would have had more bitterness in it, were it not for the fact that her naive self-sufficiency touched his sense of humor, while her dainty beauty wakened his paternal pride.

Nevertheless, it was patent that Dorothea had been too much her own mistress. Without admitting that he had been wrong in his methods hitherto, he confessed that the time had come when the duenna system must be introduced, as a matter not only of propriety, but of prudence. He assured himself of his regret that no American lady who could take the position chanced to be on the spot, but allayed his sorrow on the ground that any fairly well-mannered, virtuous woman could fulfil the functions of so mechanical a task, just as any decent, able-bodied man is good enough to be a policeman.

It was somewhat annoying that the lady in question should be young and pretty; for it was a sad proof of the crudity of human nature that the mere residence of a free man and a free woman under the same roof could not pass without comment among their friends. For himself it was a matter of no importance; and as for her, a woman who has her living to earn must often be placed in situations where she is exposed to remark.

To anticipate all possibility of mistake, it would be necessary that his attitude toward Mrs. Eveleth should be strictly that of the employer toward the employed. He must ignore the circumstance of their earlier acquaintance, with its touch of something memorable which neither of them had ever been able to explain, and confine himself as far as possible, both in her interests and his own, to such relations as he held with his stenographers and his clerks. What friendliness she required she must receive from other hands; and, doubtless, she would find sufficient.

Having intrenched himself behind his fortifications of reserve, he was able to maintain just the right shade of dignity, when, in the half-light of the midwinter afternoon, Diane glided into the big, book-lined apartment, in which the comfortable air induced through long occupancy by people of means did not banish a certain sombreness. She entered with the subdued manner of one who has been sent for peremptorily, but who acknowledges the right of summons. The perception of this called an impulse to apologize to Derek's lips; but on reflection he repressed it. It was best to assume that she would do his bidding from the first. Standing by the fireplace, with his arm on the mantelpiece, he bowed stiffly, without offering his hand. Diane bowed in return, keeping her own hands securely in her small black muff.

"Won't you sit down?"

Without changing his position he indicated the large leathern chair on the other side of the hearth. Diane sat down on the very edge - erect, silent, submissive. If he had feared the intrusion of the personal element into what must be strictly a business affair, it was plain that this pale, pinched little woman had forestalled him.

BASIL KING

Yes; she was pale and pinched. Lucilla had been right about that. There was something in Diane's appearance that suggested privation. Derek had seen such a thing before among the disinherited of mankind, but never in his own rank in life. With her air of proud gentleness, of gallant acceptance of what fate had apportioned her, she made him think of some plucky little citadel holding out against hunger. If there was no way of showing the pity, the mingled pity and approbation, in his breast, it was at least some consolation to know that in his house she would be beyond the most terrible and elemental touch of want.

"I've troubled you to come and see me," he began, with an effort to keep the note of embarrassment out of his voice, "to ask if you would be willing to accept a position in my family."

Diane sat still and did not raise her eyes, but it seemed to him that he could detect, beneath her veil, a light of relief in her face, like a sudden gleam of sunshine.

"I'm looking for a position," was all she said, "and if I could be of service - "

"I'm very much in need of some one," he explained; "though the duties of the place would be peculiar, and, perhaps, not particularly grateful."

"It would be for me to do them, without questioning as to whether I liked them or not."

"I'm glad you say that, as it will make it easier for us to come to an understanding. You've already guessed, perhaps, that I am looking for a lady to be with my daughter."

"I thought it might be something of that kind."

The difficult part of the interview was now to begin, and Pruyn hesitated a minute, considering how best to present his case. Reflection decided him in favor of frankness, for it was only by frankness on his side that Diane would be able to carry out his wishes on hers. The responsibility imposed upon him by his wife's death, he said, was one he had never wished to shirk by leaving his child to the care of others. Moreover, he had had his own ideas as to the manner in which she should be brought up, and he had put them into practice. The results had been good in most respects, and if in others there was something still to be desired, it was not too late to make the necessary changes, whether in the way of supplement or correction. Indeed, in his opinion, the psychological moment for introducing a new line of conduct had only just arrived.

"It is often better not to force things," Diane murmured, vaguely, "especially with the very young."

To this he agreed, though he laid down the principle that not to take strong measures when there was need for them would be the part of weakness. Diane having no objection to offer to this bit of wisdom, it was possible for him to go on to explain the emergency she would be called on to meet. Briefly, it arose from his own error in allowing Dorothea too much liberty of judgment. While he was in favor of a reasonable freedom for all young people, it was evident that in this case the pendulum had been suffered to swing so far in one directionthat it would require no small amount of effort on his part and Diane's - chiefly on Diane's - to bring it back. In the interest of Dorothea's happiness it was essential that the proper balance should be established with all possible speed, even though they raised some rebellion on her part in doing it.

He explained Dorothea's methods in creating her body-guard of young men, as far as he understood them; he described the young people whose society she frequented, and admitted that he was puzzled as to the precise quality in them that shocked his views; coming to the affair with Carli Wappinger, he spoke of it as "a bit of preposterous nonsense, to which an immediate stop must be put." There were minor points in his exposition; and at each one, as he made it, Diane nodded her head gravely, to show that she followed him with understanding, and was in sympathy with his opinion that it was "high time that some step should be taken."

Encouraged by this intelligent comprehension, Derek went on to define the good offices he would expect from Diane. She should come to his house not only as Dorothea's inseparable companion, but as a sort of warder-in-chief, armed, by his authority, with all the powers of command. There was no use in doing things by halves; and if Dorothea needed discipline she had better get it thoroughly, and be done with it. It was not a thing which he, Derek, would want to see last forever; but while it did last it ought to be effective, and he would look to Diane to make it so. As it was not becoming that a daughter of his should need a bodyguard of youths, Diane would undertake the task of breaking up Dorothea's circle. Young men might still be permitted "to call," but under Diane's supervision, while Dorothea sat in the background, as a maiden should. Diane would make it a point to know the lads personally, so as to discriminate between them, and exclude those who for one reason or another might not be desirable friends. As for Mr. Carli Wappinger, the door was to be rigorously shut against him. Here the question was not one of gradual elimination, but of abrupt termination to the acquaintanceship. He must request Diane to see to it that, as far as possible, Dorothea neither met the young man, nor held communication with him, on any pretext whatever. He laid down no rule in the case of Mrs. Wappinger, but it would follow as a natural consequence that the mother should be dropped with the son. These might seem drastic measures to Dorothea, to begin with; but she was an eminently reasonable child, and would soon come to recognize their wisdom. After all, they were only the conditions to which, as he had been given to understand, other young girls were subjected, so that she would have nothing to complain of in her lot. The probability of his own departure for South America, with an absence lasting till the spring, would make it necessary for Diane to use to the full the powers with which he commissioned her. He trusted that he made himself clear.

For some minutes after he ceased speaking Diane sat looking meditatively at the fire. When she spoke her voice was low, but the ring of decision in it was not to be mistaken.

"I'm afraid I couldn't accept the position, Mr. Pruyn."

Derek's start of astonishment was that of a man who sees intentions he meant to be benevolent thrown back in his face.

"You couldn't - ? But surely - ?"

"I mean, I couldn't do that kind of work."

"But I thought you were looking for it - or something of the sort."

"Yes; something of the sort, but not precisely that."

"And it's precisely that that I wish to have done," he said, in a tone that betrayed some irritation; "so I suppose there is no more to be said."

"No; I suppose not. In any case," she added, rising, "I must thank you for being so good as to think of me; and if I feel obliged to decline your proposition, I must ask you to believe that my motives are not petty ones. Now I will say good-afternoon."

Keeping her hands rigidly within her muff, and with a slight, dignified inclination of the head, she turned from him.

She was half-way to the door before Derek recovered himself sufficiently to speak.

"May I ask," he inquired, "what your objections are?"

She turned where she stood, but did not come back toward him.

"I have only one. The position you suggest would be intolerable to your daughter and odious to me."

"But," he asked, with a perplexed contraction of the brows, "isn't it what companions to young ladies are generally engaged for?"

"I was never engaged as a companion before, so I'm not qualified to say. I only know - "

She stopped, as if weighing her words.

"Yes?" he insisted; "you only know - what?"

"That no girl with spirit - and Miss Pruyn *is* a girl with spirit - would submit to that kind of tyranny."

"It wouldn't be tyranny in this case; it would be authority."

"She would consider it tyranny - especially after the freedom you've allowed her."

"But you admit that it's freedom that ought to be curbed?"

"Quite so; but aren't there methods of restriction other than those of compulsion?"

"Such as - what?"

"Such as special circumstances may suggest."

"And in these particular circumstances - ?"

"I'm not prepared to say. I'm not sufficiently familiar with them."

"Precisely; but I am."

"You're familiar with them from a man's point of view," she

smiled; "but it's one of those instances in which a man's point of view counts for very little."

"Admitting that, what would be your advice?"

"I have none to give."

"None?"

She shook her head. Leaving his fortified position by the mantelpiece, he took a step or two toward her.

"And yet when I began to speak you seemed favorably inclined to the offer I was making you. You must have had ideas on the subject, then."

"Only vague ones. I made the mistake of supposing that yours would be equally so."

"And with your vague ideas, your intention was - ?"

"To adapt myself to circumstances; I couldn't tell beforehand what they would be. I imagined that what you wanted for your daughter was the society of an experienced woman of the world; and I am that, whatever else I may not be."

"You're very young to make the claim."

"There are other ways of gaining experience than by years; and," she added, with the intention to divert the conversation from herself, "the small store I happen to possess I was willing to share with your daughter, in whatever way she might have need of it."

"But not in my way."

"Not in your way, perhaps, but for the furthering of your purposes."

"How could you further my purposes when you wouldn't do what I wanted?"

"By getting her to do it of her own accord."

"Could you promise me she would?"

"I couldn't promise you anything at all. I could only do my best, and see how she would respond to it."

"She's a very good little girl," he hastened to declare.

"I'm sure of that. Though I don't know her well, I've seen her often enough to understand that whatever mistakes she may make, they are those of youth and independence. She is only a motherless girl who has been allowed - who, in a certain way, has been obliged - to look after herself. I've noticed that underneath her self-reliant manner she's very much a child."

"That's true."

"But I should never treat her as a child, except - except in one way."

"Which would be - ?"

"To give her plenty of affection."

"She's always had that."

"Yes, yours; she hasn't had her mother's. Don't think me cruel in saying it, but no girl can grow up nourished only by her father's love, and not miss something that the good God intended her to have. The reason women are so essential to babies and men is chiefly because of their faculty for understanding the inarticulate. With all your daughter has had, there is one great thing that she hasn't had; and if you had placed me near her, my idea, which I call vague, would have been - as far as any one could do it now - to supply her with some of that."

Derek retreated again to the fireside, alarmed by a language suspiciously like that he had heard on other occasions concerning the motherless condition of his child. Was it going to turn out that all women were alike? There had been minutes during the last half-hour when, as he looked into Diane's face, it seemed to him that here at last was one as honest as air and as straightforward as light. But no experienced woman of the world, as she declared herself to be, could forget that this was a ludicrously delicate topic with a widower. She must either avoid it altogether, or expose herself to misinterpretation in pursuing it. It took him a few minutes to perceive that Diane had chosen the latter course, and had done it with a fine disdain of anything he might choose to think. She was not of the order of women who hesitate for petty considerations, or who stoop to small manoeuvrings.

"I'm afraid I must go now," she said, when he had stood some time without speaking.

"Don't go yet. Sit down."

His tone was still one of command, but not of the same quality of command as that which he had used on her entry. He brought her a chair, and she seated herself again.

"You said just now," he began, resuming his former attitude, with his arm on the mantelpiece, "that you didn't expect me to be so definite. Suppose I had been indefinite; then what would you have done?"

"I should have been indefinite, too."

"That's all very well; but, you see, I have to look at things from the point of view of business."

"And is there never anything indefinite in business?"

"Not if we can help it."

"And what happens when you can't help it?"

"Then we have to look for some one to whose discretion we can trust."

"Exactly; and, if you'll allow me to say it, Miss Pruyn is at an age and in a position where she needs a friend armed with discretion rather than authority."

"Well, suppose we were agreed about everything - the discretion and all - what would you begin by doing?"

"I shouldn't begin by doing anything. I should try to win your daughter's confidence; and if I couldn't do that I should go away."

"So that in the end it might happen that nothing would be accomplished."

"It might happen so. I shouldn't expect it. Good hearts are generally sensitive to good influences; and beneath her shell of manner Miss Pruyn strikes me as neither more nor less than a dear little girl."

Again he was suspicious of a bid for favor; but again Diane's air of almost haughty honesty negatived the thought.

"I'm glad you see that," was the only comment he made. "But," he added, once more taking a step or two toward her, "when you had won her confidence, then you would do things that I suggested, wouldn't you?"

"I shouldn't have to. She would probably do them herself, and a great deal better than you or I."

"I don't see how you can be sure of that. If you don't make her - "

"When you've watered your plant and kept it in the sunshine you don't have to make it bloom. It will do that of itself."

"But all these young men? - and this young Wappinger - ?"

"I should let them alone."

"Not young Wappinger!"

"What harm is he doing? I admit that the present situation has its foolish aspects from your point of view and mine; but I can think of things a great deal worse. At least you know there is nothing clandestine going on; and young people who have the virtue of being open have the very first quality of all. If you let them alone - or leave them to sympathetic management - you will probably find that they will outgrow the whole thing, as children outgrow an inordinate love of sweets."

There was a brief pause, during which he stood looking down at her, a smile something like that of amusement hovering about his lips.

"So that, in your judgment," he began again, "the whole thing resolves itself into a matter of discretion. But now - if you'll pardon me for asking anything so blunt - how am I to know that you would be discreet?"

For an instant she lifted her eyes to his, as if begging to be spared the reply.

"If it's not a fair question - " he began.

"It *is* a fair question," she admitted; "only it's one I find difficult to answer. If it wasn't important - urgently important - that I should obtain work, I should prefer not to answer it at all. I must tell you that I haven't always been discreet. I've had to learn discretion - by bitter lessons."

"I'm not asking about the past," he broke in, hastily, "but

about the future."

"About the future one cannot say; one can only try."

"Then suppose we try it?"

His own words took him by surprise, for he had meant to be more cautious; but now that they were uttered he was ready to stand by them. Once more, as it seemed to him, he could detect the light of relief steal into her expression, but she made no response.

"Suppose we try it?" he said again.

"It's for you to decide," she answered, quietly. "My position places me entirely at the disposal of any one who is willing to employ me."

"So that this is better than nothing," he said, in some disappointment at her lack of enthusiasm.

"I shouldn't put it in that way," she smiled; "but then I shouldn't put it in any way, until I saw whether or not I gave you satisfaction. You must remember you're engaging an untried person; and, as I've told you, I have nothing in the way of recommendations."

"We will assume that you don't need them."

"It's a good deal to assume; but since you're good enough to do it, I can't help being grateful. Is there any particular time when you would like me to begin?"

"Perhaps," he suggested, drawing up a small chair and seating himself nearer her, "it would be best to settle the business part of our arrangement first. You must tell me frankly if there is anything in what I propose that you don't find satisfactory."

"I'm sure there won't be, " Diane murmured, faintly, with a

feeling akin to shame that any one should be offering to pay for such feeble services as hers. She was thankful that the winter dusk, creeping into the room, hid the surging of the hot color in her face, as Derek talked of sums of money and dates of payment. She did her best to pretend to give him her attention, but she gathered nothing from what he said. If she had any coherent thought at all, it was of the greatness, the force, the authority, of one who could control her future, and dictate her acts, and prescribe her duties, with something like the power of a god. In times past she would have tried to weave her spell around this strong man, in sheer wantonness of conquest, as Vivian threw her enchantments over Merlin; now she was conscious only of a strange willingness to submit to him, to take his yoke, and bow down under it, serving him as master.

She was glad when he ended, leaving her free to rise and say his arrangements suited her exactly. She had promised to join Miss Lucilla van Tromp and Mrs. Eveleth at tea, and perhaps he would come with her.

"No, I'll run away now," he said, accompanying her to the door, "if you'll be good enough to make my excuses to Lucilla. But one word more! You asked me when you had better begin. I should say as soon as you can. As I may leave for Rio de Janeiro at any time, it would be well for things to be in working order before I go."

So it was settled, and as she departed he opened the door for her and held out his hand. But once more the little black muff came into play, and Diane walked out as she had come in, with no other salutation than a dignified inclination of the head.

Derek closed the door behind her and stood with his hand on the knob. He took the gentle rebuke like a man.

"I'm a cad," he said to himself. "I'm a cad."

Returning to his former place on the hearth, he remained long, gazing into the dying embers, and rehearsing the points of the interview in his mind. The gloaming closed around him, and he took pleasure in the fancy that she was still sitting there - silent, patient, erect, with that pinched look of privation so gallantly borne.

"By Jove! she's a brave one!" he murmured, under his breath. "She's a brick. She's a soldier. She's a lady. She's the one woman in the world to whom I could intrust my child."

Then, as his head sank in meditation, he shook himself as though to wake up from sleep into actual day.

"I've been dreaming," he said - "I've been dreaming. I must get away. I must go back to the office. I must get to work."

But instead of going he threw himself into one of the deep arm-chairs. Dropping off into a reverie, he conjured up the scene which had long been the fairest in his memory.

It was the summer. It was the country. It was a garden. In the long bed the carnations of many colors were bending their beauty-drunken heads, while over them a girl was stooping. She picked one here, one there, in search of that which would suit him best. When she had found it - deep red, with shades in the inner petals nearly black - she turned to offer it. But when she looked at him, he saw it was - Diane.

VIII

It had apparently been decreed that Derek Pruyn was not to go to South America that year. On more than one occasion he had been delayed on the eve of sailing. From February the voyage was postponed to May, and from May to September. In September it had ceased for the moment to be urgent, while remaining a possibility. It was the February of a year later before it became a definite necessity no longer to be put off.

In the mean while, under the beneficent processes of time, sunshine, and Diane Eveleth's cultivation, Miss Dorothea Pruyn had become a "bud." The small, hard, green thing had unfolded petals whose delicacy, purity, and fragrance were a new contribution to the joy of living. Society in general showed its appreciation, and Derek Pruyn was proud.

He was more than proud; he was grateful. The development that had changed Dorothea from a forward little girl into a charming maiden, and which might have been the mere consequence of growth, was to him the evident fruit of Diane's influence. The subtle differences whereby his own dwelling was transformed from a handsome, more or less empty, shell into an abode of the domestic amenities sprang, in his opinion, from a presence shedding grace. All the more strange was it, therefore, that both presence and influence remained as remote from his own personal grasp as music on the waves of sound or odors in the air. Of the many impressions produced by a year of Diane's residence beneath his roof, none perplexed him more than her detachment. Moreover, it was a detachment as difficult to comprehend in quality as to define in words. There was in her attitude nothing of the retreating nymph or of the self-effacing sufferer. She took her place equally without obtrusiveness and without affectation. Such effects as she brought about came without noise, without effort, and without laboriousness of good intention. Simple and straightforward in all her ways, she nevertheless contrived to throw into her relations with himself an element as impersonal as sunshine.

In the first days of her coming it was he who, in pursuance of his method of reserve, had held aloof. He had been frequently absent from New York, and, even when there, had lived much at one or another of his clubs. Weeks had already passed when the perception stole on him that his goings and comings meant little more to her than to the trees waving in the great Park before his door.

The discovery that he had been taking such pains to abstract himself from eyes which scarcely noticed whether he was there or not brought with it a little bitter raillery at his own expense. He was piqued at once in his self-love and in his masculine instinct for domination. It seemed to be out of the natural order of things that his thoughts should dwell so much on a woman to whom he was only a detail in the scheme of her surroundings - superior to the butler, and more animate than the pictures on the wall, but as little in her consciousness as either. It was certainly an easy opportunity in which to display that self-restraint which he had undertaken to make his portion; but when the heroic nature finds no obstacles to overcome, it has a tendency to create them.

Without obtruding himself upon Diane, Derek began to dine more frequently at his own house. On those occasions when Dorothea went out alone it was impossible for the two who remained at home to avoid a kind of conversation, which, with the topics incidental to the management of a common household, often verged upon the intimate. When Diane accompanied his daughter to the opera, he adopted the habit of dropping into the box, and perhaps taking them, with some of Dorothea's friends, to a restaurant for supper. He planned the little parties and excursions for which Dorothea's "budding" offered an excuse; and, while he recognized the subterfuge, he made his probable journey, with the long absence it would involve, serve as a palliation. Since, too, there was no danger to Diane, there could be the less reason for stinting himself in the pleasure of her presence, so long as he was prepared to pay for it afterward in full.

Thus the first winter had gone by, until with the shifting of the environment in summer a certain change entered into the situation. The greater freedom of country life on the Hudson made it requisite that Diane should be more consciously circumspect. In her detachment Derek noticed first of all a new element of intention; but since it was the first sign she had given of distinguishing between him and the dumb creation, it did not displease him. While he could not affirm that she avoided him, he saw less of her than when in town. During those difficult moments when they had no guests and Dorothea was making visits among her friends, Diane found pretexts for slipping away to New York, on what she declared to be business of her own - availing herself of the seclusion of the little French hostelry that had first given her shelter.

It was at times such as these that Derek began to perceive what she had become to him. As long as she was near him he could keep his feelings within the limitations he had set for them; but in her absence he was restless and despondent till she returned. The brutality of life, which made him master of the beauty of the country and the coolness of the hills, while it drove her to stifle in the town, stirred him with alternate waves of indignation and compassion.

There was a torrid afternoon in August when the sight of her, trudging along the dusty highway to the station, almost led him to betray himself by his curses upon fate. Dorothea having left for Newport in the morning, Diane was, as usual, seeking the privacy of University Place for the two weeks the girl's visit was to last. Understanding her desire not to be alone with him for even a few hours when there was no third person in the house, Derek had taken the opportunity to motor for lunch to a friend's house some miles away. With the intention of not returning till after she had gone, he had ordered a carriage to be in readiness to drive her to her train; but his luncheon was scarcely ended when the thought occurred to him that, by hurrying back, he might catch a last glimpse of her before she started.

He had already half smothered her in dust when he perceived that the little woman in black, under a black parasol, was actually Diane. To his indignant queries as to why she should be plodding her way on foot, with this scorching sun overhead, her replies were cheerful and uncomplaining. A series of small accidents in the stable - such had constantly happened at her own little chateau in the Oise - having made it inadvisable to take the horses out, one of the men had conveyed her luggage to the station, while she herself preferred to walk. She was used to the exigencies of country life, in both France and Ireland; and as for the heat, it was a detail to be scorned. Dust, too, was only matter out of place, and a necessary concomitant of summer. Would he not drive on, without troubling himself any more about her?

No; decidedly he would not. She must get in and let him take her to the station. There he could work off his wrath only by buying her ticket and seeing to her luggage; while his charge to the negro porter to look to her comfort was of such a nature that during the whole of the journey she was pelted with magazine literature and tormented with glasses of ice-water.

That night he found himself impelled by his sense of honor as a gentleman to write a letter of apology for the indignity she had been exposed to while in his house. When it had gone he considered it insufficient, and only the reflection that he ought to have business in town next day kept him from following it up with a second note.

Arrived in New York, where the city was burning as if under a sun-glass, he found his chief subject for consideration to be the choice of a club at which to lunch. There, in the solitude of the deserted smoking-room, where the heat was tempered, the glare shut out, and the very footfall subdued, he thought of the little hotel in University Place. Because human society had mysterious unwritten laws, the woman he loved was forced to steal away from the freshness and peace of green fields and sweeping river, to take refuge amid the noisome ugliness from which, in spite of her courage, her exquisite nature must shrink. He, whose needs were simple, as his tastes were comparatively coarse, could command the sybaritic luxury of a Roman patrician, while she, who could not lift her hand without betraying the habits of inborn refinement, was exposed not only to vulgar contact, but to a squalor of discomfort as odious as vice. The thought was a humiliation. Even if he had not loved her, it would have seemed almost the duty of a man of honor to step in between her and the cruel pathos of her lot.

It was a curious reflection that it was the very fact that he did love her which held him back. Could he have turned toward Paradise and said to the sweet soul waiting for him there, "This woman has need of me, but you alone reign in my heart," he would have felt more free to act. But the time when that would have been possible had gone by. Anything he might do now would be less for her need than his own; and his own he could endure if loyalty to his past demanded it. None the less was it necessary to find a way in which to come to Diane's immediate relief; and by the time he had finished his cigar he thought he had discovered it.

"Having been obliged to run up to town," he explained, when she had received him in the little hotel parlor, "I've dropped in to tell you that I'm going away for a few weeks into Canada."

"Isn't it rather hot weather for travelling?" she asked, with that clear, smiling gaze which showed him at once that she had seen through his pretext for coming.

"It won't be hot where I'm going - up into the valley of

the Metapedia."

"It's rather a sudden decision, isn't it?"

"N - no. I generally try to get a little sport some time during the year."

"Naturally you know your own intentions best. I only happen to remember that you said, yesterday morning, you hoped not to leave Rhinefields till the middle of next month."

"Did I say that? I must have been dreaming?"

"Very likely you were. Or perhaps you're dreaming now."

"Not at all; in fact, I'm particularly wide awake. I see things so clearly that I've looked in to tell you some of them. You must get out of this stifling hole and go back to Rhinefields at once."

"I don't like that way of speaking of a place I've become attached to. It isn't a stifling hole; it's a clean little inn, where the service is the very law of kindness. The art may be of a period somewhat earlier than the primitive," she laughed, looking round at the highly colored chromos of lake and mountain scenery hanging on the walls, "and the furniture may not be strictly in the style of Louis Quinze, but the host and hostess treat me as a daughter, and every garcon is my slave."

"I can quite understand that; but all the same it's no fit place for you."

"I suppose the fittest place for any one is the place in which he feels at home."

"Don't say that," he begged, with sudden emotion in his voice.

"I think I ought to say it," she insisted, "first of all because it's true; and then because you would feel more at ease about me if you knew just how it's true."

"You know that I'm not at ease about you."

"I know you think I must be discontented with my lot, when - in a certain sense - I'm not at all so. I don't pretend that I prefer working for a living to having money of my own; but I've found this" - she hesitated, as if thinking out her phrase - "I've found that life grows richer as it goes on, in whatever way one has to live it. It's as if the streams that fed it became more numerous the farther one descended from the height."

"I'm glad you're able to say that - "

"I can say it very sincerely; and I lay stress upon it, because I know you're kind enough to be worried about me. I wish I could make you understand how little reason there is for it, though you mustn't think that I'm not touched by it, or that I mistake its motive. I've come to see that what I've often heard, and used scarcely to believe, is quite true, that American men have an attitude toward women entirely different from that of our men. Our men probably think more about women than any other men in the world; but they think of them as objects of prey - with joys and sorrows not to be taken seriously. You, on the contrary, are willing to put yourself to great inconvenience for me, merely because I am a woman."

"Not merely because of that," Derek permitted himself to say.

"We needn't weigh motives as if they were golddust. When we have their general trend we have enough. I only want you to see that I understand you, while I must ask you not to be hurt if I still persist in not availing myself of your courtesy. I wish you wouldn't question me any more about it, because there are situations in which one cheapens things by the very effort to put them into words. If you were a woman, you'd comprehend my feeling - "

"Let us assume that I do, as it is. I have still another suggestion to make. Admitting that I stay at Rhinefields, why can't you ask your mother-in-law to come and make you a couple of weeks' visit there?"

For a moment Diane forgot the restraint she made it a habit to impose upon herself in the new conditions of her life, and slipped back into the spontaneous manner of the past.

"How tiresome you are! I never knew any one but a child twist himself in so many directions to get his own way."

"You see, I'm accustomed to having my own way. You ought not to think of resisting me."

"I'm not resisting you; I'm only eluding your grasp. There's one great obstacle to what you've just been good enough to propose: my mother-in-law couldn't come. Miss Lucilla van Tromp couldn't spare her. As a matter of fact, she - Miss Lucilla - asked me to go to Newport and stay with her all the time Dorothea is with the Prouds; but I declined the invitation. You see now that I don't lack cool and comfortable quarters because I couldn't get them."

"I see," he nodded. "You evidently prefer - this."

"I'll tell you what I prefer: I prefer a breathing-space in which to commune with my own soul."

"You could commune with your own soul at Rhinefields."

"No, I couldn't. It's an exercise that requires not only solitude and seclusion, but a certain withdrawal from the world. If I were in France, I should go and spend a fortnight in my old convent at Auteuil; but in this country the nearest approach I can make to that is to be here where I am. After all that has happened in the last year and more, I am trying to find myself again, so to speak - I'm trying to re-establish my identity with the Diane de la Ferronaise, who seems to me to have faded back into the distant twilight of time. Won't you let me do it in my own way, and ask me no more questions? Yes; I see by your face that you will; and we can be friends again. Now," she added, briskly, springing up and touching a bell, "you're going to have some of my iced coffee. I've taught them to make it, just as I used to have it at the Mauconduit - that was our little place near Compiegne - and I know you'll find it refreshing."

It was half an hour later, while he was taking leave of her, that a thought occurred to him which promised to be fruitful of new resources.

"Very well," he declared, as they were parting, "if you persist in staying here, I, too, shall persist in looking in whenever I come to town - which will have to be pretty often just now - to see that you're not down with some sort of fever."

"But," she laughed, "I thought you were going away - to Canada?"

"I'm not obliged to; and you've rather succeeded in dissuading me."

"Then let me succeed in dissuading you from everything. Don't come here again - please don't."

"I certainly shall."

"I'm generally out."

"In that case I shall stay till you come in."

"Of course I can't keep you from doing that. I will only say that the American man I've had in mind for the past few months - wouldn't."

The fact that he did not go back to University Place, either on this or any subsequent occasion when she thought it well to withdraw there, emphasized his helplessness to aid her. By the time autumn returned, and the household was once more settled in town, he had grown aware that between Diane and himself there was an impalpable wall of separation, which he could no more pass than he could transcend the veil between material existence and the Unseen World. He began to perceive that what he had called detachment of manner, more or less purposely maintained, was in reality an element in the situation which from the beginning had precluded friendship. Diane and he could not be friends in any of the ordinary senses of the word. As employer and employed their necessary dealings might be friendly; but to anything more personal, under the present arrangement, there was attached the impossible condition of stepping off from terra firma into space.

The obvious method of putting their mutual relationship on a basis richer in future potentialities Derek still felt himself unable to adopt of his own initiative act. The vow which bound him to his dead wife was one from which circumstances - and not merely his own fiat - must absolve him; but as winter advanced it seemed to him that life had begun to speak on the subject with a voice of imperative command.

It was the middle of January, when a small, accidental happening drew all his growing but still debatable intentions into one sharp point of resolution. It was such an afternoon as comes rarely, even in the exhilarating winter of New York - an afternoon when the unfathomable blue of the sky overhead runs through all the gamut of tones from lavender to indigo; when the air has the living keenness of that which the Spirit first breathed into the nostrils of man; when the rapture of the heart is that of neither passion, wine, nor nervous excitement, but comes nearer the exaltation of deathless youth in a deathless world than anything else in a temporary earth. It was a day on which even the jaded heart is in the mood to begin all over again, in renewed pursuit of the happiness which up to now has been elusive. To Derek, whose heart was by no means jaded, it was a day on which the instinctive hope of youth, which he supposed he had outlived, proved itself of one essence with the conscious passion of maturity.

When, as he walked homeward along Fifth Avenue, he overtook Diane, also making her way homeward, the happy occurrence seemed but part of the general radiance permeating life. The chance meeting on the neutral ground of out-of-doors took Diane by surprise; and before she had time to put up her guards of reserve she had betrayed her youth in a shy heightening of color. Under the protection of the cheerful, slowly moving crowd she felt at liberty to drop for a minute the subdued air of his daughter's paid companion, and in her replies to what he said she spoke with some of her old gayety of verve. It was an unfortunate moment in which to yield to this temptation, for it was, perhaps, the only occasion since her coming to New York on which she was closely observed.

Engrossed as they were, the one with the other, they had insensibly relaxed their pace, becoming mere strollers on the outside edge of the throng. The sense of being watched came to both of them at once, and, looking up at the same moment, they saw, approaching at a snail's pace, an open Victoria, in which were two ladies, to whom they were objects of plainly expressed interest. The elder was an insignificant little woman, who looked as though she were being taken out by her costly furs, while the younger was a girl of some two or three and twenty, of a type of beauty that would have been too imperious had it not been toned down by that air which to the unintelligent means boredom, though the wise know it to spring from something gone amiss in life. Both ladies kept their eyes fixed so exclusively on Diane that they had almost passed before remembering to salute Derek with a nod.

"I've seen those ladies somewhere," Diane observed, when they had gone by.

"I dare say. They've probably seen you, too. The elder is Mrs. Bayford, sister of Mr. Grimston, my uncle's partner in Paris. The girl is Marion Grimston, his daughter."

"I remember perfectly now. They used to come to our charity sales, and - and - anything of that kind."

Pruyn laughed.

"Anything, you mean, that was open to all comers. Mrs. Grimston would be flattered."

"I didn't mean to speak slightingly," she hastened to say. "There were plenty of nice people in Paris whom I didn't know."

"And plenty, I imagine, who thought you ought to have known them. Mrs. Grimston, and Mrs. Bayford, too, would have been among that number."

"Well, you see I do know them - by sight. I recall Miss Grimston especially. She's so handsome."

"I shall tell her that to-night."

"To-night?"

"Yes; it's with them that Dorothea and I are dining. The name conveying nothing to you, you probably didn't remember it. The fact is that, as Mrs. Bayford is the sister of my uncle's partner - my partner, too - I make it a point to be very civil to her twice a year - once when I dine with her, and once when she dines with me. The annual festivals have been delayed this season because she has only just returned from a long visit to Japan and India, with Marion in her wake."

There had been so much to say which, in the glamour of that glorious afternoon, was more important that no further time was spent on the topic. Derek forgot the meeting till Mrs. Bayford recalled it to him as he sat beside her in the evening. She was one of those small, ill-shapen women whose infirmities are thrown into more conspicuous relief by dress and jewels and *decolletage*. Seated at the head of her table, she produced the impression of a Goddess of Discord at a feast of well-meaning, hapless mortals.

"I want a word with you," she said, parenthetically, to Derek, on her left, before turning her attention to the more important neighbor on her right.

"One is scant measure," he laughed, in reply, "but I must be grateful even for that."

It was the middle of dinner before she took notice of him again, but when she did she plunged into her subject boldly.

"I suppose you didn't think I knew who you were walking with this afternoon?"

"Yes, I did, because the lady recognized you. She said you and Mrs. Grimston were among the nice people in Paris whom she hadn't met - but whom she knew very well by sight."

If Derek thought this reply calculated to appease an angry deity, he discovered his mistake.

"Did she have the indecency to say she hadn't met me?"

"I think she did; but she probably didn't know that the word indecency could apply to anything connected with you."

"Why, I was introduced to her four times in one season!"

"I suppose she hasn't as good a memory as yours."

"Oh, as for that, it wasn't a matter of memory. Nobody was permitted to forget her - she was quite notorious."

"I've always heard that in Paris the mere possession of beauty is enough to keep any one in the public eye."

"It wasn't beauty alone - if she *has* beauty; though for my part I can't see it."

"It *is* of rather an elusive quality."

BASIL KING

"It must be. But if it exists at all, I can tell you that it's of a dangerous quality."

"Hasn't that always been the peculiarity of beauty ever since the days of Helen of Troy?"

"I'm sure I can't say. I've always tried to steer clear of that sort of thing - "

"That must be an excellent plan; only it deprives one of the power of speaking as an authority, doesn't it?"

"I don't pretend to speak as an authority. If I say anything at all, it's what everybody knows."

"What everybody knows is generally - scandal."

"This was certainly scandal; but it wasn't the fact that everybody knew it that made it so."

"Then I'm sure you wouldn't wish to repeat it."

"I don't see why you should be sure of anything of the kind. I consider it my duty to repeat it."

"Then you won't be surprised if I consider it mine to contradict it."

"Certainly not. I shouldn't be surprised at anything you could do, Derek, after what I've heard since I came home."

"I won't ask you what that is - "

"No; your own conscience must tell you. No one can go on as you've been doing, and not know he must be talked about."

"I've always understood that that was more flattering than to be ignored."

"It depends. There's such a thing as receiving that sort of flattery first, only to be ignored in the sequel. I speak as your friend, Derek - "

"I thoroughly understand that; but may I ask if it's in the way of warning or of threat?"

"It's in the way of both. You must see that, whatever risks I may be prepared to run myself, as long as I have Marion with me I can't expose her to - "

"To what?"

Notwithstanding his efforts to keep the conversation to a tone of banter, acrimonious though it had to be, Derek was unable to pronounce the two brief syllables without betraying some degree of anger. Glancing up at him as she shrank under her weight of jewels, Mrs. Bayford found him very big and menacing; but she was a brave woman, and if she shrivelled, it was only as a cat shrivels before springing at a mastiff.

"I can't expose her to the chance of meeting - "

She paused, not from hesitation, but with the rhetorical intention of making the end of her phrase more telling.

"My future wife," he whispered, before she had time to go on. "It's only fair to tell you that."

"Good heavens! You're not going to marry the creature!"

Mrs. Bayford brought out the words with the dramatic action and intensity they deserved. In the hum of talk around and across the table it was doubtful whether or not they were heard, and yet more than one of the guests glanced up with a look of interrogation. Dorothea caught her father's eyes in a gaze which he had some difficulty in returning with the proper amount of steadiness; but Mrs. Berrington Jones came to the rescue of the company by asking Mrs. Bayford to tell the amusing story of how her bath had been managed in Japan.

So the incident passed by, leaving a sense of mystery in the air; though for Derek, all sense of annoyance disappeared in the knowledge that he was Diane's champion.

He was thinking over the incident in the luxurious semi-darkness of the electric brougham as they were going home-ward, when the clear voice of Dorothea broke in on his meditation.

"Are you going to be married, father?"

The question could not be a surprise to him after the occurrence at the table, but he was not prepared to give an affirmative answer on the spur of the moment.

"What makes you ask?" he inquired, after a second's reflection.

"I heard what Mrs. Bayford said."

"And how should you feel if I were?"

"It would depend."

"On what?"

"On whether or not it was any one I liked."

"That's fair. And if it was some one whom you did like?"

"Then it would depend on whether or not it was - Diane."

"And if it was Diane?"

"I should be very glad."

"Why?"

She slipped her arm through his and snuggled up to him.

"Oh, for a lot of reasons. First, because I've always supposed you'd be getting married one day; and I've been terribly afraid you'd pick out some one I couldn't get along with."

"Have I ever shown any symptom to justify that alarm?"

"N - no; but you never can tell - with a man."

"Can you be any surer with a woman?"

"No; and that's one of my other reasons. I'm not very sure about myself."

"You don't mean that it's to be young Wap - ?" he began, uneasily.

"I suppose it will have to be he - or some one else. They keep at me."

"And you don't know how long you may be able to hold out."

"I'm holding out as well as I can," she laughed, "but it can't go on forever. And then - if I do - "

"Well - what?"

"You'd be left all alone, and, of course, I should be worried about that - unless you - you - "

"Unless I married some one."

"No; not some one; no one - but Diane."

They were now at their own door, but before she sprang out she drew down his face to hers and kissed him.

IX

During the succeeding week Derek Pruyn, having practically announced an engagement which did not exist, found himself in a somewhat ludicrous situation. Too proud to extort a promise of secrecy from Mrs. Bayford, he knew the value of his indiscretion - if indiscretion it were - to any purveyor of tea-table gossip; and while Diane and he remained in the same relative positions he was sure it was being bruited about, with his own authority, that they were to become man and wife. It did not diminish the absurdity of the situation that he was debarred from proposing and settling the affair at once by the grotesque fact that he actually had not time.

There was certainly little opportunity for lovemaking in those hurried days of preparing for his long absence in South America. He was often obliged to leave home by eight in the morning, rarely returning except to go wearily to bed. Though nothing had been said to him, he had more than one reason for suspecting that Mrs. Bayford was at work; and, at the odd minutes when he saw Diane, it seemed to him as if her clearness of look was extinguished by an expression of perplexity.

He would have reproached himself more keenly for his lack of energy in overcoming obstacles had it not been for the fact that, owing to their peculiar position as members of one household, and that household his, he was planning to ask Diane to become his wife on that occasion when he would also be bidding her adieu. She would thus be spared the difficulties of a trying situation, while she would have the season of his absence in which to adjust her mind to the revolution in her life. He resolved to adhere to this intention, the more especially as a small family dinner at Gramercy Park, from which he was to go directly to his steamer, would give him the exact combination of circumstances he desired.

When, after dinner, Miss Lucilla's engineering of the company allowed him to find himself alone with Diane in the library, he made her sit down by the fireside, while he stood, his arm resting on the mantelpiece, as on the afternoon of their first serious interview, over a year before. As on that other occasion, so, too, on this, she sat erect, silent, expectant, waiting for him to speak. What was coming she did not know; but she felt once more his commanding dominance, with its power to ordain, prescribe, and regulate the conditions of her life.

"Doesn't this make you think of - our first long talk together?"

"I often think of it," Diane said, faintly, trying to assume that they were entering on an ordinary conversation. "As you didn't agree with me - "

"I do now," he said, quickly. "I see you were right, in everything. I want to thank you for what you've done for Dorothea - and for me. I didn't dream, a year ago, that the change in both of us could be so great."

"Dorothea was a sweet little girl, to begin with - "

"Yes; but I don't want to talk about that now. She will express her own sense of gratitude; but in the mean while I want to tell you mine. You will understand something of its extent when I say that I ask you to be my wife."

Diane neither spoke nor looked at him. The only sign she gave of having heard him was a slight bowing of the head, as of one who accepts a decree. The first few instants' stillness had the ineffable quality which might spring from the abolition of time when bliss becomes eternity. There was a space, not to be reckoned by any terrestrial counting, during which each heart was caught up into wonderful spheres of emotion - on his side the relief of having spoken, on hers the joy of having heard; and though it passed swiftly it was long enough to give to both the vision of a new heaven and a new earth. It was a vision that never faded again from the inward sight of either, though the mists of mortal error began creeping over it at once.

"If I take you by surprise - " he began, as he felt the clouds of reality closing round him.

"No," she broke in, still without looking up at him; "I heard you intended to ask me."

Though he made a little uneasy movement, he knew that this was precisely what she might have been expected to say.

"I thought you had possibly heard that," he said, in her own tone of quiet frankness, "and I want to explain to you that what happened was an accident."

"So I imagined."

"If I spoke of you as my future wife, I must ask you to believe that it was in the way of neither ill-timed jest nor foolish boast."

"You needn't assure me of that, because I could never have thought so. If I want assurance at all it's on other points."

"If I can explain them - "

"I can almost explain them myself. What I require is rather in the way of corroboration. Wasn't it much as the knight of old threw the mantle of his protection over the shoulders of a distressed damsel?"

"I know what you mean; but I don't admit the justice of the simile."

"But if you did admit it, wouldn't it be something like what actually occurred?"

"You're putting questions to me," he said, smiling down at her; "but you haven't answered mine."

"I must beg leave to point out," she smiled, in return, "that you haven't asked me one. You've only stated a fact - or what I presume to be a fact. But before we can discuss it I ought to be possessed of certain information; and you've put me in a position where I have a right to demand it."

After brief reflection Derek admitted that. As nearly as he could recall the incident at Mrs. Bayford's dinner-party, he recounted it.

"You see," he explained, in summing up, "that, as a snobbish person, she could hardly be expected to forgive you for forgetting her, when she had been introduced to you four times in a season. She not unnaturally fancied you forgot her on purpose, so to speak - "

"I suppose I did," she murmured, penitently.

"What?" he asked, with sudden curiosity. "Would you - "

"I wouldn't now. I used to then. Everybody did it, when people were introduced to us whom we didn't want to know. I've done it when it wasn't necessary even from that point of view - out of a kind of sport, a kind of wantonness. I've really forgotten about Mrs. Bayford now - everything except her face - but I dare say I remembered perfectly well, at the time. It would have been nothing unusual if I had."

"In that case," he said, slowly, "you can't be surprised - "

"I'm not," she hastened to say. "If Mrs. Bayford retaliates, now that she has the power, she's within her right - a right which scarcely any woman would forego. It was perfectly natural for

Mrs. Bayford to speak ill of me; and it was equally natural for you to spring to my defence. You'd have sprung to the defence of any one - "

"No, no," he interjected, hurriedly.

"Of any one whom you - respected, as I hope you respect me. You've offered me," she went on, her eyes filling with sudden tears - "you've offered me the utmost protection a man can give a woman. To tell you how deeply I'm touched, how sincerely I'm grateful, is beyond my power; but you must see that I can't avail myself of your kindness. Your very willingness to repeat at leisure what you said in haste makes it the more necessary that I shouldn't take advantage of your chivalry."

"Would that be your only reason for hesitating to become my wife?"

The deep, vibrant note that came into his voice sent a tremor through her frame, and she looked about her for support. He himself offered it by taking both her hands in his. She allowed him to hold them for a second before withdrawing behind the intrenched position afforded by the huge chair from which she had risen, and on the back of which she now leaned.

"It's the reason that looms largest," she replied - "so large as to put all other reasons out of consideration."

"Then you're entirely mistaken," he declared, coming forward in such a way that only the chair stood between them. "It's true that at Mrs. Bayford's provocation I spoke in haste, but it was only to utter the resolution I had taken plenty of time to form. If I were to tell you how much time, you'd be inclined to scorn me for my delay. But the truth is I'm no longer a very young man; in comparison with you I'm not young at all. You yourself, as a woman of the world, must readily understand that at my age, and in my position, prudence is as honorable an element in the offer I am making you as romance would be in a boy's. I make no apology for being prudent. I state the fact that I've been so only that you may know that I've tried to look at this question from every point of view - Dorothea's as well as yours and mine. I took my time about it, and long before I warned Mrs. Bayford that she was speaking of one who was dear to me, my mind was made up. With such hopes as I had at heart it would have been wrong to have allowed her to go on without a word of warning."

"I can see that it would have that aspect."

"Then, if you can see that, you must see that I speak to you now in all sincerity. My desire isn't new. I can truthfully say that, since the first day I saw you, your eyes and voice have haunted me, and the longing to be near you has never been absent from my heart. I'll be quite frank with you and say that, before you came here, it was my avowed intention not to marry again. Now I have no desire on earth - my child apart - so strong as to win you for my wife. The year we've spent under the same roof must have given you some idea of the man whom you'd be marrying; and I think I can promise you that with your help he would be a better man than in the past. Won't you say that I may hope for it?"

With arms supported by the high back of the chair and cheek on her clasped hands, she gazed away into the dimness of the room, as if waiting for him to continue; but during the silence that ensued it seemed to Derek as if a shadow crossed her features, while her bright look died out in a kind of wistfulness. She had, perhaps, been hoping for a word he had not spoken - a word whose absence he had only covered up by phrases.

"Well? Have you nothing to say to me?" he asked, when some minutes had gone by.

"I'm thinking."

"Of what?"

"Of what you say about prudence. I like it. It seems to me I ought to be prudent, too."

"Undoubtedly," he agreed, in the dry tone of one who assents to what he finds slightly disagreeable.

"I mean," she said, quickly, "that I ought to be prudent for you - for us all. There are a great many things to be thought of, things which people of our age ought not to let pass unconsidered. Men *think* the way through difficulties, while women *feel* it. I'm afraid I must ask for time to get my instincts into play."

"Do you mean that you can't give me an answer to-night - before I go on this long journey?"

"I couldn't give you an affirmative one."

"But you could say, No?"

"If you pressed the matter - if you insisted - that's what I should have to say."

"Why?"

"That would be - my secret."

"Is it that you think you couldn't love me?"

For the first time the color came to her cheek and surged up to her temples, not suddenly or hotly, but with the semi-diaphanous lightness of roseate vapor mounting into winter air. As he came nearer, rounding the protective barrier of the arm-chair, she retreated.

"I should have to solve some other questions before I could answer that," she said, trying to meet his eyes with the necessary steadiness.

"Couldn't I help you?"

She shook her head.

"Then couldn't you consider it first?"

"A woman generally does consider it first, but she speaks about it last."

"But you could tell me the result of what you think, as far as you've drawn conclusions?"

"No; because whatever I should say you would find misleading. If you're in earnest about what you say to-night, it would be better for us both that you should give me time."

"I'm willing to do that. But you speak as if you had a doubt of me."

"I've no doubt of you; I've only a doubt about myself. The woman you've known for the last twelve months isn't the woman other people have known in the years before that. She isn't the Diane Eveleth of Paris any more than she is the Diane de la Ferronaise of the hills of Connemara, or of the convent at Auteuil. But I don't know which is the real woman, or whether the one who now seems to me dead mightn't rise again."

"I shouldn't be afraid of her."

"But I should. You say that because you didn't know her; and I couldn't let you marry me without telling you something of what she was."

"Then tell me."

"No, not now; not to-night. Go on your long journey, and come back. When it's all over, I shall be sure - sure, that is, of myself - sure on the point about which I'm so much in doubt, as to whether or not the other woman could return."

"I should be willing to run the risk," he said, with a short laugh, "even if she did."

"But I shouldn't be willing to let you. You forget she ruined one rich man; she might easily ruin another."

"That would depend very much upon the man."

"No man can cope with a woman such as I was only a few years ago. You can put fetters on a criminal, and you can quell a beast to submission, but you can't bind the subtle, mischievous woman-spirit, bent on doing harm. It's more ruthless than war; it's more fatal than disease. You, with your large, generous nature, are the very man for it to fasten on, and waste him, like a fever."

She moved back from him, close to the bookshelves against the wall. The eyes which Derek had always seen sad and lustreless glowed with a fire like the amber's.

"You must understand that I couldn't allow myself to do the same thing twice," she hurried on, "and, if I married you, who knows but what I might? I'm not a bad woman by nature, but I think I must need to be held in repression. You'd be giving me again just those gifts of money, position, and power which made me dangerous."

"Suppose you were to let me guard against that?" he said.

"You couldn't. It would be like fighting a poisonous vapor with the sword. The woman's spell, whether for good or ill, is more subtle and more potent than anything in the universe but the love of God."

"I can believe that, and still be willing to trust myself to yours," he answered, gravely. "I know you, and honor you as men rarely do the women they marry, until the proof of the years has tried them. In your case the trial has come first. I've watched you bear it - watched you more closely than you've ever been aware of. I've stood by, and seen you carry your burden, when it was harder than you imagine not to take my part in it. I've looked on, and seen you suffer, when it was all I could do to keep from saying some word of sympathy you might have resented. But, Diane," he cried, his voice taking on a strange, peremptory sharpness, "I can't do it any longer! My power of standing still, while you go on with your single-handed fight, is at an end. If ever God sent a man to a woman's aid, He has sent me to yours; and you must let me do what I'm appointed for. You must come to me for comfort in your loneliness. You must come to me for care in your necessity. I have both care and comfort for you here; and you must come."

Without moving toward her he stood with open arms.

"Come!" he cried again, commandingly.

The tears coursed down her cheeks, but she gave no sign of obeying him, except to drag one hand from the protecting bookcase ledge, to which she seemed to cling.

"Come, Diane!" he repeated! "Come to me!"

The other hand fell to her side, while she gazed at him piteously, as though in reluctant submission to his will.

"Come!" he said once more, in a tone of authority mingled with appeal.

Drawn by a force she had no power to withstand, she took one slow, hesitating step toward him.

"I haven't yielded," she stammered. "I haven't consented. I can't consent - yet."

"No, dearest, no," he murmured, with arms yearning to her as she approached him; "nevertheless - come!"

X

Notwithstanding the fact that she had wept in his arms - wept as women weep who are brave in the hour of trial, only to break down in the moment of relief - Diane would give Derek Pruyn no other answer. She could not consent - yet. With this reply he was obliged to sail away, getting what comfort he might from its implications.

During the three months of his absence Diane took knowledge of herself, appraising her strength and probing her weakness. She was too honest not to own that there were desires in her nature which leaped into newness of life at the thought that there might again be means to support them. Diane de la Ferronaise was not dead, but sleeping. Her love of luxury and pleasure - her joy in jewels, equipage, and dress - her woman's elemental weaknesses, second only to the instinct for maternity - all these, grown lethargic from hunger, were ready to awake again at the mere possibility of food. She was forced to confront the fact that, with the same opportunities, she had it in her to go back to the same life. It was a humiliating fact, but it stared her in the face, that experience had shown her a creature for a man to be afraid of. Derek Pruyn had seen her subdued by circumstances, as the panther is subdued by famine; but it was not yet proved that the savage, preying thing was tamed.

There was only one force that would tame her; but there *was* that force, and Diane knew that she had submitted to its domination. From weeks of tortuous self-examination she emerged into this knowledge, as one comes out of a labyrinthine cavern into sunshine. Even here in the open, however, was a problem still to solve. Could she marry the man who had never told her that he loved her, even though she herself loved him? Had she the power to give herself without stint, while asking of him only what he chose to offer her? Would she, who had made men serve her, with little more than smiles for their reward, be content to serve in her own turn, getting nothing but a half-loaf for her heart's sustenance? She asked herself these questions, but put off answering them - waiting for him to force decision on her.

So the rest of the winter passed, and by the time Derek came back the hyacinths were fading from the gardens and parks, and the tulips were coming into bloom. To both Diane and Dorothea spring was bringing a new motive for looking forward together with a new comprehension of the human heart's capacity for joy.

Perhaps no day of their patient waiting was so long in passing as that on which it was announced to them that Derek Pruyn had landed that afternoon. He had sent word that he could not come home at once, as business required his immediate presence at the office. Having already exhausted their ingenuity in adorning the house, and putting everything he could possibly want in the place where he could most easily find it, there was nothing to do but to sit through the long hours in an impatience which even Diane found it difficult to disguise. The visits of the postman were welcomed as affording the additional task of arranging Derek's letters on the desk in the small, book-lined room specially devoted to his use; and when, in the evening, a cablegram arrived, Diane herself propped it in a conspicuous place, with a tiny silver dagger, for opening the envelope, beside it. The act, with its suggestion of intimate life, gave her a stealthy pleasure; and when Dorothea glided in and caught her sitting in Derek's own chair at the desk, she blushed like a school-girl detected in a crime. It was perhaps this acknowledgment of weakness that enabled Dorothea to speak out, and say what had been for some time on her mind.

"Diane," she asked, dropping among the cushions of a divan, "are you going to marry father?"

Diane felt the color receding from her face as suddenly as it had come, while she gained time in which to collect her astonished wits by putting the silver dagger down beside the telegram with needless exactitude before attempting a response.

"Do you remember what Sir Walter Scott said, in the days when the authorship of *Waverley* was still a secret, to the indiscreet people who asked him if he had written it? 'No,' he answered; 'but if I had I should give you the same reply.'"

"That means, I suppose, that you don't want to tell me?"

"It might be taken to imply something of the sort."

"As a matter of fact, I suppose it would be more delicate on my part not to ask you."

"I won't attempt to contradict you there."

"I shouldn't do it if I didn't wish you *were* going to marry him. I've wanted it a long time; but I want it more than ever now."

"Why more than ever now?"

"Because I expect to be married before very long myself."

"May I venture to inquire to which of the many - "

"To none of the many. There's never, really, been more than one."

"And his name - ?"

"Is Carli Wappinger."

"Oh, Dorothea!"

"That's just it. That's why I want you to marry father. I want to put a stop to the 'Oh, Dorotheas!' and you're the only person in the world who can help me do it."

"How?"

"I don't have to tell you that. It's one of the reasons why I rely on you so thoroughly that you always know exactly what to do without having to receive suggestions. I put myself in your hands entirely."

"You mean that you're going to marry a man to whom your father will be bitterly opposed, and you expect me to win his joyful benediction."

"That's about it," Dorothea sighed, from the depth of her cushions.

"Of course, I must be grateful to you, dear, for this display of confidence; but you won't be surprised if I find it rather overwhelming."

"I shall be very much surprised, indeed. I've never seen you find anything overwhelming yet; and you've been put in some difficult situations. You only have to *live* things in order to make other people take them for granted. You've never done anything to specially please father, and yet he listens to you as if you were an oracle. It's the same way with me. If any one had told me two years ago that I should ever come to praying for a stepmother I should have thought them crazy; and yet I have come to it, just because it's you."

After that it was not unnatural that Diane should go and sit on the divan beside Dorothea for any exchange of such confidences as could not be conveniently made from a distance. If she admitted anything on her own part, it was by implication rather than by direct assertion, and though she did not promise in words to come to the aid of the youthful lovers, she allowed the possibility that she would do so to be assumed.

So, in soft, whispered, broken confessions the evening slipped away more rapidly than the day had done, and by ten o'clock they knew he must be near. The last touch of welcome came when they passed from room to room, lighting up the big house in cheerful readiness for its lord's inspection. When all was done Dorothea stationed herself at a window near the street; while Diane, with a curious shrinking from what she had to face, took her seat in the remotest and obscurest corner in the more distant of the two drawingrooms. When the sound of wheels, followed by a loud ring at the bell, told her that he was actually at the door, she felt faint from the violence of her heart's beating.

Dorothea danced into the hail, with a cry and a laugh which were stifled in her father's embrace. Diane rose instinctively, waiting humbly and silently where she stood. At their parting she had torn herself, weeping and protesting, from his arms; but when he came in to find her now, he would see that she had yielded. The door was half open through which he was to pass - never again to leave her!

"Diane is in there."

It was Dorothea's voice that spoke, but the reply reached the far drawing-room only as a murmur of deep, inarticulate bass.

"What's the matter, father?"

Dorothea's clear voice rose above the noise of servants moving articles of luggage in the hall; but again Diane heard nothing beyond a confused muttering in answer. She wondered that he did not come to her at once, though she supposed there was some slight prosaic reason to prevent his doing so.

"Father" - Dorothea's voice came again, this time with a distinct note of anxiety - "father, you don't look well. Your eyes are bloodshot."

"I'm quite well, thank you," was the curt reply, this time perfectly audible to Diane's ears. "Simmons, you fool, don't leave those steamer rugs down here!"

Diane had never heard him speak so to a servant, and she knew that something had gone amiss. Perhaps he was annoyed that she had not come to greet him. Perhaps it was one of the duties of her position to receive him at the door. She had known him to give way occasionally to bursts of anger, in which a word from herself had soothed him. Leaving her place in the corner, she was hurrying to the hall, when again Dorothea's voice arrested her.

"Aren't you going in to see Diane?"

"No."

From where she stood, just within the door, Diane knew that he had flung the word over his shoulder as he went up the hail toward the stairway. He was going to his room without speaking to her. For an instant she stood still from consternation, but it was in emergencies like this that her spirit rose. Without further hesitation she passed out into the hall, just as Derek Pruyn turned at the bend in the staircase, on his way upward. For a brief second, as, standing below, she lifted her eyes to his in questioning, their glances met; but, on his part, it was without recognition.

XI

Half an hour after Derek's return Diane was summoned into his presence in the little room where she had arranged his letters in the afternoon. The door was standing open, and she went in slowly, her head high. She was dressed as when she had parted from him; and the whiteness of her neck and shoulders, free from jewels, collar, or chain, was the more brilliant from contrast with the severe line of black. In her pale face all expression was focussed into the pained inquiry of her eyes.

She entered so silently that he did not hear her, or lift his head from the hand on which it leaned wearily, as he rested his elbow on the desk. Pausing in the middle of the room, she had time to notice that he had opened a few of the letters lying before him, but had thrust them impatiently from him, evidently unread. The cablegram she had laid where his glance would immediately fall upon it was between his fingers, but the envelope was unbroken. His attitude was so much that of a man tired and dispirited that her heart went out to him.

It was perhaps the involuntary sigh that broke from her lips that caused him to look up. When he did so his eyes fixed themselves on her with a dazed stare, as though he wondered whence and for what she had come. In the eager attention with which she regarded him she noted subconsciously that he was unshaven and ill-kempt, and that his eyes, as Dorothea had said, were bloodshot.

He dragged himself to his feet, and with forced courtesy asked her to sit down. She allowed herself to sink mechanically to the edge of the divan where, only an hour ago, Dorothea and she had exchanged happy confidences. In the minutes of silence that followed, when he had resumed his own seat, she felt as if she were in some queer nightmare, where nothing could be explained.

"Did you ever hear of a young French explorer named Persigny?"

She nodded, without speaking. The irrelevancy of the question was in keeping with the odd horror of the dream.

"Did you know he was exploring in Brazil?"

"I think I may have heard so."

"He came up from Rio with me - on the same steamer."

She listened, with eyes fixed fast upon him, wondering what he meant.

"He wasn't alone," Derek went on, speaking in a lifeless monotone. "There were others of his party with him. There was one, especially, with whom I became on terms that were almost - intimate."

For the first time it occurred to her that he was trying to see through her thoughts; but in her bewilderment at his words, she met his gaze steadily.

"There was something about this young man that attracted me," he continued, in the same dull voice, "and I listened to his troubles. In particular he told me why he had fled from Paris to hide himself in the forests of the Amazon. Shall I tell you the reason?"

"If you like."

"It was an old story; in some respects a vulgar story. He had got into the toils of an unscrupulous woman."

Her sudden perception of what he was leading up to forced her into a little involuntary movement.

"I see you understand," he said, quickly, with the glimmer of a smile. "I thought you would; for, as a matter of fact, much of what he said brought back our conversation on the night before I sailed. There was not a little in it that was mystery to me at the time, which he - illumined."

She sat with lips parted and bosom heaving, her hands clasped tightly in her lap. If she was conscious of any sensation, it was of terrible curiosity to know how the tale was to be turned.

"What you said to me then," he pursued, in the same cruel quietness of tone - "what you said to me then, as to the influence of a bad woman in a man's life, seemed to me - what shall I say? - not precisely exaggerated, but somewhat over-wrought. I didn't know it could be so true to the actual facts of experience. My friend's words at times were almost an echo of your own. He had been the lover of a woman - "

Once more she started, raising her hand in silent protest against the words.

"He - had - been - the - lover - of - a - woman," he repeated, with slow emphasis, "who, after having ruined her husband's life, was preparing to ruin his. She would have ruined his as she had ruined the lives of other men before him. When he endeavored to elude her, she set on her husband to call him out. There was a duel - or the semblance of a duel. My friend fired into the air. The poor devil of a husband shot himself. It appears that he had every reason for doing so."

"My husband didn't shoot himself."

"Your husband?" he asked, with an ironical lifting of the eyebrows. "What makes you think I've been speaking of him?"

"The man whom you call your friend is the Marquis de Bienville - "

"He didn't mention your name; but I see you're able to tell me his. It's what I was afraid of. I've repeated only a very little of what he said; but since you recognize its truth already, it isn't necessary to continue."

She passed her hand over her forehead, with the gesture of one trying desperately to see aright.

"I must ask you to tell me plainly: Was I the - the unscrupulous woman into whose toils Monsieur de Bienville fell?"

"He didn't say so."

"Then why - why have you spoken of this to me?"

"Because what I heard from him fitted in so exactly with what I had heard from you that it made an entire story. It was like the two parts of a puzzle. The one without the other is incomplete and perplexing; but having both, you can see the perfect whole. I will be frank enough to tell you that many of your sayings were dark to me until I had his to lend them light."

"Would it be of any use to say that what he told you wasn't true?"

"I don't know that it would be of any use to say it, unless it could be proved."

"Did you ask him to give you proof?"

"No; because you had already provided me with that.

"How?"

"Surely you must remember telling me that you had ruined

one rich man, and might ruin another: that no man could cope with a woman such as you were two or three years ago. There were these things - there were other things - many other things - "

"And that's what you understood from them?"

"I understood nothing whatever. If I thought of such words at all, it was to attribute them to a morbid sensibility. It wasn't until I got their interpretation that they came back to me. It wasn't until I had met some one who knew you before I did, and better than I did - "

"It wasn't till then that you thought of me what no man ever thinks of a woman until he is ready to trample her in the mire, under his feet."

Straightening himself up, as a man who defends his position, he took an argumentative tone.

"What motive would Bienville have for lying? - to a stranger? - and about a stranger? There are moments when you know a man is telling you the truth, as if he were in the confessional. He wasn't speaking of you, but of himself. Not only were no names mentioned, but he had no reason to think I had ever heard of the woman he talked to me about, nor has he yet. If it hadn't been for your own half-hints, your own half-confessions, I doubt if I should ever have had more than a suspicion of - of - the truth."

"I could have explained everything," she said, with a break in her voice. "I've never concealed from you the fact that there was a time in my life when I was very indiscreet. I lived like the women of fashion around me. I was inconsiderate of other people. I did things that were wrong. But before I knew you I had repented of them."

"Quite so; but, unfortunately, what is conventionally known as a repentant woman is not the sort of person I would have chosen to be near my child."

She rose, wearily, dragging herself toward the desk. "Now that I've heard your opinion of me," she said, quietly, "I suppose you have no reason for detaining me any longer."

"Are you going away?" he asked, sharply.

"What else is there for me to do?"

"Have you nothing to say in your own defence?"

"You haven't asked me to say anything. You've tried and condemned me unheard. Since you adopt that method of justice I'm forced to abide by it. I'm not like a person who has rights or who can claim protection from any outside authority. You're not only judge and jury to me, but my final court of appeal. I must take what you mete out to me - and bear it."

"I don't want to be hard on you," he groaned.

"No; I can believe that. I dare say the situation is just as cruel for you as for me. When circumstances become so entangled that you can't explain them, everybody has to suffer."

"I'm glad you can do me that justice. My life for the past week - ever since Bienville began to talk to me - has been hell."

"I'm sorry for that. I'm sorry to have brought it on you. I'm afraid, too, that the future may be harder for you still; for no man can do a woman such wrong as you're doing me, and not pay for it."

"Wrong? Can you honestly say I'm doing you wrong, Diane? Isn't it true - you'll pardon me if I put my questions bluntly, the circumstances don't permit of sparing either your feelings or my own - isn't it true that for two or three years before your husband's death your name in Paris was nothing short of a byword?"

"I'm not sure of what you mean by a byword. I acknowledge that I braved public opinion, and that much ill was said of me - often, more than I deserved."

"Isn't it true that your name was connected with that of a man called Lalanne, and that he was killed in a duel on your account?"

"It's true that Monsieur Lalanne made love to me; it's also true that he was killed in a duel; but it's not true that it was on my account. The instance is an excellent illustration of the degree to which the true and the false are mixed in Parisian gossip - perhaps in all gossip - and a woman's reputation blasted. Unhappily for me, I felt myself young and strong enough to be indifferent to reputation. I treated it with the neglect one often bestows upon one's health - not thinking that there would come a day of reckoning."

"If there had been only one such case it might have been allowed to pass; but what do you say of De Cretteville? what of De Melcourt? What of Lord Wendover?"

"I have nothing to say but this: that for such scandal I've a rule, from which I have no intention of departing even now: I neither tell it, nor listen to it, nor contradict it. If it pleases the Marquis de Bienville to repeat it, and you to give it credence, I can't stoop to correct it, even in my own defence."

"God knows I'm not delving into scandal, Diane. If I bring up these miserable names, it's only that you may have the opportunity to right yourself."

"It's an opportunity impossible for me to use. If I were to attempt to unravel the strand of truth from the web of falsehood, it would end in your condemning me the more. The canons of conduct in France are so different from those in America that what is permissible in one country is heinous in the other. In the same way that your young girls shock our conceptions of propriety, our married women shock yours. It would be useless to defend myself in your eyes, because I should be appealing to a standard to which I was never taught to conform."

"I thought I had taken that into consideration. I'm not entirely ignorant of the conditions under which you've lived, and I meant to have allowed for them. But isn't it true that you exceeded the very wide latitude recognized by public opinion, even in a place like Paris?"

"I didn't take public opinion into account. I was reckless of its injustice, as I was careless of its applause. I see now, however, that indifference to either brings its punishment."

"Those are abstract ideas, and I'm trying to deal with concrete facts. Isn't it true that George Eveleth was a rich man when you married him, and that your extravagance ruined him?"

"It helped to ruin him. I plead guilty to that. I had no knowledge of the value of money; but I don't offer that as an excuse."

"Isn't it true that the Marquis de Bienville was your lover, and that you were thinking of deserting your husband to go with him?"

"It's true that the Marquis de Bienville asked me to do so, and that I was rash enough to turn him into ridicule. I shouldn't have done it if I had known that there was a man in the world capable of taking such a revenge upon a woman as he took on me."

"What revenge?"

"The revenge you're executing at this minute. He said - what very few men, thank God, will say of a woman, even when it's true, and what it takes a dastard to say when it's not true. Even in the case of the fallen woman there's a chivalrous human pity that protects her; while there's something more than that due to the most foolish of our sex who has not fallen. I took it for granted that, at the worst, I could count on that, until I met your friend. His cup of vengeance will be full when he learns that he has given you the power to insult me."

"I don't mean to insult you," he said, in a dogged voice, "but I mean, if possible, to know the truth."

"I'm not concealing it. I'm ready to tell you anything."

"Then, tell me this: isn't it the case that when George Eveleth discovered your relations with Bienville, he challenged him?"

"It's the case that he challenged him, not because of what he discovered, but of what Monsieur de Bienville said."

"At their encounter, didn't Bienville fire into the air - ?"

"I've never heard so."

"And didn't George Eveleth fall from a self-inflicted shot?"

"No. He died at the hand of the Marquis de Bienville."

"So you told me once before, though you didn't tell me the man's name. But, Diane, aren't you convinced in your heart that George Eveleth knew that which made his life no longer worth the living?"

"Do you mean that he knew something - about me?"

"Yes - about you."

"That's the most cruel charge Monsieur de Bienville has invented yet."

"Suppose he didn't invent it? Suppose it was a fact?"

" Have you any purpose in subjecting me to this

needless torture?"

"I have a purpose, and I'm sorry if it involves torture; but I assure you it isn't needless. I must get to the bottom of this thing. I've asked you to marry me; and I must know if my future wife - "

"But I'm not - your future wife."

"That remains to be seen. I can come to no decision - "

"But I can."

"That must wait. The point before us is this: Did, or did not, George Eveleth kill himself?"

"He did not."

"You must understand that it would prove nothing if he did."

"It would prove, or go far to prove, what you said just now - that I had made his life not worth the living."

"His money troubles may have counted for something in that. What it would do is this: it would help to corroborate Bienville's word against - yours."

"Fortunately there are means of proving that I'm right. I can't tell you exactly what they are; but I know that, in France, when people die the registers tell just what they died of."

"I've already sent for the necessary information. I've done even more than that. I couldn't wait for the slow process of the mails. I cabled this morning to Grimston, one of my Paris partners, to wire me the cause of George Eveleth's death, as officially registered. This is his reply."

He held up the envelope Diane had placed on the desk earlier in the evening.

"Why don't you open it?" she asked, in a whisper of suspense.

"I've been afraid to. I've been afraid that it would prove him right in the one detail in which I'm able to put his word to the test. I've been hoping against hope that you would clear yourself; but if this is in his favor - "

"Open it," she pleaded.

With the silver dagger she had laid ready to his hand he ripped up the envelope, and drew out the paper.

"Read it," he said, passing it to her, without unfolding it.

Though it contained but one word, Diane took a long time to decipher it. For minutes she stared at it, as though the power of comprehension had forsaken her. Again and again she lifted her eyes to his, in sheer bewilderment, only to drop them then once more on the all but blank sheet in her hand. At last it seemed as if her fingers had no more strength to hold it, and she let it flutter to the floor.

"He was right?"

The question came in a hoarse undertone, but Diane had no voice in which to reply. She could only nod her head in dumb assent.

It grew late, and Derek Pruyn still sat in the position in which Diane had left him. His hands rested clinched on the desk before him, while his eyes stared vacantly at the cluster of electric lights overhead. He was living through the conversations with Bienville on shipboard. He began with the first time he had noticed the tall, brown-eyed, black-bearded young Frenchman on the day when they sailed out of the harbor of Rio de Janeiro. He passed on to their first interchange of casual remarks, leaning together over the deck-rail, and watching the lights of Para recede into the darkness. It was in the hot, still evenings in the Caribbean Sea that, smoking in neighboring deck-chairs, they had first drifted into intimate talk, and the young man had begun to unburden himself. They had been distinctly interesting to Derek, these glimpses of a joyous, idle, light-o'-love life, with a tragic element never very far below its surface, so different from his own gray career of business. They not only beguiled the tedious nights, but they opened up vistas of romance to an imagination growing dull before its time, in the seriousness of large practical affairs. In proportion as the young Frenchman showed himself willing to narrate, Derek became a sympathetic listener. As Bienville told of his pursuit, now of this fair face, and now of that, Derek received the impression of a chase, in which the hunted engages not of necessity, but, like Atalanta, in sheer glee of excitement. Like Atalanta, too, she was apt to over-estimate her speed, and to end in being caught.

It was not till after he had recounted a number of *petites histoires*, more or less amusing, that Bienville came to what he called "*l'affaire la plus serieuse de ma vie*," while Derek drank in the tale with all the avidity the jealous heart brings to the augmentation of its pain. To the idealizing purity of his conception of Diane any earthly failing on her part became the extremity of sin. He had placed her so high that when she fell it was to no middle flight of guilt; as to the fallen angel, there was no choice for her, in his estimation, between heaven and the nether hell.

Outwardly he was an ordinary passenger, smoking quietly in a deck-chair, in order to pass the time between dinner and the hour for "turning in." His voice, as he plied Bienville with questions, betrayed his emotions no more than the darkened surface of the sea gave evidence of the raging life within its depths. To Bienville himself, during these idle, balmy nights, there was a threefold inspiration, which in no case called for strict exactitude of detail. There was, first, the pleasure of talking about himself; there was, next, the desire to give his career the advantage of a romantic light; and there was, thirdly, the story-teller's natural instinct to hold his hearer spellbound. The little more or the little less could not matter to a man whom he didn't know, in talking about a woman whose name he hadn't given; while, on the other hand, there was the satisfaction, to which the Latin is so sensitive, of showing himself a lion among ladies.

Moreover, he had boasted of his achievements so often that he had come to believe in them long before giving Derek the detailed account of his victory on the gleaming Caribbean seas. On his part, Derek had found no difficulty in crediting that which was related with apparent fidelity to fact, and which filled up, in so remarkable a manner, the empty spaces between the mysterious, broken hints Diane had at various times given him of her own inner life. The one story helped to tell the other as accurately as the fragments of an ancient stele, when put together, make up the whole inscription. The very independence of the sources from which he drew his knowledge negatived the possibility of doubt. There was but one way in which Diane could have put herself right with him: she could have swept the charge aside, with a serene contemptuousness of denial. Had she done so, her assertion would have found his own eagerness to believe in her ready to meet it halfway. As it was, alas! her admissions had been damning. Where she acknowledged the smoke, there surely must have been the fire! Where she owned to so much culpability, there surely must have been the entire measure of guilt!

For the time being, he forgot Bienville, in order to review the conversation of the last half-hour. Diane had not carried herself like a woman who had nothing with which to reproach herself; and that a woman should be obliged to reproach herself at all was a humiliation to her womanhood. In the midst of this gross world, where the man's soul naturally became stained and coarsened, hers should retain the celestial beauty with which it came forth from God. That, in his opinion, was her duty; that was her instinct; that was the object with which she had been placed on earth. A woman who was no better than a man was an error on the part of nature; and Diane - oh, the pity of it! - had put herself down on the man's level with a naivete which showed her unconscious of ever having been higher up. She had confessed to weaknesses, as though she were of no finer clay than himself, and spoke of being penitent, when the tragedy lay in the fact that a woman should have anything to repent of.

The minutes went by, but he sat rigid, with hands clinched before him, and eyes fixed in a kind of hypnotic stare on the cluster of lights, taking no account of time or place. Throughout the house there was the stillness of midnight, broken only by the rumble of a carriage or the clatter of a motor in the street. The silence was the more ghostly owing to the circumstance that throughout the empty rooms lights were still flaring uselessly, welcoming his return. Presently there came a sound - faint, soft, swift, like the rustle of wings, or a weird spirit footfall. Though it was scarcely audible, it was certain that something was astir.

With a start Derek came back from the contemplation of his intolerable pain to the world of common happenings. He must see what could be moving at this unaccustomed hour; but he had barely risen in his place when he was disturbed by still another sound, this time louder and heavier, and characterized by a certain brusque finality. It was the closing of a door; it was the closing of the large, ponderous street-door. Some one had left the house.

In a dozen strides he was out in the hail and on the stairway. There, on the landing, where an hour or two ago he had turned to look down upon Diane, stood Dorothea in her night-dress - a little white figure, scared and trembling.

"Oh, father, Diane has gone away!"

For some seconds he stared at her blankly, like a man who puzzles over something in a strange language. When he spoke, at last, his voice came with a forced harshness, from which the girl shrank back, more terrified than before:

"She was quite right to go. You run back to bed."

BASIL KING

XII

From the shelter of the little French hostelry in University Place, Diane wrote, on the following morning, to Miss Lucilla van Tromp, telling her as briefly and discreetly as possible what had occurred. While withholding names and suppressing the detail which dealt with the manner of her husband's death, she spoke with her characteristic frankness, stating her case plainly. Though she denied the main charge, she repeated the admissions Derek had found so fatal, and accepted her share of all responsibility.

"Mr. Pruyn is not to blame," she wrote. "From many points of view he is as much the victim of circumstances as I am. I have to acknowledge myself in fault; and yet, if I were more so, my problem would be easier to solve. There are conditions in which it is scarcely less difficult to discern the false from the true than it is to separate the foul current from the pure, after their streams have run together; and I cannot reproach Mr. Pruyn if, looking only on the mingled tides, he does not see that they flow from dissimilar sources. Though I left his house abruptly, it was not because he drove me forth; it was rather because I feel that, until I have regained some measure of his respect, I cannot be worthy in his eyes - nor in my own - to be under one roof with his daughter."

*   *   *   *   *

To Miss Lucilla, in her ignorance of the world, it seemed, as she read on, as if the foundations of the great deep had been broken up and the windows of heaven opened. That such things happened in romances, she had read; that they were not unknown in real life, even in New York, she had heard it whispered; but that they should crop up in her own immediate circle was not less wonderful than if the night-blooming cereus had suddenly burst into flower in her strip of garden. Miss Lucilla owned to being shocked, to being grieved, to being puzzled, to being stunned; but she could not deny the thrill of excitement at being caught up into the whirl of a real love-affair.

When the first of the morning's duties in the sickroom were over she waylaid Mrs. Eveleth in a convenient spot and told her tale. She did not read the letter aloud, finding its phraseology at times too blunt; but, with those softening circumlocutions of which good women have the secret, she conveyed the facts. There was but one short passage which she quoted just as Diane had written it:

"'I am sure my mother-in-law will stand by me, and bear me out. She alone knows the sort of life I led with her son, and I am convinced that she will see justice done me.'"

Mrs. Eveleth listened silently, with the still look of pain that belongs to those growing old in the expectation of misfortune.

"I've been afraid something would happen," was her only comment.

"But surely, dear Mrs. Eveleth, you don't think any of it can be true!"

The elder woman began moving toward the door.

"So many things have been true, dear, that I hoped were not!"

This answer, given from the threshold, left Miss Lucilla not more aghast than disappointed. It brought into the romance features which no single woman can afford to contemplate. She would have entered into the affairs of a wronged heroine with enthusiastic interest; but what was to be done with those of a possibly guilty one? She was so ready for the unexpected that as she stood at a back window, looking into the garden, it was almost a surprise not to find the night-blooming cereus really lifting its exotic head among the stout spring shoots of the peonies. With the vague feeling that the Park might prove more fruitful ground for the phenomenon, she moved to a front window, where she was not long unrewarded. If it was not the night-blooming cereus that drove up in the handsome, open automobile, turning into the Park, it was something equally portentous; for Mrs. Bayford had already played a part in Diane's drama, and was now, presumably, about to enter on the scene again. Miss Lucilla drew back, so as to be out of sight, while keeping her visitors in view. For a minute she hoped that Marion Grimston herself might be minded to make her a call, for she liked the handsome girl, whose outspoken protests against the shams of her life agreed with her own more gentle horror of pretension. Marion, wreathed in veils, was, however, at the steering-wheel, and, as she guided the huge machine to the curbstone, showed no symptoms of wishing to alight. Beside her was Reggie Bradford, a large, fat youth, whose big, good-natured laugh almost called back echoes from the surrounding houses. As the car stopped he lumbered down from his perch, and helped Mrs. Bayford to descend. When he had clambered back to his place again the great vehicle rolled on. It was plain now to Miss Lucilla that a new act of the piece was about to begin, and she hurried back to the library in order to be in her place before the rising of the curtain. For Miss Lucilla's callers there was always an immediate subject of conversation which had to be exhausted before any other topic could be touched upon; and Mrs. Bayford tackled it at once, asking the questions and answering them herself, so as to get it out of the way.

"Well, how is Regina? Very much the same, of course. I don't suppose you'll see any change in her now, until it's for the worse. Poor thing! one could almost wish, in her own interests, that our Heavenly Father would think fit to take her to Himself. Now, I want to talk to you about something serious."

Mrs. Bayford made herself comfortable in a deep, low chair, with her feet on a footstool.

"I suppose you've never guessed," she asked, at last, "why Marion has been with me all this time?"

"I did guess," Miss Lucilla admitted, with a faint blush, "but I don't know that I guessed right."

"I expect you did. No one could see as much of her as you've done without knowing she had a love-affair."

"That's what I thought."

"It's been a great trial," Mrs. Bayford sighed, "and it isn't over yet. In fact, I don't know but what it's only just beginning."

"Wasn't he - desirable?"

"Oh yes; very much so, and is so still. It wasn't that. He was all that any one could wish - old family, position, title, good looks, everything."

"But if Marion liked him, and he liked her - ?"

"I could explain it to you better if you knew more about men."

"I do know a - a little," Miss Lucilla ventured to assert, shyly.

"There is a case in which a little is not enough. You've got to understand a man's capacity for loving one woman and being fascinated by another. I think they call it double consciousness."

"I don't think it's very honorable," Miss Lucilla declared, in disapproval.

"A man doesn't stop to think of honor, my dear, when he's in a grand passion. Bienville has honor written in his very countenance, but this was an occasion when he couldn't get it into play. It was perfectly tragic. He had already spoken to Robert Grimston in the manliest way - told all about himself - found out how much Marion would have as her *dot* - and got permission to pay her his addresses - when all came to nothing because of another woman."

With this as an introduction it was natural that Mrs. Bayford should go on to repeat the oft-told tale in its entirety, lending it a light that no one had given to it yet. With the information she already possessed from Diane's letter it was impossible for Lucilla not to recognize all the characters as readily as Derek Pruyn had done, while she had the advantage over him of knowing Marion Grimston's place in the action. It was a dreadful story, and if Miss Lucilla was not more profoundly shocked it was because Mrs. Bayford, by overshooting the mark, rendered it incredible. None the less she agreed with Mrs. Bayford on the main point she had come to urge, that Diane, on one side, and Marion and Bienville, on the other, should be kept, if possible, from meeting.

"Not that I think," Mrs. Bayford went on, "that Raoul - that's his name - would ever take up with her again. Still, you never can tell; I've seen such cases. A fire will often blaze up when you think it's out. And now that everything is going so smoothly it would be a thousand pities to throw any obstacle in the way."

"Everything is going smoothly, then? I'm glad of that, for Marion's sake."

"Yes; it's practically a settled thing. When it seemed likely that he would return to France by way of New York, Robert Grimston wrote me to say that if anything happened it would have his full consent. Things move rapidly in Paris, and the whole episode is as much a part of the past as last year's styles. Then, too, everybody there knows now that Raoul didn't kill George Eveleth; and, of course, that removes a certain unpleasant thought that some people might have about him."

"Have you seen him yet?"

"I heard from him this morning. He asked if he could call on Marion and me this afternoon. You can guess what was my reply."

The nature of this having been made clear, Mrs. Bayford went on to express her fears as to the complications which might arise from the chance meeting of Bienville and Derek on the steamer, of which the former had given her information in his note. Nothing would be more natural now than for Derek to invite Marion and Bienville to dinner; and there would be Diane!

"I think I can relieve your mind on that point," Miss Lucilla said, trying to choose her words cautiously. "There would be no danger of their meeting Mrs. Eveleth just now, as she has left Dorothea for the present."

There was so much satisfaction to Mrs. Bayford in knowing that, as far as Diane was concerned, the coast was comparatively clear, that she gathered up her skirts and departed. After she had gone, Miss Lucilla's sense of being the pivot of a romantic plot was heightened by the appearance of Diane. She came in with her usual air of confidence in her ability to meet the world, and if her pale face showed traces of tears and sleeplessness, its expression was, if anything, more courageous. Had it not been for this brave show Miss Lucilla would have wanted to embrace her and hold her hands, but, as it was, she could only retire shyly into herself, as in the presence of one too strong to need the support of friends.

"No; don't call my mother-in-law yet," Diane pleaded, as Miss Lucilla was about to touch a bell. "I want to talk to you first, and tell you things I couldn't say in writing."

Then the story was told again, and from still another point of view. Once more Diane acknowledged the weaknesses of conduct she had confessed already, but Miss Lucilla was a woman and understood her speech.

"I knew you'd believe in me," Diane said, half sobbing, as she ended her tale. "I knew you'd understand that one can be a foolish woman without having been a wicked one. Mr. Pruyn would not have been so hard on me if he had thought of that."

"Shall I go and tell him?"

"No; it's too late. The wrong that's been done needs a more radical remedy than you or I could bring to it. Bienville has lied, and I must force him to retract. Nothing else can help me."

To poor Miss Lucilla this was a new and alarming feature in the situation. If it was so, then Marion Grimston ought not to be allowed to marry him. If Diane was right - and she must be right - Mrs. Bayford was mistakenly urging on a match that would bring unhappiness to her niece. This complication was almost more than Miss Lucilla's quietly working intellect could seize, and she followed Diane's succeeding words with but a wandering attention. She understood, however, that, next to being justified by Bienville, Diane attached importance to the aid she expected from Mrs. Eveleth. Hers was the only living voice that could testify to the happy relations always existing between her son and his wife. She could tell, and would tell, that George had fallen as the champion of Diane's honor, and not as the victim of her baseness. If he died it was because he believed in her, not because he was seeking the readiest refuge from their common life. Diane would explain all to Mrs. Eveleth, to whose loyalty she could trust, and on whose love she could depend.

"I'll go and find her," Miss Lucilla said, rising. "You'd like to see her alone?"

"No; I'd rather you were present. My troubles have got beyond the stage of privacy. It's best that those who care for me should hear what can be said in my defence."

Miss Lucilla went, and returned. A few minutes later Mrs. Eveleth could be heard coming slowly down the stairs. But before she had time to enter the room Derek Pruyn, using the privilege of a relative, walked in without announcement.

XIII

If the morning had brought surprises to Miss Lucilla van Tromp, it had not denied them to the Marquis de Bienville. They were all the more astonishing in that they came out of a sky that was relatively clear. As he stood in his dressing-gown, with a cigarette between his fingers, at one of the upper windows of his tall, towerlike hotel, he would have said that his life at the moment resembled the blue dome above him, from which, after a cloudy dawn and dull early morning, the last fleecy drifts were being blown away.

There were many circumstances that combined just now to make him glad of being Raoul de Laval, Marquis de Bienville. The mere material comfort of modern hotel luxury had a certain joyous novelty after nearly two years spent amid the unprofitable splendors of the tropical forest. True, New York was not Paris; but it was an excellent distributing centre for Parisian commodities and news, and would do very well for the work he had immediately in hand. So far, all promised hopefully. His valet had joined him from France, with whatever he could wish in the way of wardrobe; and Mrs. Bayford's reply to his note contained much information beyond what was actually written down in words. Moreover, the statement he had found awaiting him from the Credit Lyonnais revealed the fact that, owing to the two years in which he had little or no need to spend money, he could now live with handsome extravagance until after he married Miss Grimston. He might even pay the more pressing of his debts, though that possibility presented itself in the light of a work of supererogation, seeing that in so short a time he should be able to pay them all.

Then would begin a new era in his life. On that point he was quite determined. At thirty-two years of age it was high time to think of being something better in the world than a mere man-beauty. His experience with Persigny had shown that he was capable of something worthier than dalliance, as his fathers had been before him.

He did not precisely blame himself for shortcomings in the past, since, according to French ideas, he had not enough money on which to be useful, while his social position precluded work. He could not serve his country for fear of serving the republic, nor live on his estates, because Bienville was too expensive to keep up. However well-meaning his nature, there had been almost nothing open to him but the career of the idle, handsome, high-born youth, with money enough to pay for the luxuries of life, while his name secured credit for its necessities.

With his looks and his address it would have been easy to find a wife who, by meeting his financial need, would have facilitated his path in virtue; but on this point he was fastidious. Rather, perhaps, he was typical of that modern, transitional phase of the French social mind which, while still acknowledging the supremacy of the family in matrimonial affairs, insists on some freedom of personal selection. That his future wife should have enough money to make her a worthy chatelaine of Bienville, as well as to meet the subsidiary expenses the position implied, was a foregone conclusion; but it was equally a matter beyond dispute that she should be some one whom he could love. He had not found this combination of essentials until he met Marion Grimston, and the hand he was thereupon prepared to offer her was not wholly empty of his heart.

In her he saw for the first time in his life the intrepid maiden who seems to dare a man to come and master her. That she should be the daughter of Robert Grimston, with his commercial primness, and Mrs. Grimston, with her pretentious snobbery, was a mystery he made no attempt to solve. It was enough for him that this proud creature was in the world, especially as her bearing toward him inspired the hope that he might win her. It was a pity that he should have turned aside from such high endeavor in a foolish dash to make himself the Hippomenes of Diane Eveleth's Atalanta. Putting little heart into the latter contest, he would have suffered little mortification from defeat, had it not been that the high spirits of the pursued lady invited the world to come and laugh with her at his expense.

Then it was that the Marquis de Bienville, in an uncontrollable access of wounded vanity, had thrown his traditions of honor to the winds, and lied. It was not such a lie as could be told - and forgotten; for there were too many people eager to believe and repeat it. Within twenty-four hours he found himself famous, all the way from the Parc Monceau to the rue de Varennes. After his conscience had given him a sleepless night he got up to see that any modification of his statement meant retraction. Retraction was out of the question, in that it involved the loss of his reputation among men. He was caught in a trap. He must lie and maintain his place, or he must confess and go out of society. It must not be supposed that he took his predicament lightly, or that he made his choice without pangs of self-pity at the cruel necessity. It was his honor, or hers! and if only the one or the other could be saved, it must be his. So he saved it - according to his lights. He saved it by being very bold in his statements by day, and heaping ignominy on himself during the black hours of sleeplessness. He found, however, that the process paid; for boldness engendered a sort of fictitious belief which paralyzed the tendency to self-upbraiding until it ceased.

The special quality of his courage was shown on that gray dawn when he stood up before George Eveleth in a corner of the Pre Catalan. He had not the moral force to confess himself a perjurer in the sight of Paris, but he could stand ready to take the bullets in his breast. In going to the encounter he had no intention of doing otherwise. He would not atone to an injured woman by setting her right in the eyes of men, but he would make her the offering of his life.

It was a satisfaction now to know, as he was assured by letters, that the incident was practically forgotten, and that Diane Eveleth had disappeared. He himself found it easier than it used to be to dismiss the subject from his mind; and if he recalled it at times, it was generally - as it had been on shipboard - when at the end of his store of confidential anecdotes. He was thinking, however, of dropping the story from his repertoire, for he had more than remarked that its effect was slightly sinister upon himself. He noticed, too, that, during the first twenty-four hours on the steamer, Derek Pruyn avoided him, while he on his part had felt a curious impulse to slink out of sight, which could only be explained by the supposition that, as often happens on long voyages, they had seen too much of each other.

Finding that he had let his cigarette go out, he threw it away, and turned from the window to complete his toilet. As he did so his valet entered with a card, stating that the gentleman who had sent it in was waiting in the hail outside.

"Ask him to come in," he said, briefly, when he had read the name. He was scarcely surprised, for Pruyn had spoken more than once of showing him some civilities when they reached New York, and putting him up at one or two convenient dubs.

"My dear sir," he cried, going forward with outstretched hand; but the words died on his lips as Derek pushed his way in brusquely, without greeting.

Again the young man attempted the ceremonious by apologizing for the informality of his surroundings and the state of his dress; but again he faltered before the haggard glare in Derek's eyes.

"I want to talk to you," Pruyn said, abruptly. Bienville made a gesture of mingled politeness and astonishment.

"Certainly; but shall we not sit down while we do it? Will you smoke? Here are cigarettes, but you probably prefer a cigar."

Educated in England, like many young Frenchmen of the upper classes, Bienville spoke English fluently and with little accent.

"I want to talk to you," Derek said again. He took no notice of the proffered seat, and they remained standing, as they were, with the round table, bestrewn with letters, between them. "You remember," Derek continued, speaking with difficulty - "you remember the story you told me on the voyage - about a woman?"

Bienville nodded. He had a sudden presentiment of what was coming.

"I must tell you that on the night before I sailed for South America, three months ago, I asked that woman to be my wife."

"In that case," Bienville said, promptly, and with a tranquillity he did not feel, "I withdraw my statements."

"Withdrawal isn't enough. You must tell me they were not true."

Bienville remained silent for a minute. He was beginning to realize the firmness of the ground he stood on. His instinct for self-preservation was strong, and he had confidence in his dexterous use of the necessary weapons.

"You must give me time to reflect on that," he said, after a pause.

"Why do you need time? If the thing isn't true, you've only got to say so."

"It's not quite so easy as that. You can't cut every difficulty with a sword, as they did the Gordian knot. One may go far in defence of a woman's honor, but there are boundaries which even a gallant man cannot pass; and, before I speak, I must see where they lie."

"I want the truth. I want no defence of a woman's honor - "

"Ah, but I do. That's the difference."

"Damn your difference! You didn't think much of a woman's honor when you began your infernal tales."

"Did you, when you let me go on?"

"No. That's where I share your crime. That's all that keeps me from striking you now."

"I let that pass. I know how you feel. I know just how hard it is for you. I've been in something like your situation myself. No man can have much to do with a woman without being put there in one way if not another. It's because I do understand you that I share your pain - and support your insults."

The tremor in his voice, coupled with the dignity of his bearing, carried a certain degree of conviction, so that when Derek spoke again it was less fiercely.

"Then I understand you to confirm what you told me on board ship?"

"On the contrary; you understand me to take it back. Why shouldn't that be enough for you - without asking further questions?"

"Because I'm not here to go through formalities, but to seek for facts."

"Precisely; and yet, wouldn't it be wise, under the circumstances, not to be too exacting? If I do my best for you - "

"It isn't a question of doing your best, but of telling me the truth."

"I can quite see that it might strike you in that way; but you'll pardon me, I know, if I see it from another point of view. No man in my situation would consider it a matter of telling you the truth, so much as of coming to the aid of a lady whose good name he had unwittingly imperilled. My supreme duty is there; and I'm willing to do it to the utmost of my power. I am willing to withdraw everything I have ever uttered that could tell against her. Can you ask me to do more?"

"Yes; I can ask you to deny it."

"Isn't that already a form of denial?"

"No; it's a form of affirmation."

"That's because you choose to take it so. It's because you prefer to go behind my words, and ascribe to me motives which, for all you know, I do not possess."

"I've nothing to do with your motives; my aim is to get at the truth."

"Since you have nothing to do with my motives," Bienville said, with a slight lifting of the brows, "you'll permit me, I am sure, to be equally indifferent to your aims. I tell you what I am prepared to do; but what is it to me whether you are satisfied or not? I am sorry to - to - inconvenience the lady; but as for you - !"

With a snap of the fingers he turned and strolled to the window, where he stood, looking out, with his back toward his guest. It was significant of their tension of feeling and concentration of mind that both gesture and attitude went unnoted by both. Derek remained silent and motionless, his slower mind trying to catch up with the Frenchman's nimble adroitness. He had not yet done so when Bienville turned and spoke again.

"Why should we quarrel? What should we gain by doing that? You and I are two men of the world, to whom human nature is as an open book. What do you expect me to do? What do you expect me to say? What more did you think to call forth from me when you came here this morning? Do me justice. Am I not going as far as a man can go when I say that I blot out of my memory the cursed evenings you and I spent together in cursed talk? That doesn't cover the ground, you think; but would any other form of words cover it any better? Would you believe me the more, whatever set of speeches I might adopt? Would you not always have in the back of your mind your expressive English phrase, that I was lying like a gentleman? You know best what you can do, as I know best what I can do; but is it not true that we have arrived at a point where the less that is spoken in words on either side, the better it will be for us all?"

When he had finished, Bienville turned again toward the window, leaning his head wearily against the frame. Derek stood a minute longer watching him. Then, as if accepting the assertion that there was nothing more that could be said, he went quietly, with bent head, from the room.

*   *   *   *   *

He was down in the street before he became fully conscious that, among the confused, strangled cries of pain within him, that which was loudest and most imploring was a wailing self-reproach. It was a self-reproach with a strain of pleading in it, akin to that with which a mother blames herself for the failings of her son, seizing on any one else's wrong to palliate the guilt of the accused. He had injured Diane himself! He had pried into her past, and laid bare her sins, and stripped her life of that covering of secrecy which no human existence could do without, least of all his own.

He walked on with bowed head, his eyes blind to the May

sunshine, his ears deaf to the city's joyous, energetic uproar, his mind closed to the fact that important business affairs were awaiting his attention. His feet strayed toward Gramercy Park, directed not so much by volition as by the primary man-instinct to be near some sweet, sympathetic woman in the hour of pain. Lucilla and he had, grown up in one family as boy and girl together, and there were moments when he found near her the peace he could get nowhere else in the world.

He pushed by the footman who admitted him and walked straight to the room where Lucilla was generally to be found. Though he could scarcely be surprised to see Diane sitting by her, he stopped on the threshold, with signs of embarrassment, and made as though he would withdraw. Overwhelmed by the responsibilities of such a moment, Miss Lucilla looked appealingly at Diane, who rose.

"Don't go, Mr. Pruyn," she said, forcing herself to show firmness. "You arrive very opportunely. I have just asked my mother-in-law to come to my aid in some of the things we discussed last night. Won't you do me the justice to hear her?"

She crossed the room to where Mrs. Eveleth appeared on the threshold, and, taking her by the hand, led her to the chair which Pruyn placed for her.

"I'd better go, Diane dear," Miss Lucilla whispered, tremblingly.

"Please don't," Diane insisted. "I'd much rather have you stay. I've no secrets from Miss Lucilla," she added, speaking to Derek. "I need a woman friend; and I've found one."

"You couldn't find a better," Pruyn murmured, while Miss Lucilla slipped her arm around Diane's waist, rather to steady herself than to support her friend.

"Miss Lucilla knows everything that you know, petite mere," Diane continued, turning to where her mother-in-law sat, slightly bowed, her extended hand resting on her cane, like some graceful Sibyl. "She knows everything that you know, and she knows one thing more. She knows what some cruel people say was the way in which - George died."

Diane uttered the last two words in a kind of sob, and Mrs. Eveleth looked up, startled.

"George - died?" she questioned, slowly, with a look of wonder.

Diane nodded, unable, for the minute, to speak.

"But we know how - he died."

"Mr. Pruyn tells me that we don't."

"I beg you not to put it in that way," Derek said, hurriedly. "I repeated only what was told me, and what was afterward verified. Do you not think we can spare Mrs. Eveleth what must be so painful?"

"There's no need to spare me, Mr. Pruyn. I think I've reached the point to which old people often come - where they can't feel any more."

"Oh, mother, don't say that," Diane wailed, with a curiously childlike cry. She had never before called Mrs. Eveleth mother, and the word sounded strangely in this room which had not heard it since Miss Lucilla was a little girl. "My mother would rather know," she declared, almost proudly, speaking again to Pruyn, "than be kept in ignorance of something in which she could help me so much."

"What is it?" Mrs. Eveleth asked, eagerly.

Then Diane told her. It had been stated, so she said, that George had not fallen in her defence, but by his own hand - to escape her; and there was no one in the world but his own mother to give this monstrous calumny the lie. During the recital Mrs. Eveleth sat with clasped hands, but with head sinking lower at each word. Once she murmured something which only Miss Lucilla was near enough to hear:

"Then that's why they wouldn't let me look at him in his coffin."

"He did love me, didn't he?" Diane cried. "He was happy with me, wasn't he, mother dear? He understood me, and upheld me, and defended me, whatever I did. He didn't want to leave me. He knew I should never have cared for the loss of the money - that we could have faced that together. Tell them so, mother; tell them."

For the first time since he had known her Derek saw Diane forget her reserve in eager pleading. She stepped forward from Miss Lucilla's embrace, standing before Mrs. Eveleth with palms opened outward, in an attitude of petition. The older woman did not raise her head nor speak.

"He was happy with me," Diane insisted. "I made him happy. I wasn't the best wife he could have had, but he was satisfied with me as I was, in spite of my imperfections. He was worried sometimes, especially toward - toward the last; but he wasn't worried about me, was he, mother dear?"

Still the mother did not speak nor raise her head. Diane took a step nearer and began again.

"I didn't know we were living beyond our means. I didn't know what was going on around me. I reproach myself for that. A wiser woman *would* have known; but I was young, and foolish, and very, very happy. I didn't know I was ruining George, though I'm ready to take all the responsibility for it now. But he never blamed me, did he, mother? never, by a word, never by a look. Oh, speak, and tell them!"

Her voice came out with a sharp note of anxiety, in which

there was an inflection almost of fear; but when she ceased there was silence.

"Petite mere," she cried, "aren't you going to say anything?"

The bowed head remained bowed; the only sign came from the trembling of the extended hand, resting on the top of the stick.

"If you don't speak," Diane cried again, "they'll think it's because you don't want to."

If there was a response to this, it was when the head bent lower.

"Mother," Diane cried, in alarm, "I've no one in the world to speak a word for me but you. If you don't do it, they'll believe I drove George to his death - they'll say I was such a woman that he killed himself rather than live with me any longer."

Suddenly Mrs. Eveleth raised her head and looked round upon them all. Then she staggered to her feet.

"Take me away!" she said, in a dead voice, to Lucilla van Tromp. "Help me! Take me away! I can't bear any more!" Leaning on Miss Lucilla's arm, she advanced a step and paused before Diane, who stood wide-eyed, and awe-struck rather than amazed, at the magnitude of this desertion. "May God forgive you, Diane," she said, quietly, passing on again. "I try to do so; but it's hard."

While Derek's eyes were riveted on Diane, she stood staring vacantly at the empty doorway through which Mrs. Eveleth and Miss Lucilla had passed on their way up-stairs. This abandonment was so far outside the range of what she had considered possible that there seemed to be no avenues to her intelligence through which the conviction of it could be brought home. She gazed as though her own vision were at fault, as though her powers of comprehension had failed her.

Derek, on his part, watched her, with the fascination with which we watch a man performing some strange feat of skill - from whom first one support, and then another, and then another, falls away, until he is left with nothing to uphold him, perilously, frightfully alone.

When at length the knowledge of what had occurred came over her, Diane looked round the familiar room, as though to bring her senses back out of the realm of the incredible. When her eyes rested on him it was simply to include him among the common facts of earth after this excursion into the impossible. She said nothing, and her face was blank; but the little gesture of the hands - the little limp French gesture: the sudden lift, the sudden drop, the soft, tired sound, as the arms fell against the sides - implied fatality, finality, inexplicability, and an infinite weariness of created things.

XIV

"Do you think he did - shoot himself?"

They continued to stand staring into each other's eyes - the width of the room between them. A red azalea on the long mahogany table, strewn with books, separated them by its fierce splash of color. The apathy of Diane's voice was not that of worn-out emotion, but of emotion which finds no adequate tones. The very way in which her inquiry ignored all other subjects between them had its poignancy.

"What do *you* think?"

"Oh, I suppose he did. Every one says so; then why shouldn't it be true? If it were, it would only be of a piece with all the rest."

"I reminded you last night that he had other troubles besides - besides - "

"Besides those I may have caused him."

"If you like to put it so. He might have been driven to a desperate act by loss of fortune."

"Leaving me to face poverty alone. No; I can't think so ill of him as that. If you suggest it by way of offering me consolation, you're making a mistake. Of the two, I'd rather think of him as seeking death from horror - horror of me - than from simple cowardice."

"It would be no new thing in the history of money troubles; and it would relieve you of the blame."

"To fasten it on him. I see what you mean; but I prefer not to accept that kind of absolution. If there's any consolation left to me, it's in the pride of having been the wife of an honorable man. Don't take it away from me as long as there's any other explanation possible. I see you're puzzled; but you'd have to be a wife to understand me. Accuse me of any crime you like; take it for granted that I've been guilty of it; only don't say that he deserted me in that way. Let me keep at least the comfort of his memory."

"I want you to keep all the comfort you can get, Diane. God forbid that I should take from you anything in which you find support. So far am I from that, that I come to offer you - what I have to offer."

There was a minute's silence before she replied:

"I don't know what that is."

"My name."

There was another minute's silence, during which she looked at him hardly.

"What for?"

"I should think you'd see."

"I don't. Will you be good enough to explain?"

"Is that necessary? Is this a minute in which to bandy words?"

"It's a minute in which I may be permitted to ask the meaning of your - generosity."

"It isn't generosity. I'm saying nothing new. I've come only for an answer to the question I asked you before going to South America, three months ago."

"Oh, but I thought that question had answered itself."

"Then perhaps it has - in that, whatever reply you might have given me under other conditions, now you must accept me."

"You mean, I must accept - your name."

"My name, and all that goes with it."

"How could you expect me to do that, after what happened last night?"

"What happened last night shall be - as though it had not happened."

"Could you ever forget it?"

"I didn't say I should forget it. I suppose I couldn't do that any more than you. I said it should be as though it hadn't been."

"And what about Dorothea?"

"That must be as it may."

"You mean that Dorothea would have to take her chance."

"She needn't know anything about it - yet."

"You couldn't keep it from her forever."

"No. But she'll probably marry soon. After that she'll understand things better."

"That is, she'll understand the position in which you've been placed - that you could hardly have acted otherwise."

"I don't want to go into definitions. There are times in life when words become as dangerous as explosives. Let us do what we see to be our obvious duty, without saying too much about it."

"Isn't it your first duty to protect your child?"

"My first duty, as I see it now, is to protect you."

"I don't see much to be gained by shielding one person when you expose another. What happens to me is a small matter compared with the consequences to her."

"Your influence hasn't hurt her in the past; why should it do so now?"

"You forget that there are other things besides my influence. Her whole position, her whole life, would be changed, if she had for a mother - if you had for a wife - a notorious woman like me."

"There are situations where the child must follow the parent."

"But there are none, as far as I know, in which the parent must sacrifice the child."

"I don't agree with you. There are moments in which we must act in a certain definite manner, no matter what may be the outcome. Don't let us talk of it any more, Diane. You must know as well as I that there is but one thing for us to do."

"You mean, of course, that I must marry you."

"You must give me the right to take care of you."

"Because it's a duty that no one else would assume. That's what it comes to, isn't it?"

"I repeat that I don't want to discuss it - "

"You must let me point out that some amount of discussion is needed. If we didn't have it before marriage, we should have it afterward, when it would be worse. You won't think I'm boasting if I say that I think my vision is a little keener than yours, and that I see what you'd be doing more clearly than you do yourself. You know me - or you think you know me - as a guilty woman, homeless, penniless, and without a friend in the world. You don't want to leave me to my fate, and there's no way of helping me but one. That way you're prepared to take, cost what it will. I admire you for it; I thank you for it; I know you would do it like a man. But it's just because you *would* do it like a man - because you *are* doing it like a man - that your kindness is far more cruel than scorn. No woman, not the weakest, not the worst, among us, would consent to be taken as you're offering to take me. A man might bring himself to accept that kind of pity; but a woman - never! You said just now that you had come to offer me - what you had to offer; but surely I'm not fallen so low as to have to take it."

"I said I offered you my name and all that goes with it. I would try to tell you what it is, only that I find something in our relative positions transcending words. But since you need words - since apparently you prefer plainness of speech - I'll tell you something: I saw Bienville this morning."

She looked up with a new expression, verging on that of curiosity.

"And - ?"

"Since then," he continued, "I've become even more deeply conscious than I was before of the ineradicable nature of what I feel for you."

"Ah?"

"I've come to see that, whatever may have happened, whatever you may be, I want you as my wife."

"Do you mean that you would overlook wrongdoing on my part, and - and - care for me, just the same?"

"I mean that life isn't a conceivable thing to me without you; I mean that no considerations in the world have any force as against my desire to get you. Whatever your life has been, I subscribe to it. Listen! When I saw Bienville this morning he withdrew what he said on shipboard - as nearly as possible, without giving himself the lie, he denied it - and yet, Diane, and yet I knew his first story was - the truth. No, don't shrink. Don't cry out. Let me go on. I swear to God that it makes no difference. I see the whole thing from another point of view. I'll not only take you as you are, but I want you as you are. I give you my honor, which is dearer than my life - I give you my child, who is more precious than my honor. Everything - everything is cheap, so long as I can win you. Don't shrink from me, Diane. Don't look at me like that - "

"How can I help shrinking from anything so base?"

Her voice rose scarcely above a whisper, but it checked the movement with which, after the minutes of almost motionless confrontation, he came toward her with eager arms.

"Base?" he echoed, offended.

"Yes - base. That a man should care for a woman whom he thinks to be bad is comprehensible; that he should wish to make her his wife is credible; that he should hope to lift her out of her condition is admirable; but that he should descend from his own high plane to stay on hers is despicably weak; while to drag down with him a girl in the very flower of her purity is a crime without a name."

The dark flush showed how quickly his haughty spirit responded to the flicker of the lash.

"If you choose to put that interpretation of my words - " he began, indignantly.

"I don't; but it's the interpretation they deserve. There's almost no indignity that can be uttered which you haven't heaped upon me; and of them all this last is the hardest to be borne. I bear it; I forgive it; because it convinces me of what I've been afraid of all along - that I'm a woman who throws some sort of evil influence over men. Even you are not exempt from it - even you! Oh, Derek, go away from me! If you won't do it for your own sake, do it for Dorothea's. I won't do battle with Bienville's accusations now. Perhaps I may never do battle with them at all. What does it matter whether he tells the truth or lies? The pressing thing just now is that you should be saved - "

"Thank you; I can take care of myself. Let's have no more fine splitting of moral hairs. Let us settle the thing, and be done with it. There's one big fact before us, and only one. You can't do without me; I can't do without you. It's a crisis at which we've the right to think only of ourselves and thrust every one else outside."

"Wait!" she cried, as he advanced once more upon her. "Wait! Let me tell you something. You mustn't be hard on me for saying it. You asked just now for my answer to your question of three months ago. My answer is - "

"Diane!" he said, lifting his hand in warning. "Be careful. Don't speak in a hurry. I'm not in a mood to plead or argue any longer. What you say now will be - the irrevocable word."

"I know it. It will not only be the irrevocable word, but the last word. Derek, I see you as you are, a strong, simple, honest man. I admire you; I esteem you; I honor you; I'm grateful to you as a woman is rarely grateful to a man. And yet I'd rather be all you think me; I'd rather earn my bread as desperate women do earn it than be your wife."

They looked at each other long and steadily. When he spoke, his words were those she had invited, but they made her gasp as one gasps at that which suddenly takes one's breath.

"As you will," he said, briefly.

XV

As the pivot of events, Miss Lucilla van Tromp was beginning to feel the responsibilities of her position. Only a woman with an inexhaustible heart could have met as she did the demands for sympathy, of various shades, made by the chief participants in the drama; while there was one phase of the action which called for a heroic display of conscience.

It was impossible now to contemplate Marion Grimston's peril without a grave sense of the duties imposed by friendship. Some people might stand by and see a girl wreck her happiness by giving her heart to an unworthy suitor, but Miss van Tromp was not among that number. It was, in fact, one of those junctures at which all her good instincts prompted her to say, "I ought to go and tell her." As a patriotic spinster, she held decided views on the question of marriage between American heiresses and impecunious foreign noblemen - and, in her eyes, all foreign noblemen were impecunious - in any case; but to see Marion Grimston become the victim of her parents' vulgar ambition gave to the subject a personal bearing which made her duty urgent. If ever there was a moment when a goddess in a machine could feel justified in descending, for active intervention, it was now. She had the less hesitation in doing so, owing to the fact that she had known Marion since her cradle; and between the two there had always existed the subtle tie which not seldom binds the widely diverse but essentially like-minded together. Accordingly, on a bright May morning, within a few days of the last meeting between Derek Pruyn and Diane Eveleth, she sallied forth to the fashionable quarter where Mrs. Bayford dwelt, coming home, some two hours later, with a considerably extended knowledge of the possibilities inherent in human nature.

The tale Miss Lucilla told was that which had already been many times repeated, each narrator lending to it the color imparted by his own views of life. As now set forth, it became the story of a girl sought in marriage by a man who has inflicted mortal wrong upon an innocent young woman. With unconscious art Miss Lucilla placed Marion Grimston herself in the centre of the piece, making the subsidiary characters revolve around her. This situation brought with it a double duty: the one explicit in righting the oppressed, the other implicit - for Miss Lucilla balked at putting it too plainly into words - in punishing a wicked marquis.

The girl sat with head slightly bowed and rich color deepening. If she showed emotion at all, it was in her haughty stillness, as though she voluntarily put all expression out of her face until the recital was ended. The effect on Miss Lucilla, as they sat side by side on a sofa, was slightly disconcerting, so that she came to her conclusion lamely.

"Of course, my dear, I don't know his side of the story, or what he may have to say in self-defence. I'm only telling you what I've heard, and just as I heard it."

"I dare say it's quite right."

The brevity and suggested cynicism of this reply produced in Miss Lucilla a little shock.

"Oh! Then, you think - ?"

"There would be nothing surprising in it. It's the sort of thing that's always happening in Paris. It's one of the peculiarities of that society that you can never believe half the evil you hear of any one - not even if it's told you by the man himself. I might go so far as to say that, when it's told you by himself you're least of all inclined to credit it."

"But how dreadful!"

"Things are dreadful or not, according to the degree in which you're used to them. I've grown up in that atmosphere, and so I can endure it. In fact, any other atmosphere seems to me to lack some of the necessary ingredients of air; just as to some people - to Napoleon, for instance - a woman who isn't rouged isn't wholly dressed."

"I know that's only your way of talking, dear. Oh, you can't shock *me*."

"At any rate, the way of talking shows you what I mean. I can quite understand how Monsieur de Bienville might have said that of Mrs. Eveleth."

Lucilla's look of pain induced Miss Grimston promptly to qualify her statement.

"I said I could understand it; I didn't say I respected it. It's only what's been said of hundreds of thousands of women in Paris by hundreds of thousands of men, and in the place where they've said it it's taken with the traditional grain of salt. If all had gone as it was going at the time - if the Eveleths hadn't lost their money - if Mr. Eveleth hadn't shot himself - if Mrs. Eveleth had kept her place in French society - the story wouldn't have done her any harm. People would have shrugged their shoulders at it, and forgotten it. It's the transferring of the scene here, among you, that makes it grave. All your ideas are so different that what's bad becomes worse, by being carried out of its milieu. Monsieur de Bienville must be made to understand that, and repair the wrong."

"You seem to think there's no question but that - there *is* a wrong?"

"Oh, I suppose there isn't. There are so many cases of the kind. Mrs. Eveleth is probably neither more nor less than one of the many Frenchwomen of her rank in life who like to skate out on the thin edge of excitement without any intention of going through. There are always women like my aunt Bayford to think the worst of people of that sort, and to say it."

"And yet I don't see how that justifies Monsieur de Bienville."

"It doesn't justify; it only explains. Responsibility presses less heavily on the individual when it's shared."

"But wouldn't the person - you'll forgive me, dear, won't you, if I'm going too far? - wouldn't the person who has to take his part in that kind of responsibility be a doubtful keeper of one's happiness?"

Miss Grimston, half lowering her eyes, looked at her visitor with slumberous suspension of expression, and made no reply.

"If a man isn't good - " Miss Lucilla began again, tremblingly.

"No man is perfect."

"True, dear; and yet are there not certain qualities which we ought to consider as essentials - ?"

"Monsieur de Bienville has those qualities for me."

"But surely, dear, you can't mean - ?"

"Yes, I do mean."

The avowal was made quietly, with the still bearing of one who gives a few drops of confession out of deep oceans of reserve. Miss Lucilla gazed at her in astonishment. That her parents should sacrifice her was not surprising; but that she should be willing to sacrifice herself went beyond the limits of thought. The revelation that Marion could actually love the man was so startling that it shocked her out of her timidity, loosening the strings of her eloquence and unsealing the sources of her maternal tenderness. There was nothing original in Miss

Lucilla's subsequent line of argument. It was the old, oft-uttered, futile appeal to the head, when the heart has already spoken. It premised the possibility of placing one's affections where one cannot give one's respect, regardless of the fact that the thing is done a thousand times a day. It reasoned, it predicted, it implored, with an effect no more disintegrating on the girl's decision than moonbeams make upon a mountain. Through it all, she sat and listened with the veiled eyes and mysterious impassivity which gave to her personality a curiously incalculable quality, as of a force presenting none of the ordinary phenomena by which to measure or compute it.

It was not till Miss Lucilla touched on the subject of honor that she obtained any sign of the effect she was producing. It was no more, on Marion's part, than an uneasy movement, but it betrayed its cause. Miss Lucilla pressed her point with renewed insistence, and presently two big tears hung on the long, black lashes and rolled down.

"I should like to see Mrs. Eveleth."

Like the hasty raising and dropping of a curtain on some jealously guarded view, the words gave to Miss Lucilla but a fleeting glimpse of what was passing in the obscure recesses of the girl's heart; but she determined to make the most of it by fixing, there and then, the day and hour when, without apparently forcing the event, the two might come face to face on the neutral ground of Gramercy Park.

It was a meeting that, when it took place, would have been attended with embarrassment had not both young women been practised in the ways of their little world. Progress in mutual understanding was made the easier by the existence, on both sides, of the European view of life, with its fusion of interests, its softness of outline, its give and take of toleration, in contradistinction to the sharp, clear, insistent American demands for a certain line of conduct and no other. Five minutes had not gone by in talk before each found in the other's presence that sense of repose which comes from similar habits of thought and a common native idiom. Whatever grounds for difference they might find, they were, at least, ranged on the same side in that battle which the two hemispheres half unconsciously wage upon each other as to the main purposes of life. Thus they were able to approach their subject without that first preliminary shock which makes it difficult for races to agree; and thus, too, Marion Grimston found herself, before she was aware of it, pouring out to Diane Eveleth that heart which, in response to Miss Lucilla's tender pleading, had been dumb.

They sat in the big, sombre library where, only a few days before, Diane had seen Derek Pruyn turn his back on her, without even a gesture of farewell. On the long mahogany table the red azalea was in almost passionate luxuriance of blossom; while through the open window faint odors of lilac came from Miss Lucilla's bit of garden.

"I don't want you to think him worse than you're obliged to," Marion said, as though in defence of the stand her heart had taken. "I've been told that very few men possess the two kinds of courage - the moral and the physical. Savonarola had the one and Nelson had the other; but neither of them had both. And of the two, for me, the physical is the essential. I can't help it. If I had to choose between a soldier and a saint, I'd take the soldier. When the worst is said of Monsieur de Bienville, it must be admitted that he's brave."

"I've always understood that he was a good rider and a good shot," Diane admitted. "I've no doubt that in battle he would conduct himself like a hero."

The girl's head went up proudly, and from the languorous eyes there came one splendid flash before the lids fell over them again.

"I know he would; and when a man has that sort of courage he's worth saving."

"You admit, then, that he needs to be - saved?" Again the heavy lids were lifted for one brief, search-light glance.

"Yes; I admit that. I believe he has wronged you. I can't tell you how I know it; but I do. It's to tell you so that I've asked you to come here. I hoped to make you see, as I do, that he's capable of doing it without appreciating the nature of his crime. If we could get him to see that - "

"Then - what?"

"He'd make you reparation."

"Are you so sure?"

"I'm very sure. If he didn't - " The consequences of that possibility being difficult of expression, she hung upon her words.

"I should be sorry to have you brought to so momentous a decision on my account."

"It wouldn't be on your account; it would be on my own. I understand myself well enough to see that I could love a dishonorable man; but I couldn't marry him."

"You have, of course, your own idea as to what makes a man dishonorable."

"What makes a man dishonorable is to persist in dishonor after he has become aware of it. Any one may speak thoughtlessly, or boastfully, or foolishly, and be forgiven for it. But he can't be forgiven if he keeps it up, especially when by his doing so a woman has to suffer."

The movement with which Diane pushed back her chair and rose betrayed a troubled rather than an impatient spirit.

" Miss Grimston , " she said, standing before the girl and

looking down upon her, "I should almost prefer not to have you take my affairs into your consideration. I doubt if they're worth it. I can't deny that I shrink from becoming a factor in your life, as well as from feeling that you must make your decisions, or unmake them, with reference to me."

"I'm not making my decisions, or unmaking them, with reference to you; it's with reference to Monsieur de Bienville. He has my father's consent to his asking me to be his wife. I understand that, according to the formal French fashion, he's going to do it to-morrow. Before I give him an answer I must know that he is such a man as I could marry."

"You would have thought him so if you hadn't heard this about me."

"Even so, it's better for me to have heard it. Any prudent person would tell you that. What I'm going to ask you to do now will not be for your sake; it will be for mine."

"You're going to ask me to do something?"

"Yes; to see Monsieur de Bienville."

Diane recoiled with an expression of dismay.

"I know it will be hard for you," Miss Grimston pursued, "and I wouldn't ask you to do it if it were not the straightest way out of a perplexing situation. I've confidence enough in him to believe that when he has seen you and heard your story, he'll act according to the dictates of a nature which I know to be essentially honorable, even if it's weak. You can see what that will mean to us all. It will not only clear you and rehabilitate him, but it will bring happiness to me."

There was something in the way in which these brief statements were made that gave them the nature of an appeal. The very difficulty of the reserved heart in speaking out, the shame-flushed cheek - the subdued voice - the halting breath - had on Diane a more potent effect than eloquence. What was left of her own hope, too, at once put forth its claim at the possibility of getting justice. It was a matter of taking her courage in both hands, in one tremendous effort, but the fact that this girl believed in her was a stimulus to making the attempt. Before they parted - with stammering expressions of mutual sympathy - she had given her word to do it.

XVI

In the degree to which masculine good looks and elegance are accessories to impressing a maid's heart, the Marquis de Bienville had reason to be sure of the effect he was producing, as he bent and kissed Miss Marion Grimston's hand, in her aunt's drawing-room, on the following afternoon. He was not surprised to detect the thrill that shot through her being at his act of homage, and communicated itself back to him; for he was tolerably certain of her love. That had been, to all intents and purposes, confessed more than two years ago; while, during the intervening time, he had not lacked signs that the gift once bestowed had never been withdrawn. He had stood for a few seconds at the threshold on entering the room, just to rejoice consciously at his great good-fortune. She had risen, but not advanced, to meet him, her tall figure, sheathed in some close-fitting, soft stuff, thrown into relief by the dark-blue velvet portiere behind her. He was not unaware of his unworthiness in the presence of this superb young creature, and as he crossed the room it was with the humility of a worshipper before a shrine.

"Mademoiselle," he said, simply, when he had raised himself, "I come to tell you that I love you."

The glance, slightly oblique, of suspended expression with which she received the words encouraged him to continue.

"I know how far what I have to give is beneath the honor of your acceptance; and yet when men love they are impelled to offer all the little that they have. My one hope lies in the fact that a woman like you doesn't love a man for what he is - but for what she can make him."

The words were admirably chosen, reaching her heart with a force greater than he knew.

"A woman," she answered, with a certain stately uplifting of the head, "can only make a man that which he has already the power to become. She may be able to point out the way; but it's for him to follow it."

"I don't think you'd see me hesitate at that."

"I'm glad you say so; because the road I should have to ask you to take would be a hard one."

"The harder the better, if it's anything by which I can prove my love."

"It is; but it's not only that; it's something by which you could prove mine."

His face brightened.

"In that case, Mademoiselle - speak."

She took an instant to assemble her forces, standing before him with a calmness she did not feel.

"You must forgive me," she said, trying to keep her voice steady, "if I take the initiative, as no girl is often called upon to do. Perhaps I should hesitate more if you hadn't told me, two years ago, what I know you've come to repeat to-day. The fact that I've waited those two years to hear you say it gives me a right that otherwise I shouldn't claim."

He bowed.

"There are no rights that a woman can have over a man which you, Mademoiselle, do not possess over me."

"Before telling me again," she continued, speaking with difficulty, "what you've told me already, I want to say that I can only listen to it on one condition."

"Which is - ?"

"That your own conscience is at peace with itself."

There was a sudden startled toss of the head, but he answered, bravely:

"Is one's conscience ever at peace with itself? A woman's, perhaps; but a man's - !"

He shook his head with that wistful smile of contrition which is already a plea for pardon.

"I'm not speaking of life in general, but of something in particular. I want you to understand, before you ask me - what you've come to ask, that you couldn't make one woman happy while you're doing another a great wrong."

He was sure now of what was in store for him, and braced himself for his part. He was one of those men who need but to see peril to see also the way of meeting it. He stood for a minute, very straight and erect, like a soldier before a court-martial - a culprit whose guilt is half excused by his very manliness.

"I have wronged women. They've wronged me, too. All I can do to show I'm sorry for it is - not to give them the same sort of offence again."

"I'm thinking of one woman - one woman in particular."

He threw back his head with fine confidence.

"I don't know her."

"It's Diane Eveleth. She says - "

"I can imagine what she says. If I were you, I wouldn't pay it more attention than it deserves."

"It deserves a good deal - if it's true."

"Not from you, Mademoiselle. It belongs to a region into which your thought shouldn't enter."

"My thought does enter it, I'm afraid. In fact, I think of it so much that I've invited Mrs. Eveleth to come here this afternoon. I hope you don't mind meeting her?"

"Certainly not. Why should I?" he demanded, with an air of conscious rectitude.

Miss Grimston touched a bell.

"Ask Mrs. Eveleth to come in," she said to the footman who answered it.

As Diane entered she greeted Bienville with a slight inclination of the head, which he returned, bowing ceremoniously.

"I've begged Mrs. Eveleth to meet us," Marion hastened to explain, "for a very special reason."

"Then perhaps she will be good enough to tell me what it is," Bienville said, with a look of courteous inquiry.

"Miss Grimston thought - you might be able - to help me."

There was a catch in Diane's voice as she spoke, but she mastered it, keeping her eyes on his, in the effort to be courageous.

"If there's anything I can do - " he began, allowing the rest of his sentence to be inferred.

He concealed his nervousness by placing a small gilded chair for Diane to sit on. He himself took a chair a few feet away, seating himself sidewise, with his elbow supported on the back, in an easy attitude of attention. Marion Grimston withdrew to the more distant part of the room, where, with her hands behind her, she stood leaning against the grand piano, with the bearing of one only indirectly, and yet intensely, concerned. Bienville left the task of beginning to Diane. In spite of his determination to be self-possessed, a trace of compunction was visible in his face as he contrasted the subdued little woman before him with the sparkling, insouciant creature to whom, two or three years ago, he had paid his inglorious court.

"I shall have to speak to you quite simply and frankly," Diane began, with some hesitation, still keeping her eyes on his, "otherwise you wouldn't understand me."

"Quite so," Bienville assented, politely.

"You may not have heard that since - my - my husband's death, I have my own living to earn?"

"Yes; I did hear something of the kind."

"I've had what people in my position call a good situation, but I have lost it."

"Ah? I'm sorry."

"I thought you would be. That's why Miss Grimston asked me to tell you the reason. She was sure you wouldn't injure me - knowingly."

"Naturally. I'm very much surprised that any one should think I've injured you at all. To the best of my knowledge your name has not passed my lips for two years, at the least. If it had it would only have been spoken - with respect."

"I'm sure of that. I'm not pretending when I say that I'm

absolutely convinced you're a man of sensitive honor. If you weren't you couldn't be a Frenchman and a Bienville. I want you to understand that I've never attributed - the - things that have happened - to anything but folly and imprudence - for which I want to take my full share of the blame."

"I've never ventured to express to you my own regret," Bienville said, in a tone not free from emotion, "but I assure you it's very deep."

"I know. All our life was so wrong! It's because I feel sure you must see that as well as I do that I hoped you'd help me now."

He said nothing in reply, letting some seconds pass in silence, waiting for her to come to her point.

"On the way up from South America," she began again, with visible difficulty, "you were on the same ship with my - my - employer. From certain things you said then - "

"But I've withdrawn them," he interrupted, quickly. "He should have told you that. Mademoiselle," he added, rising, and turning toward Marion Grimston, "wouldn't it spare you if we continued this conversation alone?"

"No; I'd rather stay," Miss Grimston said, with an inflection of request. "Please sit down again."

"He should have told you that," Bienville repeated, taking his seat once more, and speaking with some animation. "I did my best to straighten things out for him."

"Then he didn't understand you. He told me you had taken back what you had said, but only in a way that reaffirmed it."

"That's nothing but a tortuous construction put on straight-forward words."

"Quite so; but for that very reason I thought that perhaps

you'd go to him again and explain what you meant more clearly."

He took a minute to consider this before speaking.

"I don't see how I can," he said, slowly. "I've already used the plainest words of which I have command."

"Words aren't everything. It's the way they're spoken that often counts most. I'm sure you could convince him if you went the right way to work about it."

"I doubt that. I'm afraid I don't know how to force conviction on any one against his will."

"You mean - ?"

"I mean - you'll excuse me; I speak quite bluntly - I mean that he seemed very willing to believe anything that could tell against you, but less eager to credit what was said in your defence."

"You think so because you don't understand him. As a matter of fact - "

"Oh, I dare say. I don't pretend to understand the gentleman in question. But for that very reason it would be useless for me to try to enlighten him further. It would only make matters worse."

"It wouldn't if you'd put things before him just as they happened. I don't want any excuses made for me. My best defence would be - the truth."

There was a perceptible pause, during which his eyes shifted uneasily toward Marion Grimston.

"I should think you could tell him that yourself," he suggested, at last.

"It wouldn't be the same thing. You're the only person who could speak with authority. He'd accept your word, if you gave it - in a certain way."

"I'm afraid I don't know what that way is."

"Oh yes, you do, Bienville!" she exclaimed, pleadingly, leaning forward slightly, with her hands clasped in her lap. "Don't force me to speak more plainly than I need. You must know what I refer to."

He shook his head slowly, with a look of mystification.

"What you may not know," she continued, "is all it means to me. I won't put the matter on any ground but that of my need for earning money. Because Mr. Pruyn has - misunderstood you, I've had to give up my - my - place" - she forced the last word with a little difficulty - "and until something like a good name is restored to me I shall find it hard to get another. You can have no idea of what that means. I had none, until I had to face it. There's only one kind of work I'm fitted for - the kind I've been doing; but it's just the kind I can't have without the - the reputation you could give back to me."

That this appeal was not without its effect was evident from the way in which his expressive brown eyes clouded, while he stroked his black beard nervously. The fact that his pity was largely for himself - that with instincts naturally chivalrous he should be driven to these miserable verbal shifts - being unknown to Diane, she was encouraged to proceed.

"You see," she went on, eagerly, "it wouldn't only bring me happiness, but it would add to your own. You're at the beginning of a new life, just like me - or, rather, just as I could be if you'd give me the chance. Think what it would be for you to enter on it, I won't say with a clear conscience, but with the knowledge that in rising yourself you had helped an unhappy woman up, instead of thrusting her further down! It isn't as if it would be so hard for you, Bienville. I'd make it easy for you. Miss Grimston would help me. Wouldn't you?" she added, turning toward Marion. "It could all be done quite simply and confidentially between ourselves - and Mr. Pruyn."

"Oh no, it couldn't," he said, coldly. "If I were to admit what you imply, secrecy wouldn't be of any use to me."

"Does that mean," she asked, fixing her earnest eyes upon him, "that you don't admit it?"

"It means," he said, rising quietly and standing behind his chair, "that this conversation is extremely painful to me, and I must ask to be excused from taking any further part in it. I know only vaguely what you mean, Madame; and if I don't inquire more in detail, it's because I want to spare you distressing explanations. I think you must agree with me, Mademoiselle," he continued, looking toward Miss Grimston, "that we should all be well advised in letting the subject drop."

Marion came slowly forward, advancing to the side of Diane, over whose shoulder, as she remained seated, she allowed her hand to fall, in a pose suggestive of protection.

"Of course, Monsieur," she agreed, "we must let the subject drop, if you have nothing more to say."

He stood silent a minute, looking at her steadily. "I'm afraid I haven't," he said, then.

"Nor I," Miss Grimston returned, significantly.

Again there was a minute or two of silence, during which Bienville seemed to probe for the meaning of the two laconic words. If anything could be read from his countenance, it was doubt as to whether to relinquish the prize with dignity or to pay its price in humiliation. There was an instant in which he appeared to be bracing himself to do the latter; but when he spoke his interrogation threw the responsibility for decision on Miss Grimston.

"Have I received - my answer?"

She waited, finding it hard to give him his reply. It was as if forced to it against her will that her head bent slowly in assent.

"Then," he said, in a tone of dignified regret, "there's nothing for me but to wish Mademoiselle good-by."

He bowed separately to Miss Grimston and to Diane, and, with the self-possession of a man accustomed to the various turns of drawing-room drama, he left the room.

XVII

During the summer that followed these events Derek Pruyn set himself the task of stamping the memory and influence of Diane Eveleth out of his life. His sense of duty combined with his feelings of self-respect in making the attempt. In reflecting on his last interview with her, he saw the weakness of the stand he had taken in it, recoiling from so unworthy a position with natural reaction. To have been in love at all at his age struck him as humiliation enough; but to have been in love with that sort of woman came very near mental malady. He said "that sort of woman," because the vagueness of the term gave scope to the bitterness of resentment with which he tried to overwhelm her. It enabled him to create some such paradise of pain as that into which the souls of Othello and Desdemona might have gone together. Had he been a Moor of Venice he would doubtless have smothered her with a pillow; but being a New York banker he could only try to slay the image, whose eyes and voice had never haunted him so persistently as now. In his rage of suffering he was as little able to take a reasoned view of the situation as the maddened bull in the arena to appraise the skill of his tormentors.

When in the middle of May he had retired to Rhinefields it was with the intention of laying waste all that Diane had left behind in the course of her brief passage through his life. The process being easier in the exterior phases of existence than in those more secret and remote, he determined to work from the outside inward. Wherever anything reminded him of her, he erased, destroyed, or removed it. All that she had changed within the house he put back into the state in which it was before she came. Where he had followed her suggestions about the grounds and gardens he reversed the orders. Taken as outward and visible signs of the inward and spiritual change he was trying to create within himself, these childish acts gave him a passionate satisfaction. In a short time, he boasted to himself, he would have obliterated all trace of her presence.

And so he came, in time, to giving his attention to Dorothea. She, too, bore the impress of Diane; and as she bore it more markedly than the inanimate things around, it caused him the greater pain. He could forbid her to hold intercourse with Diane, and to speak of her; but he could not control the blending of French and Irish intonations her voice had caught, or the gestures into which she slipped through youth's mimetic instinct. In happier days he had been amused to note the degree to which Dorothea had become the unconscious copy of Diane; but now this constant reproduction of her ways was torture. Telling himself that it was not the child's fault, he bore it at first with what self-restraint he could; but as solitude encouraged brooding thoughts, he found, as the summer wore on, that his stock of patience was running low. There were times when some chance sentence or imitated bit of manne- rism on Dorothea's part almost drew from him that which in tragedy would be a cry, but which in our smaller life becomes the hasty or exasperated word.

In these circumstances the explosion was bound to come; and one day it produced itself unexpectedly, and about nothing. Thinking of it afterward Derek was unable to say why it should have taken place then more than at any other time. He was standing on the lawn, noting with savage complacency that the bit by which he had enlarged it, at Diane's prompting, had grown up again, in luxuriant grass, when Dorothea descended the steps of the Georgian brick house, behind him.

"Would you be afther wantin' me to-day?" she called out, using the Irish expression Diane affected in moments of fun.

"Dorothea," he cried, sharply, wheeling round on her, "drop that idiotic way of speaking. If you think it's amusing, you're mistaken. You can't even do it properly."

The words were no sooner out than he regretted them, but it was too late to take them back. Moreover, when a man, nervously suffering, has once wounded the feelings of one he loves, it is not infrequently his instinct to go on and wound them again.

"We have enough of that sort of language from the servants and the stable-boys. Be good enough in future to use your mother-tongue."

Standing where his words had stopped her, a few yards away, she looked up at him with the clear gaze of astonishment; but the slight shrug of the shoulders before she spoke was also a trick caught from Diane, and not calculated to allay his annoyance.

"Very well, father," she answered, with a quietness indicating judgment held in reserve, "I won't do it again. I only meant to ask you if you want me for anything in particular to-day; otherwise I shall go over and lunch at the Thoroughgoods'."

"The Thoroughgoods' again? Can't you get through a day without going there?"

"I suppose I could if it was necessary; but it isn't."

"I think it is. You'll do well not to wear out your welcome anywhere."

"I'm not afraid of that."

"Then I am; so you'd better stay at home."

He wheeled from her as sharply as he had turned to confront her, striding off toward a wild border, where he tried to conceal the extent to which he was ashamed of his ill temper by pretending to be engrossed in the efforts of a bee to work its way into a blue cowl of monk's-hood. When he looked around again she was still standing where he had left her, her eyes clouded by an expression of wondering pain that smote him to the heart.

Had he possessed sufficient mastery of himself he would have gone back and begged her pardon, and sent her away to enjoy herself. It was what he wanted to do; but the tension of his nerves seemed to get relief from the innocent thing's suffering. The very fact that her pretty little face was set with his own obstinacy of self-will, while behind it her spirit was rising against this capricious tyranny, goaded him into persistence. He remembered how often Diane had told him that Dorothea could be neither led nor driven; she could only be "managed"; but he would show Diane, he would show himself, that she could be both driven and led, and that "management" should go the way of the wall-fruit and the roses.

As, recrossing the lawn, he made as though he would pass her without further words, he was an excellent illustration of the degree to which the adult man of the world, capable of taking an important part among his fellow-men, can be, at times, nothing but an overgrown infant. It was not surprising, however, that Dorothea should not see this aspect of his personality, or look upon his commands as other than those of an unreasonable despotism.

"Father," she said, "I can't go on living like this."

"Living like what?"

"Living as we've lived all this summer."

"What's the matter with the summer? It's like any other summer, isn't it?"

"The summer may be like any other summer; but you're not like yourself. I do everything I can to please you, but - "

"You needn't do anything to please me but what you're told."

"I always do what I'm told - when you tell me; but you only tell me by fits and starts."

"Then, I tell you now: you're not to go to the Thoroughgoods'."

"But they expect me. I said I'd go to lunch. They'll think it very strange if I don't."

"They'll think what they please. It's enough for you to know what I think."

"But that's just what I don't know. Ever since Diane went away - "

"Stop that! I've forbidden you to speak - "

"But you can't forbid me to think; and I think till I'm utterly bewildered. You don't explain anything to me. You haven't even told me why she went away. If I ask a question you won't answer it."

"What's necessary for you to know, you can depend on me to tell you. Anything I don't explain to you, you may dismiss from your mind."

"But that's not reasonable, father; it's not possible. If you want me to obey you, I must know what I'm doing. Because I don't know what I'm doing, I haven't - "

"You haven't obeyed me?" he asked, quickly.

"Not entirely. I've meant to tell you when an occasion offered, so I might as well do it now. I've written to Diane."

"You've - !"

He strode up to her and caught her by the arm. It was not strange that she should take the curious light in his face for that of anger; but a more experienced observer would have seen that two distinct emotions crowded on each other.

"I've written to her twice," Dorothea repeated, defiantly, as he held her arm. "She didn't reply to me - but I wrote."

"What for?"

"To tell her that I loved her - that no trouble should keep me from loving her - no matter what it was."

He released her arm, stepping back from her again, surveying her with an admiration he tried to conceal under a scowling brow. The rigidity of her attitude, the lift of her head, the set of her lips, the directness of her glance, suggested not merely rebellion against his will, but the assertion of her own. It occurred to him then that he could break her little body to pieces before he could force her to yield; and in his pride in this temperament, so like his own, he almost uttered the cry of "Brava!" that hung on his lips. He might have done so if Dorothea had not found it a convenient moment at which to make all her confessions at once and have them off her mind. It was best to do it, she thought, now that her courage was up.

"And, father," she went on, "it may be a good opportunity to tell you something else. I've decided to marry Mr. Wappinger."

During the brief silence that followed this announcement he had time to throw the blame for it upon Diane, using the fact as one more argument against her. Had she taken his suggestions at the beginning, and suppressed the Wappinger acquaintance, this distressing folly would have received a definite check: As it was, the odium of putting a stop to it, which must now fall on him, was but an additional part of the penalty he had to pay for ever having known her. So be it! He would make good the uttermost farthing! In doing it he had the same sort of frenzied satisfaction as in defacing Diane's image in his heart.

"You shall not," he said, at last.

"I don't understand how you're going to stop me."

"I must ask you to be patient - and see. You can make a beginning to-day, by staying at home from the Thorough-goods'. That will be enough for the minute."

Fearing to look any longer into her indignant eyes, he passed on toward the stables. For some minutes she stood still where he left her, while the collie gazed up at her, with twitching tail and questioning regard, as though to ask the meaning of this futile hesitation; but when, at last, she turned slowly and re-entered the house, one would have said that the "dainty rogue in porcelain" had been transformed into an intensely modern little creature made of steel.

She did not go to the Thoroughgoods' that day, nor was any further reference made to the discussion of the morning. Compunction having succeeded irritation, with the rapidity not uncommon to men of his character, Derek was already seeking some way of reaching his end by gentler means, when a new move on Dorothea's part exasperated him still further. As he was about to sit down to his luncheon on the following day, the butler made the announcement that Miss Pruyn had asked him to inform her father that she had driven over in the pony-cart to Mrs. Throughgood's, and would not be home till late in the afternoon.

He was not in the house when she returned, and at dinner he refrained from conversation till the servants had left the room.

"So it's - war," he said, then, speaking in a casual tone, and toying with his wine-glass.

"I hope not, father, " she answered, promptly, making no

pretence not to understand him. "It takes two to make a quarrel, and - "

"And you wouldn't be one?"

"I was going to say that I hoped you wouldn't be."

"But you yourself would fight?"

"I should have to. I'm fighting for liberty, which is always an honorable motive. You're fighting to take it away from me - "

"Which is a dishonorable motive. Very well; I must accept that imputation as best I may, and still go on."

"Oh, then, it is war. You mean to make it so."

"I mean to do my duty. You may call your rebellion against it what you like."

"I'm not accustomed to rebel," she said, with significant quietness. "Only people who feel themselves weak do that."

"And are you so strong?"

"I'm very strong. I don't want to measure my strength against yours, father; but if you insist on measuring yours against mine, I ought to warn you."

"Thank you. It's in the light of a warning that I view your action to-day. You probably went to meet Mr. Wappinger."

In saying this his bow was drawn so entirely at a venture that he was astonished at the skill with which he hit the mark.

"I did."

He pushed back his chair; half rose; sat down again; poured out a glass of Marsala; drank it thirstily; and looked at her a second or two in helpless distress before finding words.

"And you talk of honorable motives!"

"My motive was entirely honorable. I went to explain to him that I couldn't see him any more - just now."

"While you were about it you might as well have said neither just now - nor at any other time."

She was silent.

"Do you hear?"

"Yes; I bear, father."

"And you understand?"

"I understand what you mean."

"And you promise me that it shall be so?"

"No, father."

"You say that deliberately? Remember, I'm asking you an important question, and you're giving me an equally important reply."

"I recognize that; but I can't give you any other answer."

"We'll see." He pushed back his chair again, and rose. He had already crossed the room, when, a new thought occurring to him, he turned at the door. "At least I presume I may count on you not to see this young man again without telling me?"

"Not without telling you - afterward. I couldn't undertake more than that."

"H'm!" he ejaculated, before passing out. "Then I must take

active measures."

It was easier, however, to talk about active measures than to devise them. While Dorothea was sobbing, with her elbows on the dining-room table, and her face buried in her hands, he was pacing his room in search of desperate remedies. It was a case in which his mind turned instinctively to Diane for help; but in the very act of doing so he was confronted by her theories as to Dorothea's need of diplomatic guidance. For that, he told himself, the time was past. The event had proved how impotent mere "management" was to control her, and justified his own preference for force.

Before she went to bed that night Dorothea was summoned to her father's presence, to receive the commands which should regulate her conduct toward "the young man Wappinger." They could have been summed up in the statement that she must know him no more. She was not only never to see him, or write to him, or communicate with him, by direct or indirect means; as far as he could command it, she was not to think of him, or remember his name. His measures grew more drastic in proportion as he gave them utterance, until he himself become aware that they would be difficult to fulfil.

"I will not attempt to extract a promise from you," he was prudent enough to say, in conclusion, "that you will carry out my wishes, because I know you would never bring on me the unhappiness that would spring from disobedience."

"It's hardly fair, father, to say that," she replied, firmly. "In war, no one should shrink from - the misfortunes of war."

"That means, then, that you defy me?"

She was calmer than he as she made her reply.

"It doesn't mean that I defy you. I love you too much to put either you or myself in such an odious position as that. But it does mean that one day, sooner or later, I shall marry - Mr. Wappinger."

He looked at her with a bitter smile.

"I admire your frankness, Dorothea," he said, after a brief pause, "and I shall do my best to imitate it. If it's to be war, we shall at least fight in the open. I know what you intend to do, and you know that I mean to circumvent you. The position on both sides being so pleasantly clear, you may come and kiss me good-night."

During the process of the stiff little embrace that followed it was as difficult for her not to fling herself sobbing on his breast as for him not to seize her in his arms; but each maintained the restraint inspired by the justice of their respective causes. When she had closed the door behind her, he stood for a long time, musing. That his thoughts were not altogether tragic became manifest as his brow cleared, and the ghost of a smile, this time without bitterness, hovered about his lips. Suddenly he slapped his leg, like a man who has made a discovery.

"By Gad!" he whispered, half aloud, "when all is said and done, she knows how to play the game!"

XVIII

It was, perhaps, the knowledge that Dorothea could play the game that enabled Derek, during the rest of the summer, to play it himself. This he did without flinching, finding strength in the fact that, as time went on, Dorothea seemed to enter into his plans and submit to his judgment. The first few weeks of pallor and silence having passed, she resumed her accustomed ways, and, as far as he could tell, grew cheerful. Always having credited her with common-sense, he was pleased now to see her make use of it in a way of which few girls of nineteen would have been capable. She accepted his surveillance with so much docility that, by the time they returned to town in the autumn he was able to congratulate himself on his success.

On her part, Dorothea carried out his instructions to the letter. Notwithstanding the opening of the season and the renewal of the usual gayeties, she lived quietly, accepting few invitations, and rarely going into society at all, except under her father's wing. On those accidental occasions when Carli Wappinger came within their range of vision, it was only as a distant ship drifts into sight at sea - to drift silently away again. If Dorothea perceived him, she gave no sign. It was clear to Derek that her spurt of rebellion was over, and that her little experience had done her no harm. The name of Wappinger being tacitly ignored between them, he could only express his pleasure, in the results he had achieved, by an extravagant increase of Dorothea's allowance, and gifts of inappropriate jewels. It would have taken a more weatherwise person than he to guess that behind this domestic calm the storm was brewing.

The first intuition of threatening events came to Mrs. Wappinger.

"I've seen nothing and heard nothing," she declared, in her emphatic way, to Diane, "but I know something is going on."

That was in September. They sat in the shade of the cool flag-paved pergola at Waterwild, Mrs. Wappinger's place on Long Island. The tea-table stood between them, and they lounged in wicker chairs. Framed by marble pillars, and festooned from above by vines drooping from the roof, there was a view of terraced lawns descending toward the sea. Between the slightly overcrowded urns and statues there were bright dashes of color, here of dahlias in full bloom, there of reddening garlands of ampelopsis or Virginia creeper. It was what Mrs. Wappinger called an "off-day," otherwise she could not have had Diane at Waterwild. In her loyalty toward the deserted woman she seized those opportunities when Carli was away, and she was certain of having no other guests, "to have the poor thing down for the day, and give her a good meal."

Not that people occupied themselves with Diane or her affairs! Her place in the hurrying, scrambling social throng had been so unobtrusive that, now that she no longer filled it, she was easily forgotten. Among the few who paid her the tribute of recollection there was the generally received impression that Derek Pruyn, having discovered her relations with the Marquis de Bienville - relations which, so they said, had been well known in Paris, in the days when she was still some one - had dismissed her from her position in his household. That was natural enough, and there was no further reason for remembering her. Having disappeared into the limbo of the unfortunate, she was as far beyond the mental range of those who retained their blessings as souls that have passed are out of sight of men and women who still walk the earth. For this very reason she called out in Mrs. Wappinger that motherly good-nature which was only partially warped by the ambition for social success. On more than one of her "off-days" she had lured Diane out of her refuge in University Place, treating her with all the kindness she could bestow without causing disparaging comment upon herself. On the present occasion she was the more desirous of her company because of the fact that, as she expressed it herself, she had "sniffed something going on."

"As I tell you," she repeated, "I've heard nothing, and seen nothing; I've just sniffed it. If you were to ask me how, I couldn't explain it to you any more than I can say how I get the scent of this climbing heliotrope. But I do get it; and I do know something is in the wind, more than what is told to you and I."

"One can only hope that it will be nothing foolish," Diane murmured, guardedly.

"It *will* be something foolish," Mrs. Wappinger declared, "and you may take my word for it. Derek Pruyn can't arrogate to himself the powers of the Lord above any more than we can. If he thinks he can stop young blood from running he'll find out he's wrong."

It was the first mention of his name that Diane had heard in many weeks, and at the sound her hand trembled in such a way that she was obliged to put down untasted the cup she had half raised to her lips.

"He's not an unkind man," she found voice to say; "he's only a mistaken one. He has one of those natures capable of dealing magnificently with great affairs, but helpless in the trivial matters of every day. He's like the people who see well at a distance, but become confused over the objects right under their eyes."

"Then the farther you keep away from that man the better the view he'll take of you. It's what I'd say to Carli if he'd ask for my advice."

"Does that mean," Diane ventured to inquire, "that you don't want him to marry Dorothea?"

"I certainly do not. If there were no other reason, she's the sort of girl to make me put one foot into the grave, whether I want to or no; and it stands to reason that I don't want to be squelched one hour before my time."

"Naturally; but I fancy you'd find her a sweeter girl than you might suppose."

"So she may be, dear; but I've spent too much money on Carli to wish to see him force his way into a family where he isn't wanted."

This was the text of Mrs. Wappinger's discourse, not only on the present occasion, but on the subsequent "off-days," when Diane was induced to visit Waterwild.

"Whatever is going on, Reggie Bradford's in it," she confided to Diane some few weeks later.

"Is that the fat young man with the big laugh?"

"Yes; and one of the greatest catches in New York. Carli tells me he's wild about Marion Grimston, and I can see for myself that Mrs. Bayford is playing him against that Frenchman. She'll get the title if she can, but if not, she'll fall back on the money."

"It's a pretty safe alternative," Diane smiled, making an effort to speak without betraying her feelings.

"Reggie is a good-natured boy," Mrs. Wappinger pursued, "but a regular water-pipe. If you want to get anything out of him you've only got to turn the faucet. It's just as well that he is; because whatever Carli is up to Reggie knows, and what Reggie knows Marion Grimston knows. If ever you see her - "

"Oh, but I don't - not now."

"That's a pity. If you did, you could pump her."

"I'm afraid I'm not much good at that sort of thing."

"Well, I am, when I get a chance. I'm bound to find out, somehow; and there are more ways of killing a cat than by giving it poison."

A few weeks later still Mrs. Wappinger informed Diane that Dorothea Pruyn was not happy.

"The Thoroughgoods told the Louds," she explained, "and the Louds told me. Her father thinks she has given in to him; but she hasn't - not an inch. He keeps her like a jailer; and she acts like a convict - always with an eye open for some way of escape. That man no more understands women than he does making pie."

"I've always noticed that the really strong men rarely do. There's almost invariably something petty about a man to whom a woman isn't a puzzle and a mystery."

"If it comes to a puzzle and a mystery, I don't know where you'd find a greater one than Derek Pruyn himself. After the way he's acted - and treated people - "

Diane flushed, but kept her emotions sufficiently under control to be able to follow her usual plan of straightforward speaking.

"If you mean me, Mrs. Wappinger, I ought to say that Mr. Pruyn has done nothing for which I can blame him. He was placed in a situation with which only a very subtle intelligence could have dealt, and I respect him the more for not having had it. It's generally the man who is most competent in his own domain who is most likely to blunder when he gets into the woman's; and I, for one, would rather have him do it. I've had to suffer because of it, and so has Dorothea; and yet that doesn't make me like it less."

"No, I dare say not," Mrs. Wappinger responded, sympathetically. "Mr. Wappinger himself was just such a man as that. He'd put through a deal that would make Wall Street shiver; but he understood my woman's nature just about as much as old Tiger there, wagging his tail on the grass, follows the styles in bonnets. Only, I'll tell you what, Mrs. Eveleth: it's for men like that that God created sensible, capable wives, like you and me; and they ought to have 'em."

This theme admitting of little discussion, Diane did not pursue it, but she went away from Waterwild with a deepened sense of Derek's need of her, as well as of Dorothea's. She could so easily have helped them both that the enforced impotence was a new element in her pain. To walk the town in search of work to which she was little suited, when that which no one but herself could accomplish had to remain undone, became, during the next few weeks, the most intolerable part of the irony of circumstance. The wifely, the maternal qualities of her being, of which she had never been strongly conscious till of late, awoke in response to the need that drew them forth, only to be blighted by denial.

The inactivity was the harder to endure because of the fact that, as autumn passed into early winter, there came a period when all her little world seemed to have dropped her out of sight. There were no more "off-days" at Waterwild, and Miss Lucilla's occasional letters from Newport ceased. Between her mother-in-law and herself, after a few painful attempts at intercourse, there had fallen an equally painful silence. Even her two or three pupils fell away.

From the papers she learned that one or another of those for whom she cared was back in town again. She walked in the chief thoroughfares in the hope of meeting some of them, but chance refused to favor her. In the dusk of the early descending November and December twilights she passed their houses, watching the warm glow of the lights within, against which, now and then, a shadow that she could almost recognize would pass by. She could have entered at Miss Lucilla's door, or Mrs.

Wappinger's; but a strange shyness, the shyness of the unfortunate, had taken hold of her, and she held back. In the mean time she was free to watch, with sad eyes and sadder spirit, the great city, reversing the processes of nature, awaken from the torpor of the genial months into its winter life.

No one knew better than herself that thrill of excited energy with which those born with the city instinct return from the acquired taste for mountain, seaside, and farm, to enter once more the maze of purely human relationships. It was a moment with which her own active nature was in sympathy. She liked to see the blinds being raised in the houses and the barricading doors taken down. She liked to see the vehicles begin to crowd one another in the streets and the pedestrians on the pavement wear a brisker air. She liked to see the shop-windows brighten with color and the great public gathering-spots let in and let out their throngs. She responded to the quickened animation with the spontaneity of one all ready to take her part, till the thought came that a part had been refused her. It was with a curious sensation of being outside the range of human activities that, during those days of timid, futile looking for employment, she roamed the busy thorough-fares of New York. As time passed she ceased to think much about her need of sympathetic fellowship in her anxiety to get work. She wrote advertisements and answered them; she applied at schools, and offices, and shops; she came down to seeking any humble drudgery which would give her the chance to live.

It was not till one day in early December that the last flicker of her hope went out. Chance had made her pass at midday along the pavement opposite one of the great restaurants. Lifting her eyes instinctively toward the group of well-dressed people on the steps, she saw that Mrs. Bayford and Marion Grimston were going in, accompanied by Reggie Bradford and the Marquis de Bienville. She had heard little or nothing of them during the last four empty months; but it was plain now that the lovers were agreed and her own cause abandoned. Up to this moment she had not realized how tenaciously she had clung to the belief that the proud, high-souled girl would yet see justice done her; and now she had deserted her, like the rest!

For the first time during her years of struggle she felt absolutely beaten - beaten so thoroughly that it would be useless to renew the fight. She had been on her way to see a lady who had advertised for a nursery governess; but she had no strength left with which to face the interview. In the winter-garden of the restaurant Mrs. Bayford was purring to her guests, Reggie Bradford was whispering to Miss Grimston, and the Marquis de Bienville was ordering the wines, while Diane was wandering blindly back to the poor little room she called her home, there to lie down and allow her heart to break.

But hearts do not break at the command of those who own them, and when she had moaned away the worst of her pain, she fell asleep. When she awoke it was already growing dark, and the knocking at her door, which roused her, was like a call from the peace of dreams to the desolation of reality. When she had turned on the light she received from the hands of the waiting servant that which had become a most rare visitant in the blankness of her life - a note.

The address was in a sprawling hand, which she recognized. What was written within was more sprawling still:

"For Heaven's sake, come to me at once. The expected has happened, and I don't know what to do. The motor will wait and bring you.

CLARA WAPPINGER."

XIX

As Diane entered, Mrs. Wappinger, dishevelled and distraught, was standing in the hail, a slip of yellow paper in her hand.

"Oh, my dear, I'm so glad you've come! I'm just about crazy! Read this!"

Diane took the paper and read:

> "D. and I are to be married to-night. Be ready to receive us to-morrow.
> CARLI."

"When did this come?" Diane asked, quickly.

"About half an hour ago. I sent for you at once."

"I see it's dated from Lakefield. Where's that?"

Mrs. Wappinger explained that Lakefield was a small winter health resort some two hours by train from New York. She and Carli had stayed there, more than once, at the Bay Tree Inn. He would naturally go to the same hotel, only, when she had telephoned to it, a few minutes ago, she could find no one of the name in residence. Under the circumstances, Diane suggested, he would probably not give his name at all. There followed a few minutes of silent reflection, during which Mrs. Wappinger gazed at Diane, in the half-tearful helplessness of one not used to coping with unusual situations.

"Won't you come in and sit down?" she asked, with a sudden

realization that they were still standing beneath the light in the hail.

"No," Diane answered, with decision; "it isn't worth while. May I have the motor for an hour or so?"

"Why, certainly. But where are you going?"

"I'm going first to Mr. Pruyn's, and afterward to Lakefield."

"To Lakefield? Then I'll go with you. We could go in the car."

Diane negatived both suggestions. The motor might break down, or the chauffeur might lose his way; the train would be safer. If any one went with her, it would have to be Mr. Pruyn.

"But don't go to bed," she added, "or at least have some one to answer the telephone, for I'll ring you up as soon as I have news for you."

"God bless you, dear," Mrs. Wappinger murmured. "I know you'll do your best for me, and them. Keep the auto as long as you like; and if you decide to go down in it, just say so to Laporte."

But Diane seemed to hesitate before going. A flush came into her cheek, and she twisted her fingers in embarrassment.

"I wonder", she faltered, "if - if - you could let me have a little money? I shall need some, and - and I haven't - any."

"Oh, my dear! my poor dear!"

Mrs. Wappinger bustled away, crumpling the notes she found in her desk into a little ball, which she forced into Diane's hand. To forestall thanks she thrust her toward the door, accompanying her down the steps, and kissing her as she entered the automobile.

"Why, bless my 'eart, if it ain't the madam!"

This outburst was a professional solecism on the part of Fulton, the English butler, at Derek Pruyn's, but it was wrung from him in sheer joy at Diane's unexpected appearance.

"You'll excuse me, ma'am", he continued, recapturing his air of decorum, "but I fair couldn't help it. We'll be awful pleased to see you, ma'am, if I may make so bold as to say it - right down to the cat. It hasn't been the same 'ouse since you went away, ma'am; and me and Mr. Simmons has said so time and time again. You'll excuse me, ma'am, but - "

"You're very kind, Fulton, and so is Simmons, but I'm in a great hurry now. Is Mr. Pruyn at home?"

"Why, no, he ain't, ma'am, and that's a fact. He's to dine out."

"Where?"

"I couldn't tell you that, ma'am; but perhaps Mr. Simmons would know. He took Mr. Pruyn's evening clothes to the bank, and he was to change there. If you'll wait a minute, ma'am, I'll ask him."

But when Simmons came he could only give the information that his master was going to a "sort o' business banquet" at one of the great restaurants or hotels. Moreover, Miss Dorothea had gone out, saying that she would not be home to dinner.

"Then I must write a note," Diane said, with that air of natural authority which had seemed almost lost from her manner. "Will you, Fulton, be good enough to bring me a glass of wine and a few biscuits while I write? I must ask you, Simmons, for a railway guide."

In Derek's own room she sat down at the desk where, six months ago, she had arranged his letters on the night when he had returned from South America. She had no time to indulge in memories, but a tremor shot through her frame as she took up the pen and wrote on a sheet of paper which he had already headed with a date:

"I have bad news for you, but I hope I may be in time to keep it from being worse. I have reason to think that Dorothea has gone to Lakefield to be married there to Carli Wappinger. Should there be any mistake you will forgive me for disturbing you; but I think it well to be prepared for extreme possibilities. I am, therefore, going to Lakefield now - at once. A train at seven-fifteen will get there a little after nine. There are other trains through the evening, the latest being at five minutes after ten. Should this reach you in time to enable you to take one of them, you will be wise to do so; but in case it may be too late, you may count on me to do all that can be done. Let some one be ready to answer the telephone all night. I shall communicate with the house from the Bay Tree Inn. I must ask you again to forgive me if I am interfering rashly in your affairs, but you can understand that I have no time to take counsel or reflect.

"DIANE EVELETH."

Having made a copy of this letter, she called Simmons and Fulton and gave them their instructions. There had been an accident, she said, of which she had been able to get only imperfect information, but it seemed possible that Miss Dorothea was involved in it. She herself was hurrying to Lakefield, and it would be Simmons' task to find Mr. Pruyn in time for him to catch the ten-five train, at latest. He was to pack two valises with all that Mr. Pruyn could require for a change. He was to take one of the two letters, and one of the two valises, and go from place to place, until he tracked his master down. Fulton was to say nothing to alarm the other servants, merely informing Miss Dorothea's maid that the young lady was absent for the night and that Mrs. Eveleth was with her. He would take charge of the second letter and the second valise, in case Mr. Pruyn should return to the house before Simmons could find him. The important charge of the telephone was also to be in Fulton's trust, and he was to answer all calls through the night. In concluding her directions Diane acknowledged her relief in having two lieutenants on whose silence, energy, and tact she could so thoroughly depend. She committed the matter to their hands not merely as to Mr. Pruyn's butler and valet, but as to his trusted friends, and in that capacity she was sure they would do their duty and hold their tongues.

In a similar spirit, when she arrived, about half-past nine, at the Bay Tree Inn, she asked for the manager, and took him into her confidence. A runaway marriage, she informed him, had been planned to take place that very night at Lakefield, and she had come there as the companion and friend of a motherless girl, her object being to postpone the ceremony.

The manager listened with sympathy, and promised his help. As a matter of fact, a gentleman had arrived, driving his own motor, that very afternoon. He had put the machine in the garage, and taken a room, but had not registered. Their season having scarcely begun, and the hotel being empty, they were somewhat careless about such formalities. He could only say that the young man was tall, fair, and slender, and seemed to be a person of means. He believed, too, that at this very minute he was smoking on the terrace before the door. If Diane had not come up by another way she must have met him. She could step out on the terrace and see for herself whether it was the person she was looking for or not.

Being tolerably sure of that already, Diane preferred to complete her arrangements first. She would ask for a room as near as possible to the main door of the hotel, so that when the young lady arrived she could be ushered directly into it. Fortunately the establishment was able to offer her exactly what she required, one of the invalids' suites which were a special feature of the house - a little sitting-room and bedroom for the use of persons whose infirmities made a long walk between their own apartments and the sun-parlor inadvisable.

BASIL KING

Having inspected and accepted it, Diane bathed her face and smoothed her hair, after which she stepped out to confront Mr. Wappinger.

XX

She saw him at the end of the terrace, peering through the moonlight, down the driveway. She did not go forward to meet him, but waited until he turned in her direction. She knew that at a distance, and especially at night, her own figure might seem not unlike Dorothea's, and calculated on that effect. She divined his start of astonishment on catching sight of her by the abrupt jerk of his head and the way in which he half threw up his hands. When he began coming forward, it was with a slow, interrogative movement, as though he were asking how she had come there, in disregard of their preconcerted signals. Some exclamation was already on his lips, when, by the light streaming from the windows of the hotel, he saw his mistake, and paused.

"Good-evening, Mr. Wappinger. What an extraordinary meeting!"

Priding himself on his worldly wisdom, Carli Wappinger never allowed himself to be caught by any trick of feminine finesse. On the present occasion he stood stock-still and silent, eying Diane as a bird eyes a trap before hopping into it. Though he knew her as a friend to Dorothea and himself, he knew her as a subtle friend, hiding under her sympathy many of those kindly devices which experience keeps to foil the young. He did not complain of her for that, finding it legitimate that she should avail herself of what he called "the stock in trade of a chaperon"; while it had often amused him to outwit her. But now it was a matter of Greek meeting Greek, and she must be given to understand that he was the stronger. How she had discovered their plans he did not stop to think; but he must

BASIL KING

make it plain to her that he was not duped into ascribing her presence at Lakefield to an accident.

"Is it an extraordinary meeting, Mrs. Eveleth - for you?"

"No, not for me," Diane replied, readily. "I only thought it might be - for you."

"Then I'll admit that it is."

"But I hoped, too", she continued, moving a little nearer to him, "that my coming might be in the way of a - pleasant surprise."

"Oh yes; certainly; very pleasant - very pleasant indeed."

"I'm a good deal relieved to hear you say that, Mr. Wappinger," she said, "because there was a possibility that you mightn't like it."

"Whether I like it or not", he said, warily, "will depend upon your motive."

"I don't think you'll find any fault with that. I came because I thought I could help Dorothea. I hoped I might be able indirectly to help you, too."

"What makes you think we're in need of help?"

She came near enough for him to see her smile.

"Because, until after you're married, you'll both be in an embarrassing position."

"There are worse things in the world than that."

"Not many. I can hardly imagine two people like Dorothea and yourself more awkwardly placed than you'll be from the minute she arrives. Remember, you're not Strephon and Chloe in a pastoral; you're two most sophisticated members of a most sophisticated set, who scarcely know how to walk about excepting according to the rules of a code of etiquette. Neither of you was made for escapade, and I'm sure you don't like it any more than she will."

"And so you've come to relieve the situation?"

"Exactly."

"And for anything else?"

"What else should I come for?"

"You might have come for - two or three things."

"One of which would be to interfere with your plans. Well, I haven't. If I had wanted to do that, I could have done it long ago. I'll tell you outright that Mr. Pruyn requested me more than once to put a stop to your acquaintance with Dorothea, and I refused. I refused at first because I didn't think it wise, and afterward because I liked you. I kept on refusing because I came to see in the end that you were born to marry Dorothea, and that no one else would ever suit her. I'm here this evening because I believe that still, and I want you to be happy."

"Did you think your coming would make us happier?"

"In the long run - yes. You may not see it to-night, but you will to-morrow. You can't imagine that I would run the risk of forcing myself upon you unless I was sure there was something I could do."

"Well, what is it?"

"It isn't much, and yet it's a great deal. When you and Dorothea are married I want to go with you. I want to be there. I don't want her to go friendless. When she goes back to town to-morrow, and everything has to be explained, I want her to be able to say that I was beside her. I know that mine is not a name to carry much authority, but I'm a woman - a woman who has head a position of responsibility, almost a mother's place, toward Dorothea herself - and there are moments in life when any kind of woman is better than none at all. You may not see it just now, but - "

"Oh yes, I do," he said, slowly; "only when you've gone in for an unconventional thing you might as well be hung for a sheep as a lamb."

"I don't agree with you. Nothing more than the unconventional requires a nicely discriminating taste; and it's no use being more violent than you can help. You and Dorothea are making a match that sets the rules of your world at defiance, but you may as well avail yourselves of any little mitigation that comes to hand. Life is going to be hard enough for you as it is - "

"Oh, I don't know about that. They can't do anything to us - "

"Not to you, perhaps, because you're a man. But they can to Dorothea, and they will. This is just one of those queer situations in which you'll get the credit and she'll get the blame. You can always make a poem on Young Lochinvar, when it's less easy to approve of the damsel who springs to the pillion behind him. I don't pretend to account for this idiosyncrasy of human nature; I merely state it as a fact. Society will forget that you ran away with Dorothea, but it will never forget that she ran away with you."

"H'm!"

"But I don't see that that need distress you. You wouldn't care; and as for Dorothea, she's got the pluck of a soldier. Depend upon it, she sees the whole situation already, and is prepared to face it. That's part of the difference between a woman and a man. *You* can go into a thing like this without looking ahead, because you know that, whatever the opposition, you can keep it down. A woman is too weak for that. She must count every danger beforehand. Dorothea has done that. This isn't going to be a leap in the dark for her; it wouldn't be for any girl of her intelligence and social instincts. She knows what she's doing, and she's doing it for you. She has made her sacrifice, and made it willingly, before she consented to take this step at all. She crossed her Rubicon without saying anything to you about it, and you needn't consider her any more."

"Well, I like that!" he said, in an injured tone, thrusting his hands into his overcoat pockets and beginning to move along the terrace.

"Yes; I thought you would," she agreed, walking by his side. "It shows what she's willing to give up for you. It shows even more than that. It shows how she loves you. Dorothea is not a girl who holds society lightly, and if she renounces it - "

"Oh, but, come now, Mrs. Eveleth! It isn't going to be as bad as that."

"It isn't going to be as bad as anything. Bad is not the word. When I speak of renouncing society, of course I only mean renouncing - the best. There will always be some people to - Well, you remember Dumas' comparison of the sixpenny and the six-shilling peaches. If you can't have the latter, you will be able to afford the former."

They walked on in silence to the end of the terrace, and it was not till after they had turned that the young man spoke again.

"I believe you're overdrawing it," he said, with some decision.

"Isn't it you who are overdrawing what I mean? I'm simply trying to say that while things won't be very pleasant for you, they won't be worse than you can easily bear - especially when Dorothea has steeled herself to them in advance. I repeat, too, that, poor as I am, my presence will be taken as safeguarding some of the proprieties people expect one to observe. I speak of my presence, but, after all, you may have provided yourself with some one better. I didn't think of that."

"No; there's no one."

"Then Dorothea is coming all alone?"

"Reggie Bradford is bringing her - if you want to know."

"By the ten-five train?"

"No; in his motor."

"How very convenient these motors are! And has she no companion but Mr. Bradford?"

"She hasn't any companion at all. She doesn't even know that the man driving the machine is Reggie. He thought that, going very slowly, as he promised to do, to avoid all chances of accident, they might arrive by eleven."

"And Dorothea was to be alone here with you two men?"

"Well, you see, we are to be married as soon as she arrives. We go straight from here to the clergyman's house; he's waiting for us; in ten minutes' time I shall be her husband; and then everything will be all right."

"How cleverly you've arranged it!"

"I had to make my arrangements pretty close," Carli explained, in a tone of pride. "There were a good many difficulties to overcome, but I did it. Dorothea has had no trouble at all, and will have none; that is", he added, with a sigh, at the recollection of what Diane had just said, "as far as getting down here is concerned. She went to tea at the Belfords', and on coming out she found a motor waiting for her at the door. She walked into it without asking questions and sat down; and that's all. She doesn't know whose motor it is, or where she's going, except that she is being taken toward me. I provided her with everything. She's got nothing to do but sit still till she gets here, when she will be married almost before she knows she has arrived."

"It's certainly most romantic; and if one has to do such things, they couldn't be done better."

"Well, one has to - sometimes."

"Yes; so I see."

"What do you suppose Derek Pruyn will say?" he asked, after a brief pause.

"I haven't the least idea what he'll say - in these circumstances. Of course, I always knew - But there's no use speaking about that now."

"Speaking about what now?" he asked, sharply.

"Oh, nothing! One must be with Mr. Pruyn constantly - live in his house - to understand him. You can always count on his being kinder than he seems at first, or on the surface. During the last months I was with Dorothea I could see plainly enough that in the end she would get her way."

He paused abruptly in his walk and confronted her.

"Then, for Heaven's sake," he demanded, "why didn't you tell me that before?"

"You never asked me. I couldn't go around shouting it out for nothing. Besides, it was only my opinion, in which, after all, I am quite likely to be wrong."

"But quite likely to be right."

"I suppose so. Naturally, I should have told you," she went on, humbly, "if I had thought that you wanted to hear; but how was I to know that? One doesn't talk about other people's private affairs unless one is invited. In any case, it doesn't matter now. A man who can cut the Gordian knot as you can doesn't care to hear that there's a way by which it might have been unravelled."

"I'm not so sure about that. There are cases in which the longest way round is the shortest way home, and if - "

"But I didn't suppose you would consider so cautious a route as that."

"I shouldn't for myself; but, you see, I have to think of Dorothea."

"But I've already told you that there's no occasion for that. If Dorothea has made her choice with her eyes open - "

"Good Lord!" he cried, impatiently, "you talk as if all I wanted was to get her into a noose."

"Well, isn't it? Perhaps I'm stupid, but I thought the whole reason for bringing her down here was because - "

"Because we thought there was no other way," he finished, in a tone of exasperation. "But if there *is* another way - "

"I'm not at all sure that there is," she retorted, with a touch of asperity, to keep pace with his rising emotion. "Don't begin to think that because I said Mr. Pruyn was coming round to it he's obliged to do it."

"No; but if there was a chance - "

"Of course there's always that. But what then?"

"Well, then - there'd be no particular reason for rushing the thing to-night. But I don't know, though," he continued, with a sudden change of tone; "we're here, and perhaps we might as well go through with it. All I want is her happiness; and since she can't be happy in her own home - "

Diane laughed softly, and he stopped once more in his walk to look down at her.

"There's one thing you ought to understand about Dorothea," she said, with a little air of amusement. "You know how fond I am of her, and that I wouldn't criticise her for the world. Now, don't be offended, and don't glower at me like that, for I *must* say it. Dorothea isn't unhappy because she hasn't a good home, or because she has a stern father, or because she can't marry you. She's unhappy because she isn't getting her own way, and for no other reason whatever. She's the dearest, sweetest, most loving little girl on earth, but she has a will like steel. Whatever she sets her mind on, great or small, that she is determined to do, and when it's done she doesn't care any more about it. When I was with her, I never crossed her in anything. I let her do what she was bent on doing, right up to the point where she saw, herself, that she didn't want to. If her father would only treat her like that, she - "

"She wouldn't be coming down here to-night. That's what you mean, isn't it?"

"Oh no! How can you say so?"

"I can say so, because I think there's a good deal of truth in it. I'm not without some glimmering of insight into her character myself; and to be quite frank, it was seeing her set her pretty white teeth and clinch her fist and stamp her foot, to get her way over nothing at all, that first made me fall in love with her."

"Then I will say no more. I see you know her as well as I do."

"Yes, I know her," he said, confidently, marching on again. "I don't think there are many corners of her character into which

I haven't seen."

Several remarks arose to Diane's lips, but she repressed them, and they continued their walk in silence. During the three or four turns they took, side by side, up and down the terrace, she divined the course his thought was taking, and her speech was with his inner rather than his outer man. Suddenly he stopped, with one of his jerky pauses, and when he spoke his voice took on a boyish quality that made it appealing.

"Mrs. Eveleth, do you know what I think? I think that you and I have come down here on what looks like a fool's business. If it wasn't for leaving Dorothea here with Reggie Bradford, I'd put you in the motor and we'd travel back to New York as fast as tires could take us."

"Upon my word," she confessed, "you make me almost wish we could do it. But, of course, it isn't possible. There must be some one here to meet Dorothea - and explain. I could do that if you liked."

"Oh no!" he exclaimed, with a new change of mind; "I should look as if I were showing the white feather."

"On the contrary, you'd look as if you knew what it was to be a man."

"And Derek Pruyn might hold out against me in the end."

"It would be time enough, even then, to do - what you meant to do to-night; and I'd help you."

He hesitated still, till another thought occurred to him.

"Oh, what's the good? It's too late to rectify anything now. They must know at her house by this time that she has gone to meet me."

"No; I've anticipated that. They understand that she's here, at the Bay Tree Inn - with me."

He moved away from her with a quick backward leap.

"With you? You've done that? You've seen them? You've told them? You're a wonderful woman, Mrs. Eveleth. I see now what you've been up to," he added, with a shrill, nervous laugh. "You've been turning me round your little finger, and I'm hanged if you haven't done it very cleverly. You've failed in this one point, however, that you haven't done it quite cleverly enough. I stay."

"Very well; but you won't refuse to let me stay too - for the reasons that I gave you at first."

"You're wily, I must say! If you can't get best, you're willing to take second best. Isn't that it?"

"That's it exactly. I did hope that no marriage would take place between Dorothea and you to-night. I hoped that, before you came to that, you'd realize to what a degree you're taking advantage of her wilfulness and her love for you - for it's a mixture of both - to put her in a false position, from which she'll never wholly free herself as long as she lives. I hoped you'd be man enough to go back and win her from her father by open means. Failing all that, I hoped you'd let me blunt the keenest edge of your folly by giving to your marriage the countenance which my presence at it could bestow. Was there any harm in that? Was there anything for you to resent, or for me to be ashamed of? Is a good thing less good because I wish it, or a wise thought less wise because I think it? You talk of turning you round my little finger, as though it was something at which you had to take offence. My dear boy, that only shows how young you are. Every good woman, if I may call myself one, turns the men she cares for round her little finger, and it's the men who are worth most in life who submit most readily to the process. When you're a little older, when, perhaps, you have children of your own, you'll understand better what I've done for you to-night; and you won't use toward my memory the tone of semi-jocular disdain that has entered into nearly every word you've addressed to me this evening. Now, if you'll excuse me," she added, wearily, "I think I'll go in. I'm very tired, and I'll rest till Dorothea comes. When she arrives you must bring her to me directly; and she must stay with me till I take her to - the wedding. My room is the first door on the left of the main entrance."

She was half-way across the terrace when he called out to her, the boyish tremor in his voice more accentuated than before.

"Wait a minute. There's lots of time." She came back a few paces toward him. "Shouldn't I look very grotesque if I hooked it?"

"Not half so grotesque as you'll look to-morrow morning when you have to go back to town and tell every one you meet that you and Dorothea Pruyn have run away and got married. That's when you'll look foolish and cut a pathetic figure. As things are it could be kept between two or three of us; but if you go on, you'll be in all the papers by to-morrow afternoon. Of course your mother knows?"

"I suppose so; I wired when I thought it was too late for her to spread the alarm. But I don't mind about her. She'll be only too glad to have me back at any price."

"Then - I'd go."

The light from the hotel was full on his face, and she could almost have kissed him for his doleful, crestfallen expression.

"Well - I will."

There was no heroism in the way in which he said the words, and the spring disappeared from his walk as he went back to the hotel to pay his bill and order out his "machine." Diane smiled to herself to see how his head drooped and his shoulders sagged, but her eyes blinked at the mist that rose before them. After all, he was little more than a schoolboy, and he and Dorothea were but two children at play.

She did not continue her own way into the hotel. Now that the first part of her purpose in coming had been accomplished, she was free to remember what the comedy with Carli had almost excluded from her mind - that within an hour or two Derek Pruyn and she might be face to face again. The thought made her heart leap as with sudden fright. Fortunately, Dorothea would have arrived by that time, and would stand between them, otherwise the mere possibility would have been overwhelming.

Yes; Dorothea ought to be coming soon. She looked at her watch, and found it was nearly eleven. On the stillness of the night there came a sound, a clatter, a whiz, a throb - the unmistakable noise of an automobile. She hurried to the end of the terrace; but it was not Dorothea coming; it was Carli going away. She breathed more freely, standing to see him pass, and knowing that he was really gone.

A minute later he went by in the moonlight, waving his hand to her as she stood silhouetted on the terrace above him. Then, to her annoyance, the motor stopped and he leaped out. For a moment her heart stood still in alarm, for if he was coming back the work might be to do all over again. He did come back, scrambling up the steps till he was at her feet. But it was only to seize her hand and kiss it hastily, after which, without a word, he was off again. Then once more the huge machine clattered and whizzed and throbbed, rattling its way down the drive and on into the dark, till all sound died away in the solemn winter silence.

XXI

During the next half-hour small practical tasks occupied Diane's mind and kept the thought of Derek Pruyn's arrival from becoming more than a subconscious dread. She informed the manager of her success with his mysterious young guest, and arranged that Dorothea, when she came, should spend the night with her. Then she put herself in telephonic communication, first with Mrs. Wappinger, and then with Fulton. She gave the former the intelligence that Carli had departed, and received from the latter the information that Simmons had found his master, who had been able to leave for Lakefield by the ten-five train. These steps being taken, there was nothing to do but to sit down and wait for Dorothea. Allowing thirty or forty minutes for possible delays, she calculated that the girl ought to arrive a good half-hour before her father. This would give her time to deal with each separately, clearing up misunderstandings on both sides, and preparing the way for such a meeting as would lead to mutual concessions and future peace.

Physically tired, she took off her hat and threw herself on the couch in her little sitting-room. By sheer force of will she continued to shut out Derek from her thought, concentrating all her mental faculties on the arguments and persuasions she should bring to bear on Dorothea. She had no nervousness on this account. The naughty, headstrong child that runs away from home does not get far without a realizing sense of its happy shelter. She divined that the long ride through the dark, with an unknown man, toward an unknown goal, would have already subdued Dorothea's spirits to the point where she would be only too glad to find herself dropping into familiar, feminine arms.

At eleven o'clock she got up from her couch with a vague impulse to be in a more direct attitude of welcome. At half-past eleven she went to the office to inquire of the manager how long a motor going slowly should take to reach Lakefield from New York, assuming that it had got away from the city about six o'clock. Alarmed by his reply, she begged him to keep a certain number of the servants up, and the hotel in readiness to cope with any emergency or accident, promising liberal remuneration for all unusual work. After that came another long hour of waiting. It was about half-past twelve when there was a sound of a carriage coming up the driveway. It was probably Derek; and yet there was a possibility that, the automobile having broken down, Reggie and Dorothea had been obliged to finish their journey in a humbler way than that in which they had started. Diane hurried to the terrace. The moon had disappeared, but the stars were out, and the night had grown colder. The pines surrounding the hotel shot up weirdly against the midnight sky, soughing with a low murmur, like the moan of primeval nature. Up the ascent from the main road the carriage crept wearily, while Diane's heart poured itself out in a sort of incoherent prayer that Dorothea might have arrived before her father. The horses dragged themselves to the steps, and Derek Pruyn sprang out.

Instinctively Diane fell back.

"Oh, it's you," she gasped, unable for the instant to say more.

"Yes," he returned, quickly, peering down into her face. "What news?"

"Dorothea hasn't come. The - the other person has gone."

"Gone? How - gone?"

"He went away of his own accord."

"That is, you sent him."

"Not exactly; he was willing to go. He saw he'd been doing wrong."

A porter having come from the hotel and seized Derek's valise, it was necessary for them to go in and attend to the small preliminaries of arrival. When they were finished Derek returned to Diane, who had seated herself in a wicker chair beside one of the numerous tea-tables to which a large part of the hall was given up. Under the eye of the drowsy clerk, who still kept his place at the office desk, she felt a certain sense of protection, even though the width of the hotel lay between them.

"Now, tell me," Derek said, in his quick, commanding tones; "tell me everything."

The repressed intensity of his bearing had on Diane the effect of making her more calmly mistress of herself. Quietly, and in a manner as matter-of-fact as she could make it, she told her tale from the beginning. She narrated her summons from Mrs. Wappinger, her visit to his own house, her arrangements there, her journey to Lakefield, and her interview with Carli Wappinger. Without making light of what he and Dorothea had undertaken to do, she reduced their fault to a minimum, turning it into indiscretion rather than anything more grave. She laid stress on the excellence of the young man's character, as well as on the promptness with which he had relinquished his part in the plan as soon as he saw its true nature. In spite of himself Derek began to think of the lad as of one who had sprung to his help in a moment of need, and to whom he was indebted for a service. Not until Diane ceased speaking was he able to brush this absurd impression away, in the knowledge that Dorothea, who should have arrived nearly two hours ago, was still out in the dark. That, for the moment, was the one fact to which everything else was subordinate.

"I can't understand it," he said, nervously. "If they left New

York by six, or even seven, they should have been here by eleven at the latest. That would have given them time for slow going or taking a circuitous route."

He rose nervously from his seat, interviewed the clerk at the desk, went out on the terrace, listened in the silence, walked restlessly up and down, and, returning to Diane, enumerated the different possibilities that would reasonably account for the delay. Glad of this preoccupation, since it diverted thought from their more personal relations, she pointed out the wisdom of accepting whatever explanation was least grave until they knew the certainty. When he had gone out several times more, to listen on the terrace, he came back, and, resuming his seat, said, brusquely:

"You look tired. You ought to get some rest."

The tone of intimate care reached Diane's heart more directly than words of greater import.

"I would," she said, simply - "that is, I'd go to my room if I thought you'd be kind to Dorothea when she came."

"And *don't* you think so?"

"I think you'd want to be," she smiled, "if you knew how."

"But I shouldn't know how?"

"You see, it's a situation that calls directly for a woman; and you're so essentially a man. When Dorothea arrives, she won't be a headstrong, runaway girl; she'll be a poor little terrified child, frightened to death at what she has done, and wanting nothing so much as to creep sobbing into her mother's arms and be comforted. If you could only - "

"I'll do anything you tell me."

"It's no use telling; you have to know. It's a case in which you must act by instinct, and not by rule of thumb."

In her eagerness to have something to say which would keep conversation away from dangerous themes, she spoke exhaustively on the subject of parental tact, holding well to the thread of her topic until she perceived that he was not so much listening to what she said as thinking of her. But she had gained her point, and led him to see that Dorothea was to be treated leniently, which was sufficient for the moment.

"Now," she finished, rising, "I think I'll take your advice, and go and rest till she comes. That's my door, just opposite. I chose the room for its convenience in receiving Dorothea. You'll be sure to call me, won't you, the minute you hear the sound of wheels?"

He had sat gazing up at her, but now he, too, rose. It was a minute at which their common anxiety regarding Dorothea slipped temporarily into the background, allowing the main question at issue between them to assert itself; but it asserted itself silently. He had meant to speak, but he could only look. She had meant to withdraw, but she remained to return his look with the lingering, quiet, steady gaze which time and place and circumstance seemed to make the most natural mode of expression for the things that were vital between them. What passed thus defied all analysis of thought, as well as all utterance in language, but it was understood by each in his or her own way. To her it was the greeting and farewell of souls in different spheres, who again pass one another in space. For him it was the dumb, stifled cry of nature, the claim of a heart demanding its rightful place in another heart, the protest of love that has been debarred from its return by a cruel code of morals, a preposterous convention, grown suddenly meaningless to a woman like her and to a man like him. Something like this it would have been a relief to him to cry out, had not the strong hand of custom been upon him and forced him to say that which was far below the pressure of his yearning.

"This isn't the time to talk about what I owe you," he said, feeling the insufficiency of his words; "it's too much to be disposed of in a few phrases."

"On the contrary, you owe me nothing at all."

"We'll not dispute the point now."

"No; but I'd rather not leave you under a misapprehension. If I've done anything to-night - been of any use at all - it's been simply because I loved Dorothea - and - and - it was right. When it was in my power, I couldn't have refused to do it for any one - for any one, you understand."

"Oh yes, I understand perfectly; but *any one*, in the same circumstances, would feel as I do. No, not as I do," he corrected, quickly. "No one else in the world could feel - "

"I'm really very tired," she said, hurriedly; "I'll go now; but I count on you to call me."

He watched her while she glided across the room; but it was only when her door had closed and he had dropped into his seat that he was able to state to himself the fact that the mere sight of her again had demolished all the barricades he had been building in his heart against her for the last six months. They had fallen more easily than the walls of Jericho at the blast of the sacred horn. The inflection of her voice, the look from her eyes, the gestures of her hands, had dispelled them into nothingness, like ramparts of mist. But it was not that alone! He was too much a man of affairs not to give credit to the practical abilities she had shown that night. No graces of person or charms of mind or resources of courage could have called forth his admiration more effectively than this display of prosaic executive capacity. What had to be done she had done more promptly, wisely, and easily than any man could have accomplished it. She had foreseen possibilities and forestalled accident with a thoroughness which he himself could not have equalled.

"My God!" he groaned, inwardly, "what a wife she would have made for any man! How I could have loved her, if it hadn't been for - "

He stopped abruptly and leaped to his feet, looking around dazed on the great empty hail, at the end of which a porter slept in his chair, while the clerk blinked drowsily behind his desk.

"I do love her," he declared to himself. "All summer long I have uttered blasphemies. I do love her. Whatever she may have been, she shall be my wife."

Out on the terrace the cold wind was grateful, and he stood for a minute bareheaded, letting it blow over his fevered face and through his hair. It had risen during the last hour, making the pines rock slowly in the starlight and swelling their moan into deep sobs.

As Derek Pruyn paced the terrace in strained expectation he was deceived again and again into the thought that something was approaching. Now it was the champing and stamping of horses toiling up the ascent; now it was the bray and throb of the automobile; now it was the voices of men, conversing or calling or breaking into laughter. Twenty times he hastened to the steps at the end of the terrace, sure he could not have been mistaken, only to hear the earth-forces sob and sough and shout again, as if in derision of this puny, presumptuous mortal, with his evanescent joy and pain.

So another hour passed. His mind was not of the imaginative order which invents disaster in moments of suspense, so that he was able to keep his watch more patiently than many another might have done. Once he tried to smoke; but the mere scent of tobacco seemed out of place in this curious world, alive with odd psychical suggestions, and he threw the cigar away into the darkness, where its light glowed reproachfully, like a dying eye, till it went out.

It was after three when a sudden sound from the driveway struck his ear; but he had been deceived so often that he would pay it no attention. Though it seemed like the unmistakable approach of an automobile, it had seemed so before, and he would not even look round till he had reached the distant end of the terrace. When he turned he could see through the trees, and along the dark line of the avenue, the advance of the heralding light. Dorothea had come at last. She was even close upon them. In a few more seconds she would be alighting at the steps.

He hurried inside to wake the porter and warn Diane.

"She's here!" he called, rapping sharply at her door. "Please come! Quick!"

There was a response and a hurried movement from within, but he did not wait for her to appear. When she came out of her room she could see from the light thrown over the terrace that the motor had already stopped at the steps. Some one was getting out, and she could hear men's voices. Advancing to a spot midway between her room and the main entry, she stood waiting for Derek to bring her his daughter. A moment later he sprang into the light of the doorway with features white and alarmed.

"Go back!" he cried to her, with a commanding gesture. "Go back!"

"But what's the matter?"

"Go back!" he ordered, more imperiously than before.

"Oh, Derek, it's Dorothea! She's hurt. I must go to her. I will not go back."

She rushed toward the entry, but he caught her and pushed her back.

"I tell you you must go back," he repeated.

"It's Dorothea!" she cried. "She's hurt! She's killed! Let me go! She needs me!"

"It isn't Dorothea," he whispered, forcing her over the threshold of her own room and trying to close the door upon her.

"Then what is it?" she begged. "Tell me now. You're hurting me. Let me go! You're killing me."

"It's - "

But there was no need to say more, for the main door swung open again and the Marquis de Bienville entered, followed by a porter carrying his valise.

At his appearance Derek relinquished Diane's hands, and Diane herself was so astonished that she stepped plainly into view. Not less astonished than herself, Bienville stopped stock-still, looked at her, looked into the room behind her, looked at Derek with a long, half-amused, comprehending stare, lifted his hat gravely, and passed on.

When he had gone there was a minute of dead silence. With parted lips and awe-stricken eyes Diane gazed after him till he had spoken to the clerk at the desk and passed on into the darker recesses of the hotel. When she turned toward Derek he was smiling, with what she knew was an effort to treat the situation lightly.

"Well, this time we've given him something to talk about," he laughed, bravely.

She shrugged her shoulders and spread apart her hands with one of her habitual, fatalistic gestures.

"I don't mind. He can't do me more harm than he's done already. It's not of him that I'm thinking, but of Dorothea.

She hasn't come."

"No, she hasn't come."

The fact had grown alarming, so much so as to make the incident of Bienville's appearance seem in comparison a matter of little moment. Diane remained on the threshold of her room, and Derek in the hail outside, while, for mutual encouragement, they rehearsed once more the list of predicaments in which the young people might have found themselves without serious danger.

Diane was about to withdraw, when a man ran down the hall calling:

"The telephone! - for the gentleman!"

Derek started on a run, Diane following more slowly. When she reached the office Derek had the receiver to his ear and was talking.

"Yes, Fulton. Go on. I hear.... Who has rung you up?... I didn't catch ... Miss - who? Oh, Miss Marion Grimston. Yes?... In Philadelphia, at the Hotel Belleville.... Yes; I understand... and Miss Dorothea is with her.... Good!... Did she say how she got there?... Will explain when we get back to New York to-morrow morning.... All right.... Yes, to lunch.... She said Miss Dorothea was quite well, and satisfied with her trip!... That's good.... Well, good-night, Fulton. Sorry to have kept you up."

He put up the receiver and turned to Diane.

"Did you understand?"

"Perfectly. I think I know what has happened. I can guess."

"Then, I'll be hanged if I can. What is it?"

"I'll let them tell you that themselves. I'm too tired to say anything more to-night."

She kept close to the office where the clerk was shutting books and locking drawers preparatory to closing.

"You must let me come and thank you - " he began.

"You must thank Miss Marion Grimston," she interrupted, "for any real service. All I've done for you, as you see, has been to bring you on an unnecessary journey."

"For me it has been a journey - into truth."

"I'll say good-night now. I shall not see you in the morning. You'll not forget to be very gentle with Dorothea, will you - and with him? Good-night again - good-night."

Smiling into his eyes, she ignored the hand he held out to her and slipped away into the semi-darkness as the impatient clerk began turning out the lights.

XXII

Derek Pruyn was guilty of an injustice to the Marquis de Bienville in supposing he would make the incident at Lakefield a topic of conversation among his friends. His sense of honor alone would have kept him from betraying what might be looked upon as an involuntary confidence, even if it had not better suited his purposes to intrust the matter, in the form of an amusing anecdote, told under the seal of secrecy, to Mrs. Bayford. In her hands it was like invested capital, adding to itself, while he did nothing at all. Months of insinuation on his part would have failed to achieve the result that she brought about in a few days' time, with no more effort than a rose makes in shedding perfume.

Before Derek had been able to recover from the feeling of having passed through a strange waking dream, before Dorothea and he had resumed the ordinary tenor of their life together, before he had seen Diane again, he was given to understand that the little scene on Bienville's arrival at the Bay Tree Inn was familiar matter in the offices, banks, and clubs he most frequented. The intelligence was conveyed by a score of trivial signs, suggestive, satirical, or over-familiar, which he would not have perceived in days gone by, but to which he had grown sensitive. It was clear that the story gained piquancy from its contrast with the staidness of his life; and his most intimate friends permitted themselves a little covert "chaff" with him on the event. He was not of a nature to resent this raillery on his own account; it was serious to him only because it touched Diane.

For her the matter was so grave that he exhausted his ingenuity

BASIL KING

in devising means for her protection. He refrained from even seeing her until he could go with some ultimatum before which she should be obliged to yield. An unsuccessful appeal to her, he judged, would be worse than none at all; and until he discovered arguments which she could not controvert he decided to hold his peace.

Action of some sort became imperative when he found that Miss Lucilla Van Tromp had heard the story and drawn from it what seemed to her the obvious conclusion.

"I should never have believed it," she declared, tearfully, "if you hadn't admitted it yourself. I told Mrs. Bayford that nothing but your own words would convince me that any such scene had taken place."

"Allowing that it did, isn't it conceivable that it might have had an honorable motive?"

"Then, what is it? If you could tell me that - "

"I could tell you easily enough if there weren't other considerations involved. I should think that in the circumstances you could trust me."

"Nobody else does, Derek."

"Whom do you mean by nobody else? - Mrs. Bayford?"

"Oh, she's not the only one. If your men friends don't believe in you - "

"They believe in me, all right; don't you worry about that."

"They may believe in you as men believe in one another; but it isn't the way I believe in people."

"I know how you believe in people if ill-natured women would let you alone. You wouldn't mistrust a thief if you saw him stealing your watch from your pocket."

"That's not true, Derek. I can be as suspicious as any one when I like."

"But don't you see that your suspicion doesn't only light, on me? It strikes Diane."

"That's just it."

"Lucilla! he cried, reproachfully.

"Well, Derek, you know how loyal I've been to her. It's been harder, too, than you've ever been aware of; for I haven't told you - I *wouldn't* tell you - one-half the things that people have hinted to me during the past two years."

"Yes; but who? A lot of jealous women - "

"It's no use saying that, Derek; because your own actions contradict you. Why did Diane leave your house, if it wasn't that you believed - ?"

"Don't." He raised his hand to his face, as if protecting himself from a blow.

"I wouldn't," she cried, "if you didn't make me. I say it only in self-defence. After all, you can only accuse me of what you've done yourself. Diane made me think at first that you had misjudged her; but I see now that if she had been a good woman you wouldn't have sent her away."

"I didn't send her away. She went."

"Yes, Derek; but why?"

"That has nothing to do with the question under discussion."

"On the contrary, it has everything to do with it. It all belongs together. I've loved Diane, and defended her; but I've come to the point where I can't do it any longer. After what's happened - "

"But, I tell you, what's happened is nothing! If it was only right for me to explain it to you, as I shall explain it to you some day, you'd find you owed her a debt that you never could repay."

"Very well! I won't dispute it. It still doesn't affect the main point at issue. Can you yourself, Derek, honestly and truthfully affirm that you look upon Diane as a good woman, in the sense that is usually attached to the words?"

"I can honestly and truthfully affirm that I look upon her as one of the best women in the world."

"That isn't the point. Louise de la Valliere became one of the best women in the world; but there are some other things that might be said of her. But I'll not argue; I'll not insist. Since you think I'm wrong, I'll take your own word for it, Derek. Just tell me once, tell me without quibble and on your honor as my cousin and a gentleman, that you believe Diane to be - what I've supposed her to be hitherto, and what you know very well I mean, and I'll not doubt it further."

For a moment he stood speechless, trying to formulate the lie he could utter most boldly, until he was struck with the double thought that to defend Diane's honor with a falsehood would be to defame it further, while a lie to this pure, trusting, virginal spirit would be a crime.

"Tell me, Derek," she insisted; "tell me, and I'll believe you."

He retreated a pace or two, as if trying to get out of her presence.

"I'm listening, Derek; go on; I'm willing to take your word."

"Then I repeat," he said, weakly, "that I believe her, I *know* her, to be one of the best women in the world."

"Like Louise de la Valliere?"

"Yes," he shouted, maddened to the retort, "like Louise de la Valliere! And what then?" He stood as if demanding a reply. "Nothing. I have no more to say."

"Then I have; and I'll ask you to listen." He drew near to her again and spoke slowly. "There were doubtless many good women in Jerusalem in the time of Herod and Pilate and Christ; but not the least held in honor among us to-day is - the Magdalen. That's one thing; and here's something more. There is joy, so we are told, in the presence of the angels of God - plenty of it, let us hope! - but it isn't over the ninety-and-nine just persons who need no repentance, so much as over the one poor, deserted, lonely sinner that repenteth - that repenteth, Lucilla, do you hear?-and you know whom I mean."

With this as his confession of faith he left her, to go in search of Diane. He had formed the ultimatum before which, as he believed, she should find herself obliged to surrender.

It was a day on which Diane's mood was one of comparative peace. She was engrossed in an occupation which at once soothed her spirits and appealed to her taste. Madame Cauchat, the land-lady, bewailing the continued illness of her lingere, Diane had begged to be allowed to take charge of the linen-room of the hotel, not merely as a means of earning a living, but because she delighted in such work. Methodical in her habits and nimble with her needle, the neatness, smoothness, and purity of piles of white damask stirred all those house-wifely, home-keeping instincts which are so large a part of every Frenchwoman's nature. Her fingers busy with the quiet, delicate task of mending, her mind could dwell with the greater content on such subjects as she had for satisfaction.

They were more numerous than they had been for a long time

past. The meeting at Lakefield had changed her mental attitude toward Derek Pruyn, taking a large part of the pain out of her thoughts of him, as well as out of his thoughts of her. She had avoided seeing him after that one night, and she had heard nothing from him since; but she knew it was impossible for him to go on thinking of her altogether harshly. She had been useful to him; she had saved Dorothea from a great mistake; she had done it in such a way that no hint of the escapade was likely to become known outside of the few who had taken part in it; she had put herself in a relation toward him which, as a final one, was much to be preferred to that which had existed before. She could therefore pass out of his life more satisfied than she had dared hope to be with the effect that she had had upon it. As she stitched she sighed to herself with a certain comfort, when, glancing up, she saw him standing at the door. The nature of her thoughts, coupled with his sudden appearance, drew to her lips a quiet smile.

"They shouldn't have shown you in here," she protested, gently, letting her work fall to her lap, but not rising from her place.

"I insisted," he explained, briefly, from the threshold.

"You can come in," she smiled, as he continued to stand in the doorway. "You can even sit down." She pointed to a chair, not far from her own, going on again with her stitching, so as to avoid the necessity for further greeting. "I suppose you wonder what I'm doing," she pursued, when he had seated himself.

"I'm not wondering at that so much as whether you ought to be doing it."

"I can relieve your mind on that score. It's a case, too, in which duty and pleasure jump together; for the delight of handling beautiful linen is like nothing else in the world."

"It seems to me like servants' work," he said, bluntly.

"Possibly; but I can do servants' work at a pinch - especially when I like it."

"I don't," he declared.

"But then you don't have to do it."

"I mean that I don't like it for you."

"Even so, you wouldn't forbid my doing it, would you?"

"I wish I had the right to. I've come here this afternoon to ask you again if you won't give it to me."

For a few minutes she stitched in silence. When she spoke it was without stopping her work or lifting her head.

"I'm sorry that you should raise that question again. I thought it was settled."

"Supposing it was, it can be reopened - if there's a reason."

"But there is none."

"That's all you know about it. There's a very important reason."

"Since - when?"

"Since Lakefield."

"Do you mean anything that Monsieur de Bienville may have said?"

"I do."

"That wouldn't be a reason - for me."

"But you don't know - "

"I can imagine. Monsieur de Bienville has already done me all the harm he can. It's beyond his power to hurt me any more."

"But, Diane, you don't know what you're saying. You don't know what he's doing. He's - he's - I hardly know how to put it - He's destroying your reputation."

She glanced up with a smile, ceasing for an instant to sew.

"You mean, he's destroying what's left of it. Well, he's welcome! There was so little of it - "

"For God's sake, Diane, don't say that; it breaks my heart. You must consider the position that you put me in. After you've rendered me one the greatest services one person can do another, do you think I can sit quietly by while you are being robbed of the dearest thing in life, just because you did it?"

"I should be sorry to think the opinion other people hold of me to be the dearest thing in life; but, even if it were, I'd willingly give it up for - Dorothea."

"It isn't for Dorothea; it's for me."

"Well, wouldn't you let me do it - for you? I'm not of much use in the world, but it would make me a little happier to think I could do any one a good turn without being promised a reward."

"A reward! Oh, Diane!"

"It's what you're offering me, isn't it? If it hadn't been for - for - the great service you speak about, you wouldn't he here, asking me again to be your wife."

"That's your way of putting it, but I'll put it in mine. If it hadn't been for the magnitude of the sacrifice you're willing to make for me, I shouldn't have dared to hope that you loved me. When all pretexts and secondary causes have been considered and thrust aside, that's why I'm here, and for no other reason whatever. If you love me," he continued, "why should you hesitate any longer? If you love me, why seek for reasons to justify the simple prompting of your heart? What have you and I got to do with other people's opinions? When there's a plain, straightforward course before us, why not go right on and follow it?"

She raised her eyes for one brief glance.

"You forget."

The words were spoken quietly, but they startled him.

"Yes, Diane; I do forget. Rather, there's nothing left for me to remember. I know what you'd have me recall. I'll speak of it this once more, to be silent on the subject forever. I want you to forgive me. I want to tell you that I, too, have repented."

"Repented of what?"

"Of the wrong I've done you. I believe your soul to be as white as all this whiteness around you."

"Then," she continued, questioning gently, "you've changed your point of view during the last six months?"

"I have. You charged me then with being willing to come down to your level; now I'm asking you to let me climb up to it. I see that I was a self-righteous Pharisee, and that the true man is he who can smite his breast and say, God be merciful to me a sinner!"

"A sinner - like me."

"I don't want to be led into further explanations," he said, suddenly on his guard against her insinuations. "You and I have said too much to each other not to be able to be frank. Now, I've been frank enough. You've understood what I've felt at other times; you understand what I feel to-day. Why draw me out, to make me speak more plainly?"

"I am not drawing you out," she declared. "If I ask you a question or two, it was to show you that not even the woman that you take me for - not even the forgiven penitent - could be a good wife for you. I can't marry you, Mr. Pruyn. I must beg you to let that answer be decisive."

There was decision in the way in which she folded her work and smoothed the white brocaded surface in her lap. There was decision, too, in the quickness with which he rose and stood looking down at her. For a second she expected him to turn from her, as he had turned once before, and leave her with no explanation beyond a few laconic words. She held her breath while she awaited them.

"Then that means," he said, at last, "that you put me in the position of taking all, while you give all."

"I don't put you in any position whatever. The circumstances are not of my making. They are as much beyond my control as they are beyond yours."

"They're not wholly beyond mine. If there are some things I can't do, there are some I can prevent."

"What things?"

His tone alarmed her, and she struggled to her feet.

"You're willing to make me a great sacrifice; but at least I can refuse to accept it."

"What do you mean?" She moved slightly back from him, behind the protection of one of the tables piled breast-high with its white load.

"You're willing to lose for me the last vestige of your

good name - "

"I don't care anything about that," she said, hurriedly.

"But I do. I won't let you."

"How can you stop me?" she asked, staring at him with large, frightened eyes.

"I shall tell Dorothea's part in the story."

"You'd - ?" she began, with a questioning cry.

"All who care to hear it, shall. They shall know it from its beginning to its end. They shall lose no detail of her folly or of your wisdom."

"You would sacrifice your child like that?"

"Yes, like that. Neither she nor I can remain so indebted to any one, as you would have us be to you."

"You - wouldn't - be - indebted - to - me?"

"Not to so terrible an extent. If it's a choice between your good name and hers - hers must go. She'd agree with me herself. She wouldn't hesitate for one single fraction of an instant - if she knew. She'd be grateful to you, as I am; but she couldn't profit by your magnanimity."

"So that the alternative you offer me is this: I can protect myself by sacrificing Dorothea, or I can marry you, and Dorothea will be saved."

"I shouldn't express it in just those words, but it's something like it."

"Then I'll marry you. You give me a choice of evils, and I take the least."

"Oh! Then to marry me would be - an evil?"

"What else do you make it? You'll admit that it's a little difficult to keep pace with you. You come to me one day accusing me of sin, and on another announcing my contrition, while on the third you may be in some entirely different mood about me."

"You can easily render me ridiculous. That's due to my awkwardness of expression and not to anything wrong in the way I feel."

"Oh, but isn't it out of the heart that the mouth speaketh? I think so. You've advanced some excellent reasons why I should become your wife, and I can see that you're quite capable of believing them. At one time it was because I needed a home, at another because I needed protection, while to-day, I understand, it is because I love you."

"Is this fair?"

"I dare say you think it isn't; but then you haven't been tried and judged half a dozen times, unheard, as I've been. I'll confess that you've shown the most wonderful ingenuity in trying to get me into a position where I should be obliged to marry you, whether I would or not; and now you've succeeded. Whether the game is worth the candle or not is for you to judge; my part is limited to saying that you've won. I'm ready to marry you as soon as you tell me when."

"To save Dorothea?"

"To save Dorothea."

"And for no other reason?"

"For no other reason."

"Then, of course, I can't keep you to your word."

"You can't release me from it except on one condition."

"Which is - ?"

"That Dorothea's secret shall be kept."

"I must use my own judgment about that."

"On the contrary, you must use mine. You've made me a proposal which I'm ready to accept. As a man of honor you must hold to it - or be silent."

"Possibly," he admitted, on reflection. "I shall have to think it over. But in that case we'd be just where we were - "

"Yes; just where we were."

"And you'd be without help or protection. That's the thought I can't endure, Diane. Try to be just to me. If I make mistakes, if I flounder about, if I say things that offend you, it's because I can't rest while you're exposed to danger. Alone, as you are, in this great city, surrounded by people who are not your friends, a prey to criticism and misapprehension, when it is no worse, it's as if I saw you flung into the arena among the beasts. Can you wonder that I want to stand by you? Can you be surprised if I demand the privilege of clasping you in my arms and saying to the world, This is my wife? When Christian women were thrown to the lions there was once a heathen husband who leaped into the ring, to die at his wife's side, because he could do no more. That's my impulse - only I could save you from the lions. I couldn't protect you against everything, perhaps, but I could against the worst. I know I'm stupid; I know I'm dull. When I come near you, I'm like the clown who touches some exquisite tissue, spun of azure; but I'm like the clown who would fight for his treasure, and defend it from sacrilegious hands, and spend his last drop of blood to keep it pure. It's to be put in a position where I can't do that that I find hard. It's to see you so defenceless - "

"But I'm not defenceless."

"Why not? Whom have you? Nobody - nobody in this world but me."

"Oh yes, I have."

"Who?"

She smiled faintly at the fierceness of his brief question.

"It's no one to whom you need feel any opposition, even though it's some one who can do for me what you cannot."

"What I cannot?"

"What you cannot; what no man can. *Asperges me hyssopo, et mundabor.* Thou shalt purge me with hyssop, and I shall be clean. Derek, He has purged me with hyssop, even though it has not been in the way you think. With the hyssop of what I've had to suffer He has purged me from so many things that now I see I can safely commit my cause to Him."

"So that you don't need me?"

She looked at him in silence before she replied:

"Not for defence."

"Nor for anything else?"

She tried to speak, but her voice failed her.

"Nor for anything else?" he asked again.

Her voice was faint, her head sank, her body trembled, but she forced the one word, "No."

XXIII

"Mademoiselle has sent for me?" Bienville kissed the hand that Miss Grimston, without rising from her comfortable chair before the fire, lifted toward him. The hand-screen with which she shielded her face protected her not only from the blaze, but from his scrutiny. In the same way, the winter gloaming, with its uncertain light, nerved her against her fear of self-betrayal, giving her that assurance of being mistress of herself which she lacked when he was near.

"I did send for you. I wanted to see you. Won't you sit down?"

"I've been expecting the summons," he said, significantly, taking the seat on the other side of the hearth.

"Indeed? Why?"

"I thought the day would come when you would be more just to me."

"You thought I'd - hear things?"

"Perhaps."

"I have. That's why I asked you to come."

During the brief silence before she spoke again he was able to congratulate himself on his diplomacy. He had checked his first impulse to come to her with his great news immediately on his return from Lakefield. He had seen how relatively ineffective the information would be were it to proceed bluntly from himself. He had even restrained Mrs. Bayford's enthusiasm, in order to let the intelligence filter gently through the neutral agencies of common gossip. In this way it would seem to Miss Grimston a discovery of her own, and appeal to her as an indirect corroboration of his word. He had the less scruple in taking these precautions in that he believed Diane to have justified anything he might have said of her. It was no small relief to a man of honor to know he had not been guilty of a gratuitous slander, even though it was only on a woman. He awaited Miss Grimston's next words with complacent expectancy, but when they came they surprised him.

"I wondered a little why you should have been at Lakefield."

"I'm afraid you'll think it was for a very foolish reason," he laughed, "but I'll tell you, if you want to know. I went because I thought you were there."

"I? At three o'clock in the morning?"

"It was like this," he went on. "You'll pardon me if I say anything to give you offence, but you'll understand the reason why. On the day when we all lunched together at the Restaurant Blitz - you, Madame your aunt, your friend Monsieur Reggie Bradford, and I - I was a little jealous of some understanding between you two, in which I was not included. You spoke together in whispers, and exchanged glances in such a way that all my fears were aroused. Afterward you went away with him. That evening, at the Stuyvesant Club, I heard a strange rumor. It was whispered from one to another until it reached me. Your friend Monsieur Bradford is not a silent person, and what he knows is sure to become common property. The rumor - which I grant you was an absurd one - was to the effect that he had persuaded you to run away and marry him; and that you had actually been seen on the way to Lakefield in his car."

"I was in his car. That's quite true."

"Ah? Then there was some foundation for the report. Madame your aunt will have told you how I hurried here, about eleven o'clock that night. You had disappeared, leaving nothing behind but an enigmatic note saying you would explain your absence in the morning. What was I to think, Mademoiselle? I was afraid to think. I didn't stop to think. I determined to follow you. It was too late for any train, so I took an auto. I reached the Bay Tree Inn - and saw what I saw. *Voila!*"

A smile of amusement flickered over her grave features, but she made no remark.

"If I was guilty of an indiscretion in following you, Mademoiselle," he pursued, "it was because of my great love for you. If you had chosen to marry some one else, I couldn't have kept you from it; but at least I was determined to try. Though I thought it incredible that you should take a step like that, in secrecy and flight, yet I find so many strange ways of marrying in America that I must be pardoned for my fear. As it is, I cannot regret it, since, by a miracle, it gave me proof of that which you have found it so difficult to believe. It has grieved me more than I could ever make you understand to know that during all these months you have doubted me."

"I'm sure of that," she said, softly, gazing into the fire. "But haven't you wondered where I was that night when you followed me to Lakefield?"

"If I have, I shouldn't presume to inquire."

"It's a secret; but I should like to tell it to you. I know you'll guard it sacredly, because it concerns - a woman's honor."

Though she did not look up, she felt the startled toss of the head, characteristic of his moments of alarm.

"If Mademoiselle is pleased to be satirical - "

"No. There's no reason why I should be satirical. If, in spite of everything, my confidence in you wasn't absolute, I shouldn't risk a name I hold so dear as that of Dorothea Pruyn."

"*Tiens!*" he exclaimed, under his breath.

"Miss Pruyn is a charming girl, but she's been very foolish. What she did was not quite so bad in American eyes as it would be in French ones, but it was certainly very wilful. If you heard rumors of an elopement, it was hers."

"*Mon Dieu!* With the big Monsieur Reggie?"

"Not quite. I needn't tell you the young man's name; it will be enough to say that the big Monsieur Reggie, as you call him, was in his confidence. It was Reggie who undertook to convey Dorothea to Lakefield, where she was to meet the bridegroom-elect and marry him."

"And then?"

"Then Reggie told me. It was silly of any one to intrust him with a mission of the kind, for he couldn't possibly keep it to himself. He told me while we were lunching at the Blitz. That's what he was whispering. That's why I went away with him after lunch and left you with my aunt. I saw you were annoyed, but I couldn't help it."

"You wanted to dissuade him?"

"I tried; but I saw it was too late for that. Reggie wouldn't desert his friend at the last minute. The only concession I could wring from him was that he should let me take his place in the motor."

"You?"

"I drive at least as well as Mr. Bradford. I made him see that in case of accident it would make all the difference in the world to Miss Pruyn's future life to be with a woman, rather than a man."

"Did you make her see it, too?"

"I didn't try. The arrangements these wise young people had made rendered the substitution easy. Dorothea had apparently considered it part of the romance not to know with whom she was going, or where she was being taken. At the time and place appointed she found an automobile, driven by a person in a big fur coat, a cap, and goggles. It was agreed that she should enter and ask no questions."

"And did she?"

"She fulfilled her engagement to the letter. As soon as she was seated I drove away; and for six hours I didn't hear a sound from her."

"Six hours? Did it take you all that time to reach Lakefield?"

"I didn't go to Lakefield. I took her to Philadelphia. My one object was to keep her from meeting the young man that night; but perhaps that's where I made my mistake."

"But why? It was better for her that she shouldn't."

"For her, perhaps; but not for every one else. You see, I lost my way two or three times; though, as I had been over the ground twice already, I was always able to right myself after a while. Near Trenton, Dorothea got frightened, and when I peeped inside I could see she was crying. As all danger was over then, I stopped and let her see who I was."

"Was she angry?"

"Quite the contrary! The poor child was terrified at her own rashness, and very much relieved to find she had been kept from being as foolish as she had intended. I got in beside her, and let her have her cry out in comfort. After that we ate some sandwiches and took heart. It was weird work, in the dead of night and along the lonely roads; but we pushed on, and crept into Philadelphia between one and two in the morning."

"That was a very brave, act, Mademoiselle." Bienville's eyes glistened and his face lighted up with an ardor that was not dampened by the casual, almost listless, air with which she told her story.

"It might have been better if I had let the whole thing alone."

"Why so?"

"You can rarely interfere in other people's affairs without doing more harm than good. If I had let them go their own way, Diane Eveleth wouldn't have been put in a false position."

"Ah?"

"That's the other part of the story. If I had known, I should have left the matter in her hands. She would have managed it better than I. As it was, she made my bit of help superfluous."

"I should find it hard to credit that," he said, twisting his fingers nervously

"You won't when I tell you."

In the quiet, unaccentuated manner in which she had given her own share in the action she gave Diane's. Shading her eyes with the hand-screen, she was able to watch his play of feature, and note how the first forced smile of bravado faded into an expression of crestfallen gravity.

"You see," she concluded, "they were frantic at Dorothea's failure to appear. When you arrived they naturally thought it was she; and if Derek Pruyn hadn't lost his head when he saw you, he wouldn't have tried to thrust her out of sight as though she were caught in a crime. It was so like a man to do it; a woman would have had a dozen ways of disarming your suspicion, while he did the very thing to arouse it. I don't blame you for thinking what you did - not in the least. I don't even blame you for telling it, since it would seem to bear out - what you said before. I should only blame you - "

"Yes, Mademoiselle? You would only blame me - ?"

"I should only blame you if - now that you know the truth - you didn't correct the impression you have given."

"Are you going to begin on that again?" he asked, in a tone of disappointment.

"I'm not beginning again, because I've never ceased. If I say anything new on the subject, it is this - that it's time the final word was spoken."

"I agree with you there; it *is* time for that word; but you must speak it."

There was a ring of energy in his voice which caused her to turn from her contemplation of the fire and look at him. When she did he had taken on a new air of resolution.

"I think it's time we came to a definite understanding," he went on, "and that you should see how the matter looks from my point of view. You speak of doing right, Mademoiselle, as if it were an easy thing. You don't realize that, for me, it would have to be the last act but one in life."

In spite of the shock, she ignored his implied confession, going on to speak in the tone of ordinary conversation.

"The last act but one? I don't understand you."

"Really? I'm surprised at that. You're so good a sportsman that I should think you'd see that if I do what you ask there will be only one more thing left for me."

For a few minutes she looked at him silently, with fixed gaze, taking in the full measure of his meaning.

"That's folly," she said at last.

"Is it? Not for me. It might be for some people, but - not for me. You must remember who I am. I'm a Frenchman. I'm an aristocrat. I'm a Bienville. I'm a member of a class, of a clan, that lives and breathes on - honor. I can do without almost everything in the world but that. I can do without money, I can do without morals, I can do without most kinds of common honesty, I can do without nearly all the Christian virtues, and still keep my place among my friends; but I can't do without that particular shade of conduct which they and I understand by the word honor."

"But aren't you doing without it as it is?"

"No; because there again our code is special to ourselves. With us the crime is not in suspicion or supposition; it isn't even in detection. It's in admission. It's in confession. All sorts of things may be thought of you, and said of you, and even known of you, and you can bluff them out; but when you have acknowledged them - you're doomed."

"Even so, isn't it better to acknowledge them - and *be* doomed?"

"That's the question. That's what I have to decide. That's where you must help me decide. If you had allowed me, I should have made up my own mind, on my own responsibility; but you won't let me. Now that the incident at Lakefield is no good as evidence, I see that you will never rest until we come to the plainest of plain speech. The problem I've had to solve is this: Is Diane Eveleth to be happy, or am I? Is she to rise while I go under, or shall I keep her down and stay on the surface? Since it's her life or mine, which is it to be? The alternative may be a brutal one, but there it is."

"And you've decided in your own favor?"

"So far. I've been actuated by the instinct of self-preservation."

"And are you going to persist in it?"

"That's for you to tell me. But I should like to remind you first of this, that if I don't - I go."

"And what if - if I went with you?"

"You couldn't. The journey would be too long."

"But you needn't go so far if I'm there."

"I couldn't take you with me. You must understand that. I once knew an American girl who married a man who cheated at cards, and buried herself alive with him. I wouldn't let a woman do that for me."

"But if she wanted to?"

"In that case she ought to be protected from herself. There's no use in ruining two lives where one will do."

"There's such a thing as losing your life to find it."

"If so, it's something for me to do - alone."

"Isn't it a kind of moral cowardice to say that?"

"I don't think so. To me it seems only looking things squarely in the face. I'm not the sort of man for whom there's any possibility of beginning life anew. A man like me can't live things down. When once, by his own confession, he has lost his honor, there's no rehabilitation that can make him a man again. Like Cain, he has got to go out from the presence of the Lord; only, unlike Cain, there's no land of Nod waiting to receive him. There's no place for him anywhere on earth. A few years ago, when I was motoring in the Black Forest with the d'Aubignys, we dropped into a little hole of an inn as nearly out of the world as anything could be. As we approached the door a man got up from a bench and shambled away. When he had got to what he considered a safe distance he turned to look at us. I knew him. It was Jacques de la Tour de Lorme."

"Really?"

"The poor wretch had hidden himself in that God-forsaken spot, where he supposed no one would be able to track him down; but we had done it. I've never forgotten his weary gait or the woe-begone look in his eyes. It is what would come to me if I waited for it."

"I don't see why. There's no similarity between the cases. Jacques de La Tour de Lorme did wrong he never could put right. You'd be doing the very thing he found impossible." He shook his head. "It wouldn't make any difference in my world. Nobody there would think of the right or the wrong; they'd only consider what I'd owned to. It's the confession that would ruin me."

"Surely you exaggerate. You could do it quietly, No one need know - outside Derek Pruyn and two or three more of us."

"I don't do things in that way," he said, with an odd return of his old-time pride. "If I put the woman right, it shall be in the eyes of the world. I don't ask to have things made easy for me. If I do it at all, I shall do it thoroughly. I'm not afraid of it or of anything it entails. It's a curious thing that a man of my make-up is afraid of being ridiculed or being given the cold shoulder, but he's not afraid to die."

Though he was looking straight at her, he was too deeply engrossed in his own thoughts to see how proudly her head went up, or to note the flash of splendid light in which her glance enveloped him.

"I was all ready to die," he pursued, in the same meditative tone, "that morning in the Pre Catalan. George Eveleth could have had my life for the asking. I'd never known him to miss his mark, and he wouldn't have missed me - if he hadn't had another destination for his bullet. I've regretted it more than once. I've had pretty nearly all that life could give me - and I've made a mess of it."

"You haven't had - love," she ventured.

"Love?" he echoed, with a short laugh. "I've had every kind of love but one; and that I'm not worthy of."

"We get a good many things we're not worthy of; but they help us just the same."

"This wouldn't help me," he returned, speaking very slowly. "I shouldn't know what to do with it. It would be as useless to me in my new conditions as a chaplet of pearls to a slave in the galleys. So, what would you do?"

"I'd do right at any cost."

She scarcely knew that the words were spoken, so intent was her thought on the strange mixture of elements in his personality. It was not until she had waited in vain for a response that she found the echo of her speech still in her mental hearing and recognized its import. Her first impulse was to cry out and take it back; but she restrained herself and waited. It was an instant in which the love of daring, that was so instinctive in her nature, blew, as it were, a trumpet-challenge to the same passion in his own, while they sat staring at each other, wide-eyed and speechless, in the dancing firelight.

XXIV

On the following day the Marquis de Bienville found the execution of any intentions he might have had toward Derek Pruyn postponed by the circumstance that Miss Regina van Tromp was dead. The helpless, inarticulate life, which for three years had served as a bond to hold more active existences together, had failed suddenly, leaving in the little group a curious impression of collapse. It became perceptible that the hushed sick-room, where Miss Lucilla and Mrs. Eveleth were the only ministrants, had in reality been a centre for those who never entered it. Now that the living presence was withdrawn, there came the consciousness of dispersing interests, inseparable from the passing away of the long established, which gives the spirit pause. The days before the funeral became a period of suspended action, in which Life refrained from too marked a manifestation of its energies, out of reverence for Death. Even when the grave was filled in, and the will read, and the family face to face with its new conditions, there was a respectful absence of hurry in beginning the work of reconstruction. The lull lasted, in fact, till James van Tromp arrived from Paris; and it was broken then only by the banker's desire "to get things settled" with all possible speed, so that he might return to the Rue Auber.

The first sign of real disintegration came from Mrs. Eveleth. She had waited for the arrival of the man whom she looked upon now as her confidential adviser, to make the announcement that, since Miss Lucilla would no longer need her, she meant to have a home of her own. The economies she had been able to practise during the last two years, together with a legacy from Miss van Tromp, would, when added to "her own income," provide her with modest comfort for the rest of her days. There was something triumphant in the way in which she proclaimed her independence of the daughter-in-law who had been the author of so many of her woes. It was the old banker himself who brought this intelligence to Diane.

During the fortnight he had been in New York he had formed an almost daily habit of dropping in on her. She was the more surprised at his doing so from the fact that her detachment from the rest of the circle of which she had formed a part was now complete. She had gone to see Miss Lucilla with words of sympathy, but her reception was such that she came away with cheeks flaming. Miss Lucilla had said nothing; she had only wept; but she had wept in a way to show that Diane herself, more than the departed Miss Regina, was the motive of her grief. After that Diane had remained shut up in her linen-room, finding in its occupied seclusion something of the peace which the nun seeks in the cloister.

There was no one but the old man to push his way into her sanctuary, and for his visits she was grateful. They not only relieved the tedium of her days, but they brought her news from that small world into which her most vital interests had become absorbed.

"So the old lady is set up for life on your money," he observed, as he watched Diane hold a white table-cloth up to the light and search it for imperfections.

"It isn't my money now; and even if it were I'd rather she had the use of it. She would have had much more than that if it hadn't been for me."

"She might; and then again she mightn't. Who told *you* what would have happened - if everything had been different from what it is? There are people who think they would have had plenty of money if it hadn't been for me; but that doesn't prove they're right."

"In any case I'm glad she has it."

"That's because you're a very foolish little woman, as I told you when you came to me three years ago. I said then that you'd be sorry for it some day - "

"But I'm not."

"Tut! tut! Don't tell me! Can't I see with my own eyes? No woman could lose her good looks as you've done and not know she's made a mistake. How old are you now?"

"I'm twenty-seven."

"Dear me! dear me! You look forty."

"I feel eighty."

"Yes; I dare say you do. Any one who's got into so many scrapes as you have must feel the burden of time. I don't think I ever saw a young woman make such poor use of her opportunities. Why didn't you marry Derek Pruyn?"

Diane kept herself quite still, her needle arrested half-way through its stitch. She took time to reflect that it was useless to feel annoyed at anything he might say, and when she formed her answer it was in the spirit of meeting him in his own vein.

"What makes you think I ever had the chance?"

"Because I gave it to you myself."

"You, Mr. van Tromp?"

"Yes; me. I did all that wire-pulling when you first came to New York; and I did it just so that you might catch him."

"Oh?"

"I did," he declared, proudly. "And if you had been the woman I took you for, you could have had him."

"But suppose I - didn't want him?"

"Oh, don't tell me that," he said, pityingly. "Why shouldn't you want him? - just as much as he'd want you?"

"Well, I'll put it that way if you like. Suppose he didn't want me?"

"Then the more fool he. I picked you out for him on purpose."

"May I ask why?"

"Certainly. I saw he was getting on in life, and, as he'd been a good many years a widower, I imagined he'd had some difficulty in getting any one to have him. If he's good-looking, he's not what you'd call very bright; and he's got a temper like - well, I won't say what. I'd pity the woman who got him, that's all; and so - "

"And so you thought you'd pity me."

"I did pity you as it was. It seemed to me you couldn't be worse off, not even if you married Derek Pruyn."

"It was certainly good of you to give me the opportunity; and if I had only known - "

"You would have let it slip through your fingers just the same. You're one of the young women who will always stand in their own light. I dare say, now, that if I told you I was willing to marry you myself, you wouldn't profit by the occasion."

"I should never want to profit by your loss, Mr. van Tromp."

"But suppose I could afford - to lose?"

Unable to answer him there, she held her peace, though it was a relief that, before he had time to speak again, a page-boy knocked at the door and entered with a card. Diane took it hastily and read the name.

"Tell the gentleman I can't see him," she said, with a visible effort to speak steadily.

"Wait!" the banker ordered, as the boy was about to turn. "Who is it?" Without ceremony he drew the card from Diane's hand and looked at it. "Heu!" he cried. "It's Bienville, is it? Of course you'll see him; of course you will; of course! Here, boy, I'll go with you."

Returning to Gramercy Park after this interview, the banker pottered about his apartment until, on hearing the door-bell ring, he looked out of the window and recognized Derek Pruyn's chauffeur. On the stairs, as he went down, he heard Miss Lucilla's voice in the hall.

"Oh, come in, Derek. Marion isn't here yet, but she won't be long. I asked you to come punctually, because I gathered from her note that she wanted to see you very particularly, and without Mrs. Bayford's knowledge. She has evidently something on her mind that she wants to tell you."

"Hello, dears!" the old man interrupted suddenly, as, leaning heavily on the baluster, he descended the stairs. "I've got good news for you."

"Good news, Uncle James?" Miss Lucilla said, reproachfully. With her long, grave face, and in her heavy crape, she looked as though she found good news decidedly out of place.

"The very best," the banker declared, reaching the hall and taking his nephew and niece each by an arm. "Come into the library and I'll tell you. There!" he went on, pushing Miss Lucilla into an arm-chair. "Sit down, Derek, and make yourself comfortable. Now, listen, both of you. Perhaps you're going to have a new aunt."

"Oh, Uncle James!" Miss Lucilla cried, in the voice of a person about to faint.

"You're going to be married!" Derek roared, with the fury of a father addressing a wayward son.

"The young woman," the banker went on to explain, "is of French extraction, but Irish on the mother's side."

Derek grasped the arms of his chair and half rose, making an inarticulate sound.

"'Sh! 'Sh!" the old man went on, lifting a warning hand. "She'd had reverses of fortune; but that wasn't the reason why she came to me. Though her husband had just died, leaving nothing, she had her own *dot*, on the income of which she could have lived. But that didn't suit her. Her husband had left a mother, who had neither *dot* nor anything else in the world. At the age of sixty the old woman was a pauper. My little lady came to see me in order to transfer all her own money secretly to her mother-in-law, and face the world herself with empty hands."

"My God!" Derek breathed, just audibly. Miss Lucilla sat upright and tense, hot tears starting to her eyes.

"Plucky, wasn't it?" the uncle went on, complacently. "I didn't approve of it at first, but I let her do it in the end, knowing that some good fellow would make it up to her."

"Don't joke, uncle," Derek cried, nervously. "It's too serious for that."

"I'm not joking. It's what I did think. And if the world wasn't full of idiots who couldn't tell diamonds from glass, a little woman like that would have been snapped up long ago."

Derek sprang up and strode across the room.

"Do you mean to tell me," he demanded, turning abruptly, "that she made over all her money to Mrs. Eveleth - a woman who has deserted her, like the rest of us?"

"That's what she did; but there's this to be said for the old lady, that she doesn't know it. She thinks it's the wreck of her own fortune, and Diane wouldn't let me tell her the truth. Since you seem to be interested in the little story," he added, with sarcasm, "you may hear all about it."

With tolerable accuracy he gave the details of his first interview with Diane, three years previous. Long before he finished, Lucilla was weeping silently, while Derek stood like a man turned to stone. Even the banker's own face took on an expression of whimsical gravity as he said in conclusion:

"And so I've decided to give her a home - that is," he added, significantly, "if no one else will."

"Do you mean that for me?" Derek asked, in a tone too low for Lucilla to hear it.

"Oh no - not particularly. I mean it for - any one."

"Because," Derek went on, "as for me - I'm not worthy to have her under my roof."

The banker made no comment, sitting in a hunched attitude and humming to himself in a cracked voice while Derek stared down at him.

They were still in this position when Marion Grimston was shown in.

XXV

Greetings having been exchanged, it was Miss Lucilla's policy to draw her uncle away to some other room, leaving Marion free to have her conference with Pruyn; but the old man settled himself in his chair again, with no intention of quitting the field. Derek, too, entered on the task of dislodging him, but without success. Nursing his knee, and peering at Marion with bulgy, short-sighted eyes, the banker kept her answering questions as to Mrs. Bayford's health, blind to her obvious nervousness and distress.

The cousins exchanged baffled, impatient glances, while Lucilla managed to say in an undertone: "Take Marion to the drawing-room. We'll never get him to go."

Derek was about to comply with this suggestion, when the footman threw open the library door again. For a moment no one appeared, though a sound of smothered voices from the hall caused the four within the room to sit in strangely aroused expectancy.

"No, no; I can't go in," came a woman's whispered protest. "You can do it without me."

"You must!" was the man's response; and a second later Bienville was on the threshold, standing aside as Diane Eveleth entered.

Derek sprang to his feet, but, as if petrified by a sense of his own impotence, stood still. Miss Lucilla, with the instincts of the hostess awake, even in these strange conditions, went

BASIL KING

forward, with her hand half outstretched and the words "Monsieur de Bienville" on her lips. The old banker rose, and, taking Diane's hand, drew it within his arm in a protecting way for which she was grateful, while she suffered him to lead her some few steps apart. Marion Grimston alone, seated in a distant corner, did not move. With her arm resting on a small table, she watched the rapidly enacted scene with the detachment of a spectator looking at a play. She had thrown back her black veil over her hat, and against the dark background her face had the grave, marble whiteness of classic features in stone.

During the minute of interrogatory silence that ensued, Bienville, with quick reversion to the habits of the drawing-room, was able to re-establish his self-control. With his hat, his gloves, and his stick, he had that air of the casual visitor which helped to give him back the sensation of having his feet on accustomed ground.

"I must beg your pardon, Miss van Tromp, for disturbing you," he said, addressing himself to Miss Lucilla, who stood in the foreground. "I shouldn't have done so if I hadn't something of great importance to say."

His voice was so calm that Miss Lucilla could not do otherwise than reply in the same vein of commonplace formality.

"I'm very glad to see you, Monsieur de Bienville. Won't you sit down? I was just going to ring for tea."

"Thank you," he said, with a wave of the hand that declined without words the proffered entertainment. "Perhaps I had better say what I have to say - and go."

"Oh, if you think so - !"

Having fulfilled her necessary duties as mistress of the house, she felt at liberty to fall back, leaving Bienville isolated in the doorway.

"Mr. Pruyn," he said, after further brief hesitation, "I come to make a confession which can scarcely be a confession to any one in this room - but you."

Derek grew white to the lips, but remained motionless, while Bienville went on.

"On the way up from South America last spring I said certain things about a certain lady which were not true. I said them first out of thoughtless folly; but I maintained them afterward with deliberate intent. When I pretended to take them back, I did so in a way which, as I knew, must convince you further."

"It did."

As he brought out the two words, Derek tried to look at Diane, but she was clinging to the arm of old James van Tromp, while her frightened eyes were riveted on Bienville.

"I'm telling you the truth to-day," Bienville continued, "partly because circumstances have forced my hand, partly because some one whom I greatly respect desires it, and partly because something within myself - I might almost call it the manhood I've been fighting against - has made it imperative. I've come to the point where my punishment is greater than I can bear. I'm not so lost to honor as not to know that life is no longer worth the living when honor is lost to me."

He spoke without a tremor, leaning easily on the cane he held against his hip.

"I must do myself the justice to say that the wrong of which I was guilty had its origin, at the first, in a sort of inadvertence. I had no intention of doing any one irreparable harm. I was taking part in a game, but I meant to play it fairly. The lady of whom I speak would bear me out when I say that the people among whom she and I were born - in France - in Paris - engage in this game as a sort of sport, and we call it - love. It isn't love in any of the senses in which you understand it here.

We give it a meaning of our own. It's a game that requires the combination of many kinds of skill, and, if it doesn't call for a conspicuous display of virtues, it lays all the greater emphasis on its own few, stringent rules. Like all other sports, it demands a certain kind of integrity, in which the moralist could easily pick holes, but which nevertheless constitutes its saving grace. Well, in this game of love I - cheated. I said, one day, that I had won, when I hadn't won. I said it to people who welcomed my victory, not through friendship for me, but from envy of - her." The perspiration began to stand in beads upon Bienville's forehead, but he held himself erect and went on with the same outward tranquillity. His eyes were fixed on Pruyn's, and Pruyn's on his, in a gaze from which even the nearest objects were excluded. "In the little group in which we lived her position was peculiar. She was both within our gates and without them. While she was one of us by birth, she was a stranger by education and by marriage. She was admitted with a welcome, and at the same time with a question. She was a mark for enmity from the very first. There was something about her that challenged our institutions. In among our worn-out passions and moribund ideals she brought a freshness we resented. She made our prejudices seem absurd from contrast with her own sanity, and showed our moral standards to be rotten by the light of the something clear and virginal in her character. I can't tell you how this effect was brought about, but there were few of us who weren't aware of it, as there were few of us who didn't hate it. There was but one impulse among us - to catch her in a fault, to make her no better than ourselves. The daring of her innocence afforded us many opportunities; and we made use of them. One man after another confessed himself defeated. Then came my turn. I wasn't merely defeated; I was put to utter rout, with ridicule and scorn. That was too much for me. I couldn't stand it; and - and - I lied."

"Oh, Bienville, that will do!" Diane cried out, in a pleading wail. "Don't say any more!"

"I'm not sure that there's any more I need to say. The rest can be easily understood. Every one knows how a man who lies once is obliged to lie again, and again, and yet again, unless he frees himself as I do. When I began I thought I had it in me to go on heroically - but I hadn't. I can't keep it up. I'm not one of the master villains, who command respect from force of prowess. I'm a weakling in evil, as in good, fit neither for God nor for the devil. But that's my affair. I needn't trouble any one here with what only concerns myself. It's too late for me to make everything right now; but I'll do what I can before - before - I mean," he stammered on, "I'll write. I'll write to the people - there were only a few of them - to whom I actually used the words I did. I'll ask them to correct the impression I have given. I know they'll do it, when they know - "

He stopped helplessly. The lustre died out of his eyes, and his pallor became sallowness.

"But I've said enough," he began again, making a tremendous effort to regain his self-mastery. "You can have no doubt as to my meaning; and you will be able to fill in anything I may have left unspoken. Now," he added, sweeping the room with a look - "now - I'd better - go."

"No, by God! you infernal scoundrel," shouted Derek Pruyn, "you shall not go."

All the suffering of months shot out in the red gleam of his eyes, while the muscular tension of his neck was like that of an infuriated mastiff. In three strides he was across the room, with clinched fist uplifted. Bienville had barely time in which to fold his arms and stand with feet together and head erect, awaiting the blow.

"Go on," he said, as Derek stood with hand poised above him. "Go on."

There was a second of breathless stillness. Then slowly the clinched fingers began to relax and the open hand descended, softly, gently, on Bienville's shoulder. Between the two men there passed a look of things unspeakable, till, with bent head and drooping figure, Derek wheeled away.

"I'll say good-by - now."

Bienville's voice was husky, but he bowed with dignity to each member of the company in turn and to Marion Grimston last. "Raoul!" The name arrested him as he was about to go. He looked at her inquiringly. "Raoul," she said again, without rising from her place, "I promised that if you ever did what you've done to-day I would be your wife."

"You did," he answered, "but I've already given you to understand that I claim no such reward."

"It isn't you who would be claiming the reward; it's I. I've suffered much. I've earned it."

"The very fact that you've suffered much would be my motive in not allowing you to suffer more."

"Raoul, no man knows the sources of a woman's joy and pain. How can you tell from what to save me?"

"There's one thing from which I *must* save you: from uniting your destiny with that of a man who has no future - from pouring the riches of your heart into a bottomless pit, where they could do no one any good. I thank you, Mademoiselle, with all my soul. I've asked you many times for your love; and of the hard things I've had to do to-day, the hardest is to give it back to you, now, when at last you offer it. Don't add to my bitterness by urging it on me."

"But, Raoul," she cried, raising herself up, "you don't understand. We regard these things differently here from the way in which you do in France. It may be true, as you say, that in losing your honor you've lost all - in French eyes; but we don't feel like that. We never look on any one as beyond redemption. We should consider that a man who has been brave enough to do what you've done to-day has gone far to establish his moral regeneration. We can honor him, in certain ways - in *certain* ways, Raoul - almost more than if he had never done wrong at all. None of us would condemn him, or cast a stone at him - should we, Lucilla? - should we, Mr. Pruyn?"

"No, no," Miss Lucilla sobbed. "We'd pity him; we'd take him to our hearts."

"She's right, Bienville," Derek muttered, nodding toward Marion. "Better do just as she says."

"I'm a Frenchman. I'm a Bienville. I can't accept mercy."

"But you can bestow it," the girl cried, passionately. "Any one would tell you that, after all that has happened - after this - I should be happier in sharing your life than in being shut out of it. I appeal to you, Miss Lucilla! I appeal to you, Diane! - wouldn't any woman be proud to be the wife of Raoul de Bienville after what he has done this afternoon, no matter how the world turned against him?"

"These ladies, in the goodness of their hearts, might say anything they chose; but nothing would alter their conviction that for you to be my wife would be only to add misery to mistake."

"That's so," the old banker corroborated, smacking his lips, "but you wouldn't be much worse when you'd done that than you are now; so why not just let her have her way?"

Bienville tried to speak again, but his dry lips refused to frame the words.

"Noble ... impossible ... drag you down," came incoherently from him, when by a quick backward movement he stepped over the threshold into the semi-obscurity of the hail.

The act was so sudden that seconds had already elapsed before Marion Grimston uttered the cry that rent her like the wail of some strong, primordial creature without the power of tears.

"Raoul, come back!"

With rapid motion she glided across the room and was in the hail.

"Raoul, come back!"

She had descended the hail, and had almost reached him as he opened the door to pass out.

"Raoul, I love you!"

But the door closed as, falling against it, she sank to the floor. Before Miss Lucilla and James van Tromp could reach her she was already losing consciousness.

XXVI

"No; stay where you are; I'll go." Derek spoke with the terse command of subdued excitement, almost pushing Diane back, as she, too, attempted to go to Marion's assistance. She sank obediently into one of the great chairs, too dazed even for curiosity as to what was passing in the hail. Derek closed the door behind him, and, though confused sounds of voices and shuffling feet reached her, she gave them but a dulled attention. It was not till he came back that her stunned intelligence revived sufficiently to enable her to think.

He closed the door again, throwing himself wearily into another of the big leathern chairs.

"They've taken her into Lucilla's room. She'll be all right now. It was better that it should end like that."

"I'm not so sure. I'm afraid for him."

"Oh, he'll survive it."

"You don't know our Frenchmen. They're not like you, nor any of your men. With their sensitiveness to honor and their indifference to moral right, it's difficult for you to understand them. I shouldn't be surprised at anything he might do."

"I'll go and see him to-morrow and try to knock a little reason into him."

"If it isn't too late."

"Oh, I dare say it will be. Everything seems to be - too late."

"It's better that some things should come too late rather than not at all."

"What things do you mean?"

"I suppose I mean the same things as you do." He gave a long sigh that was something of a groan, slipping down in his chair into an attitude, not of informality, but of dejection. For the moment neither was equal to facing the great subjects that must be met.

"I wonder what Bienville will do to himself?" he asked, suddenly, changing his position with nervous brusqueness, leaning forward now, with his elbows on his knees. "I wish you'd go and see him to-night." "Well, perhaps I will. I've a good deal of fellow-feeling with him. I can't help thinking that he and I are in much the same box, and that he has shown me the way Out."

"Derek!"

She sprang up with a cry of alarm, standing, with hands crossed on her breast, in a sudden access of terror.

"Oh, don't be afraid," he laughed, grimly, staring up at her. "I'm not his sort. There are no heroics about me. Men of my stamp don't make theatrical exits; we're too confoundedly sane. Whether we do well or whether we do ill, we plod along on our treadmill round, from the house to the office, and from the office to the grave, as if we never had anything on the conscience. But if I had the spirit of Bienville, do you know what I should do?"

"No, no, no!" she burst out. "Don't say it! Don't say it!"

"Then I won't. But if Bienville thought of it, why shouldn't I? What has he done that is worse than what I've done? What has he done that's as bad? For, after all, you were little or nothing to him, when you were everything to me. I knew you as he didn't know you. I had lived in one house with you, watched you, studied you, tried you, put you to tests that you never knew anything about, and had seen you come through them successfully. I had seen how you bore misfortune; I had seen how you carried yourself in difficult situations; I had seen the skill with which you ruled my house, and the wisdom with which you were more than a mother to my child; I had seen you combine with all that is most womanly the patience and fortitude of a man; and it wasn't enough for me - it wasn't enough for me!"

He threw himself back into his seat, with a desperate flinging out of the hands, letting his arms drop heavily over the sides of his chair till his fingers touched the floor.

"My God! My God!" he groaned, ironically. "It wasn't enough for me! I doubted her. I doubted her on the first idle word that came my way. I did more than doubt her. I haled her into my court, and tried her, and condemned her, and, as nearly as might be, put her to death. I, with my ten hundred thousand sins - all of them as black as Erebus - found her not pure enough for me! It ought to make one die of laughter. Diane," he went on, in another tone - a tone of ghastly jocularity - "didn't it amuse you, knowing yourself to be what you are - knowing what you had done for Mrs. Eveleth - knowing the things Bienville has just said of you - didn't it amuse you to see me sitting in judgment on you?"

"It doesn't amuse me to see you sitting in judgment on yourself."

"Doesn't it? I should think it would. It seems to me that if I saw a man who had done me so much harm visited with such awful justice as I'm getting now, it would make up to me for nearly everything I ever had to suffer."

"In my case it only adds to it. I wish you wouldn't say these things. If you ever did me wrong, I always knew it was - by mistake."

"Oh, Lord! Oh, Lord!" He laughed outright, getting up from his chair and dragging himself heavily across the room, where, with his hands in his pockets and his back against the bookshelves, he stood facing her. "What do you think of Bienville's attitude toward Marion Grimston?" he asked, with an inflection that would have sounded casual if it had not been for all that lay behind.

"I can understand it; but I think he was wrong."

"You think he ought to allow her to marry him?"

"Weighing one thing with another - yes."

"Would you marry a man who had shown himself such a hound?"

"It would depend."

"On what?"

"Oh, on a good many things."

"Such as - ?"

She hesitated a minute before deciding whether or not to walk into his trap, but, as his eyes were on the ground and she felt stronger than a minute or two ago, she decided to do it.

"It would depend, for one thing, on whether or not I loved him."

"And if you did love him?"

Again she hesitated, before making up her mind to speak.

"Then it would depend on whether or not he loved me."

She had given him his chance. The word he had never uttered must come now or never. For an instant he seemed about to seize his opportunity; but when he actually spoke it was only to say:

"Would *you* marry *me?*"

"No." She gave her answer firmly.

"No?"

"No."

"Why?"

She shrugged her shoulders and threw out her hands, but said nothing in words.

"Is it because I haven't expressed regret for all the things I have - to regret?"

She shook her head.

"Because if it is," he went on, "I haven't done it only for the reason that the utmost expression would be so inadequate as to become a mockery. When a man has sinned against light, as I've done, no mere cries of contrition are going to win him pardon. That must come as a spontaneous act of grace, as it wells out of the heart of the Most High - or it can't come at all."

"That isn't the reason."

"Then there's another one?"

"Yes; another one."

"One that's insurmountable?"

"Yes, as things are - that's insurmountable."

With a look of dumb, unresenting sadness, he turned away, and, leaning on the mantelpiece, stood with his back toward her, and his face buried in his hands.

Minutes went by in silence. When he spoke it was over his shoulder, and, as it were, parenthetically:

"But, Diane, I love you."

He stood as he was, listening, but as if without much expectation, for a response. When none came, and he turned round inquiringly, he beheld in her that radiant change which was visible to those who saw the martyred Stephen's face as he gazed straight into heaven.

For a long minute he stood spellbound and amazed.

"Was it that?" he asked, in a whisper.

She gave him no reply.

"It was that," he declared, in the tone of a man making a discovery. "It *was* that."

"Why didn't you tell me so before?" she found strength to say.

"Tell you, Diane? What was the use of telling you - when you knew? My life has been open, for you to look into as you would."

"Yes, but not to go into. There's only one key that unlocks the inner shrine of all - the word you've just spoken. A woman knows nothing till she hears it."

He looked at her with the puzzled air of a man getting

strange information.

"Well," he said, after a long pause, "you've heard it. So what - now?"

"Now I'm willing to say that I love you."

"Oh, but I knew that already," he returned. "A man doesn't need to be told what he can see. That isn't what I'm asking. What I want to learn is, not what you feel, but what you'll - do."

She smiled faintly.

"I'm asking what you'll - do?" he repeated.

"If you insist on my telling you that," she said glancing up at him shyly, "I'll say that - since the inner shrine is unlocked - at last - I'll go in."

"Then, come, come."

He stood with arms open, his tone of petition still blended with a suggestion of command, as she crossed the room toward him.

Choose from Thousands of 1stWorldLibrary Classics By

Adolphus WilliamWard
Aesop
Agatha Christie
Alexander Aaronsohn
Alexander Kielland
Alexandre Dumas
Alfred Gatty
Alfred Ollivant
Alice Duer Miller
Alice Turner Curtis
Alice Dunbar
Ambrose Bierce
Amelia E. Barr
Andrew Lang
Andrew McFarland Davis
Anna Sewell
Annie Besant
Annie Hamilton Donnell
Annie Payson Call
Anton Chekhov
Arnold Bennett
Arthur Conan Doyle
Arthur Ransome
Atticus
B. M. Bower
Basil King
Bayard Taylor
Ben Macomber
Booth Tarkington
Bram Stoker
C. Collodi
C. E. Orr
C. M. Ingleby
Carolyn Wells
Catherine Parr Traill
Charles A. Eastman
Charles Dickens
Charles Dudley Warner
Charles Farrar Browne
Charles Ives
Charles Kingsley
Charles Lathrop Pack
Charles Whibley
Charles Willing Beale
Charlotte M. Braeme
Charlotte M.Yonge
Clair W. Hayes
Clarence Day Jr.
Clarence E. Mulford

Clemence Housman
Confucius
Cornelis DeWitt Wilcox
Cyril Burleigh
D. H. Lawrence
Daniel Defoe
David Garnett
Don Carlos Janes
Donald Keyhole
Dorothy Kilner
Dougan Clark
E. Nesbit
E.P.Roe
E. Phillips Oppenheim
Edgar Allan Poe
Edgar Rice Burroughs
Edith Wharton
Edward J. O'Biren
John Cournos
Edwin L. Arnold
Eleanor Atkins
Elizabeth Cleghorn
Gaskell
Elizabeth Von Arnim
Ellem Key
Emily Dickinson
Erasmus W. Jones
Ernie Howard Pie
Ethel Turner
Ethel Watts Mumford
Eugenie Foa
Eugene Wood
Evelyn Everett-Green
Everard Cotes
F. J. Cross
Federick Austin Ogg
Ferdinand Ossendowski
Francis Bacon
Francis Darwin
Frances Hodgson Burnett
Frank Gee Patchin
Frank Harris
Frank Jewett Mather
Frank L. Packard
Frederick Trevor Hill
Frederick Winslow Taylor
Friedrich Kerst
Friedrich Nietzsche
Fyodor Dostoyevsky

Gabrielle E. Jackson
Garrett P. Serviss
Gaston Leroux
George Ade
Geroge Bernard Shaw
George Ebers
George Eliot
George MacDonald
George Orwell
George Tucker
George W. Cable
George Wharton James
Gertrude Atherton
Grace E. King
Grant Allen
Guillermo A. Sherwell
Gulielma Zollinger
Gustav Flaubert
H. A. Cody
H. B. Irving
H. G. Wells
H. H. Munro
H. Irving Hancock
H. Rider Haggard
H. W. C. Davis
Hamilton Wright Mabie
Hans Christian Andersen
Harold Avery
Harold McGrath
Harriet Beecher Stowe
Harry Houidini
Helent Hunt Jackson
Helen Nicolay
Hendy David Thoreau
Henrik Ibsen
Henry Adams
Henry Ford
Henry Frost
Henry James
Henry Jones Ford
Henry Seton Merriman
Henry Wadsworth
Longfellow
Henry W Longfellow
Herbert A. Giles
Herbert N. Casson
Herman Hesse
Homer
Honore De Balzac

Horace Walpole
Horatio Alger, Jr.
Howard Pyle
Howard R. Garis
Hugh Lofting
Hugh Walpole
Humphry Ward
Ian Maclaren
Israel Abrahams
J.G.Austin
J. Henri Fabre
J. M. Barrie
J. Macdonald Oxley
J. S. Knowles
J. Storer Clouston
Jack London
Jacob Abbott
James Allen
James Lane Allen
James Andrews
James Baldwin
James DeMille
James Joyce
James Oliver Curwood
James Oppenheim
James Otis
Jane Austen
Jens Peter Jacobsen
Jerome K. Jerome
John Burroughs
John F. Kennedy
John Gay
John Glasworthy
John Habberton
John Joy Bell
John Milton
John Philip Sousa
Jonathan Swift
Joseph Carey
Joseph Conrad
Joseph Jacobs
Julian Hawthrone
Julies Vernes
Justin Huntly McCarthy
Kakuzo Okakura
Kenneth Grahame
Kate Langley Bosher
L. A. Abbot
L. T. Meade
L. Frank Baum
Laura Lee Hope

Laurence Housman
Leo Tolstoy
Leonid Andreyev
Lewis Carroll
Lilian Bell
Lloyd Osbourne
Louis Tracy
Louisa May Alcott
Lucy Fitch Perkins
Lucy Maud Montgomery
Lydia Miller Middleton
Lyndon Orr
M. H. Adams
Margaret E. Sangster
Margaret Vandercook
Maria Edgeworth
Maria Thompson Daviess
Mariano Azuela
Marion Polk Angellotti
Mark Overton
Mark Twain
Mary Austin
Mary Cole
Mary Rowlandson
Mary Wollstonecraft
Shelley
Max Beerbohm
Myra Kelly
Nathaniel Hawthrone
O. F. Walton
Oscar Wilde
Owen Johnson
P.G.Wodehouse
Paul and Mable Thorn
Paul G. Tomlinson
Paul Severing
Peter B. Kyne
Plato
R. Derby Holmes
R. L. Stevenson
Rabindranath Tagore
Rahul Alvares
Ralph Waldo Emmerson
Rene Descartes
Rex E. Beach
Richard Harding Davis
Richard Jefferies
Robert Barr
Robert Frost
Robert Gordon Anderson
Robert L. Drake

Robert Lansing
Robert Michael Ballantyne
Robert W. Chambers
Rosa Nouchette Carey
Ross Kay
Rudyard Kipling
Samuel B. Allison
Samuel Hopkins Adams
Sarah Bernhardt
Selma Lagerlof
Sherwood Anderson
Sigmund Freud
Standish O'Grady
Stanley Weyman
Stella Benson
Stephen Crane
Stewart Edward White
Stijn Streuvels
Swami Abhedananda
Swami Parmananda
T. S. Ackland
The Princess Der Ling
Thomas A. Janvier
Thomas A Kempis
Thomas Anderton
Thomas Bailey Aldrich
Thomas Bulfinch
Thomas De Quincey
Thomas H. Huxley
Thomas Hardy
Thomas More
Thornton W. Burgess
U. S. Grant
Valentine Williams
Victor Appleton
Virginia Woolf
Walter Scott
Washington Irving
Wilbur Lawton
Wilkie Collins
Willa Cather
Willard F. Baker
William Makepeace
Thackeray
William W. Walter
Winston Churchill
Yei Theodora Ozaki
Young E. Allison
Zane Grey